MW01673383

Cast Upon the Tide

Wendy Hamilton

Copyright © 2026 Wendy Hamilton
All rights reserved. No part of this publication may be reproduced, listributed, or transmitted in any form or by any means, including photocopying, recording, or other electronic or mechanical methods, without the prior written permission of the publisher, except in the case of brief quotations embodied in critical reviews and certain other noncommercial uses permitted by copyright law.
ISBN: 979-8-9957444-0-5 (Paperback)
ISBN: 979-8-9957444-1-2 (Hardcover)
ISBN: 979-8-9957444-2-9 (eBook)
Any references to historical events, real people, or real places are used fictitiously. Names, characters, and places are products of the author's imagination.
Printed in the United States of America.
First edition 2026

Prologue

Boston, 1836

Brenna Whitmore had just celebrated her twelfth year.

The house still carried the remnants of it, flowers not yet removed, ribbons trailing from banisters, the quiet echo of laughter that had only just faded. Julia lingered at her side, as she always did, the two of them unwilling to let the moment pass too quickly into something ordinary

"You mustn't forget," Brenna's father had said that morning, his tone unusually firm, "we are receiving a guest today of the utmost importance."

Julia had straightened immediately. Brenna had tried. They had both promised to be on their best behavior.

At a little past the noon hour, the guest arrived.

The sound of carriage wheels carried across the front drive, followed by the measured steps of a man who did not hesitate as he entered. Brenna stood just beyond the doorway, curiosity outweighing instruction, as it often did.

Her father greeted him briefly before ushering him toward the study. The door had nearly closed when Brenna caught a glimpse.

Dark hair. Tall. Young, far younger than she expected for a man her father would call *important*. And, to her twelve-year-old mind, the most handsome man she had ever seen.

The door shut.

Julia's hand closed around her sleeve at once. "Come," she whispered, tugging her back. "Before you are seen."

Brenna allowed herself one last glance toward the study door before she turned away. Julia led her outside, down the stone steps and into the gardens where the air was lighter and the rules far less strict.

They slipped easily into familiar patterns. Julia wandered toward the flower beds, already inspecting what needed tending, her fingers brushing leaves and petals with quiet care.

"You've neglected these," she murmured, though she smiled as she said it.

"I have not," Brenna replied, though she made no move to prove otherwise. Her attention had already drifted, beyond the gardens, beyond the estate, toward the distant line of the sea.

Julia loved the grounds. The order of them. The way everything could be shaped, tended, improved.

Brenna loved the opposite. The horizon. The unknown. The promise of something just beyond reach.

She leaned lightly against the low stone wall, her gaze fixed on the water in the distance. "Do you think he'll stay long?" she asked.

Julia glanced up. "The gentleman?"

"Yes."

Julia considered it. "If he is as important as your father says, I imagine he will not linger."

Brenna nodded faintly. Still watching the sea. She did not know why the thought disappointed her.

Behind them, the study door remained closed. And inside, decisions were being made that would follow her far beyond Boston, far beyond childhood, and into a future she could not yet imagine.

Chapter 1

The night before their departure, the lamps along the Boston wharf burned low and smokey, casting long shadows over the stacked trunks and coils of rope. Brenna stood with her cloak pulled tight, fingers worrying the folded letter hidden in her reticule. The letter that had arrived without warning and with a seal she had never seen before.

England, it declared. A betrothal long arranged. A name she did not know. A future decided in ink and wax.

In 1848, a Whitmore daughter was not simply born.

She was positioned.

Brenna Whitmore had understood this since childhood, though no one had ever said it plainly. The Whitmore fortune had been built on shipping, three generations of Atlantic trade routes, tobacco, textiles and investments so vast that even London bankers spoke the name with careful respect.

Her father once joked, "The ocean answers to us, Brenna."

But the oceans she learned, answered to no one.

Two years before her twenty-first birthday, everything changed. Her father died suddenly, a fever that turned swift. With no sons to inherit, the Whitmore shipping empire passed into trusteeship, until Brenna married.

And that is when the letters began. Anonymous at first. Then threatening.

The trustees dismissed them as extortion attempts. Competitors trying to frighten the family. But a month later, one of their smaller merchant vessels vanished between Charleston and Boston.

No wreckage. No survivors. No cargo recovered.

The message was clear. The Whitmore fortune was vulnerable. And so was its sole heiress.

The trustees did not say so outright, but fear altered them. Where once they had spoken of markets and tariffs, they now spoke in lowered tones behind closed doors. Insurance claims were filed but not aggressively pursued. Shipping routes were adjusted. Armed escorts were quietly added to certain voyages.

And Brenna noticed something else. Guards. Not announced. Not uniformed, but present. One lingered too long outside her carriage one afternoon. Another followed at a polite distance during her afternoon outing at Battery Park. When she asked her guardian about it, he smiled too quickly.

"Precaution, my dear."

Precaution meant threat. The missing vessel had not been the Whitmores' largest ship. It had not carried their most valuable cargo. But it had carried something far more important, confidence.

Investors grew restless. Competitors circled. Rumors spread that Whitmore ships were no longer safe passage. That perhaps the dynasty built on the Atlantic dominance had grown complacent.

They did not summon Brenna at first. They deliberated alone.

The proposal had not, in truth, been new. It had been revealed.

When the trustees finally summoned Brenna into her late fathers study, the room felt unchanged. There was the large mahogany desk with ledgers aligned and the faint scent of pipe tobacco lingering in the grain of wood. But the men waiting inside looked, uneasy.

"You are aware," her guardian began carefully, "that certain understandings were reached during your father's lifetime."

Brenna folded her gloved hands before her. "Understandings?"

"A betrothal," another trustee supplied, voice gentler than the word deserved.

The world did not tilt. It narrowed.

Brenna stood near the tall window of the study, her arms folded tightly as she stared out at the distant harbor beyond the glass. Ships rocked gently at their moorings below, sails furled and waiting for the next tide.

Behind her the two trustees exchanged a brief glance, clearly relieved their duty had finally been done.

"You mean to tell me," Brenna said slowly, turning back toward them, "that my future was arranged years ago, and I am only now hearing of it?"

Mr. Talbot cleared his throat. "It was your father's wish."

"My father's wishes seem to involve a great many decisions I was not consulted on."

The older trustee sighed patiently. "The arrangement was made when you were quite young, negotiated when you were twelve."

"Your father believed it would secure your future should anything happen to him," another trustee added.

Brenna's brows lifted. "And now something has."

"Yes." Mr. Talbot folded his hands together. "The gentleman in question resides in England."

Brenna stared at him. "England."

"You are expected there."

She laughed once, a short incredulous sound. "Expected."

The study door opened suddenly. Julia stepped inside, her cheeks flushed from having clearly hurried through the house. "I heard raised voices," she said brightly. "Should I be concerned or intrigued?"

Brenna turned toward her. "Both."

Julia looked between the trustees. "What have you done now?"

Mr. Talbot spoke carefully. "Miss Whitmore has just been informed of her father's... previous arrangement."

Julia blinked. "What arrangement?"

Brenna sighed. "I'm apparently betrothed."

Julia stared. "You're what?"

"Betrothed."

"To whom?"

"That," Brenna said dryly, "is precisely the question I asked."

Mr. Talbot cleared his throat again. "Lord Edmund Ashcombe of Hampshire."

The name hovered between them, foreign and binding all at once. Brenna searched her memory, faint recollections of an English gentleman visiting years ago, discussions behind closed doors.

Julia's eyes widened. "A lord?"

Brenna shot her a look. "That seems to excite you more than it does me." Turning back to the trustees she added quietly, "You never told me."

"It was not to burden you so young," her guardian replied. "The formal announcement was to be made when you came of age."

Her father had been many things, ambitious, visionary and shrewd in the matters of trade.

But he also believed in permanence. Contracts. Alliances. Legacies. He had secured his daughter's future the same way he secured shipping routes, decisively.

"The Ashcombe estate was struggling at the time," the trustee continued. "Your father extended considerable financial assistance. In return, the families entered into a binding agreement."

Binding. The word struck deeper than *marriage*.

"It ensured protection," her guardian pressed. "The Whitmore name tied to an English title strengthens both positions. Particularly now."

Now that ships vanished.

Now that investors whispered.

Now that Brenna's unmarried status made her fortune dangerously vulnerable. She rose and crossed to the window, looking out towards the distant Atlantic.

"You waited to tell me," she said.

"We waited until it became necessary."

And there it was. Not romance. Not courtship. Necessity. Her life had been charted like a trade route long before she even touched the helm. He had known for years while she had lived freely. The agreement had existed quietly for years, dormant, sealed in legal ink and sealed again in family pride. But only now, amid missing ships and rising threats, had the trustees chosen to enforce it.

If someone meant to destabilize Whitmore trade, eliminating the heiress before the marriage would shatter the alliance before it formed.

If someone meant to claim the holdings through chaos, removing her at sea would accomplish precisely that.

Julia stepped closer, lowering her voice. "You mean to say you're sailing to England to meet a mysterious nobleman your father promised you to years ago?"

"Yes."

Julia's smile spread slowly. "That sounds wonderfully adventurous."

Brenna looked unimpressed. "It sounds inconvenient."
Julia laughed. "Oh Brenna, imagine it." She gestured toward the window and the harbor beyond. "A voyage across the Atlantic. England. London society."

Brenna folded her arms. "A stranger who apparently believes I belong to him."

Julia waved that away. "You don't know that."

"The trustees seem quite confident."

Mr. Talbot spoke gently. "Miss Whitmore, the arrangements for your passage have already been made."

Brenna turned sharply. "You booked my passage before telling me?"

"It seemed… efficient."

Julia laughed again. "Well if nothing else, you must admit they are committed."

Brenna pinched the bridge of her nose. "Do I even have time to pack?"

"The ship sails with tomorrow's tide."

Julia clapped her hands softly. "Oh this is perfect."

Brenna stared at her. "For whom?"

"For us."

Brenna blinked. "Us?"

Julia grinned. "You're not crossing the ocean alone."

Brenna narrowed her eyes. "You're inviting yourself."

"Obviously."

Brenna sighed. "You realize we know absolutely nothing about this man."

Julia shrugged. "That's half the fun."

Brenna walked toward the desk, already resigned to the chaos unfolding around her. "We take only what we can carry," she said decisively. "The rest can follow later."

Julia nodded eagerly. "Minimal trunks then."

Brenna gave her a look. "Your definition of minimal worries me."

Julia was already moving toward the door. "Oh Brenna, we're sailing to England." She paused, her grin widening. "This is the beginning of an adventure."

The study was steeped in the faint memory of him. Leather. Ink. The quiet weight of decisions made behind closed doors.

Alone now, Brenna stood near his desk, the letter resting in her hands, though her eyes had long since drifted past the words.

Julia had gone to pack. She had insisted.

We'll need very little to start. The rest can follow later.

Julia hadn't argued.

Brenna traced the edge of the paper with her fingers, stopping where the signature lay. Her father's hand. Familiar. Certain.

"Why?" she whispered.

The room offered nothing in return. She let out a slow breath, her gaze lifting to the chair behind the desk, the one he had always occupied.

"You would have told me," she said quietly. "You told me everything."

"Didn't you?" Silence settled heavier.

Brenna stepped closer, resting her hand against the back of the chair as though it might anchor something that had already slipped away.

"I would have listened," she continued. "I would have tried to understand."

Her voice softened. "But this..." She glanced back down at the letter. "This you kept from me."

The realization stung more than she expected. Not the agreement. Not even the journey. But the absence of trust. Or perhaps, the absence of time.

Brenna closed her eyes briefly. "Was I truly meant to go to England," she said, barely above a breath, "and marry a man I have never met?"

No answer. Only the faint creak of the house settling around her. She opened her eyes again, steadier now.

"You must have had a reason."

Her fingers tightened slightly around the letter before she folded it once more, precise, controlled. "I wish you had told me."

Whatever answer she had hoped for, it would not come. Brenna set the letter down on the desk, her hand lingering there for just a moment.

Then she straightened. "England," she said softly into the empty room.

The word no longer sounded distant. Or impossible. Only inevitable.

Brenna looked once more toward the harbor. The ships below rocked gently in the morning light. She had the sudden, unsettling feeling that Julia might be right.

And though the study remained unchanged, everything else had already begun to shift. Just not in the way either of them expected.

Chapter 2

The carriage had barely come to a full stop before Julia was already reaching for the door."Do you see it?" she said, practically breathless. "Oh, Brenna, look at her!"

Brenna leaned just enough to glimpse past the window, the towering masts cutting into the gray Boston sky. "I see a great deal of rope and an alarming number of men shouting at one another."

Julia laughed as the footman opened the door. "It is magnificent."

"It is large," Brenna corrected, though she allowed Julia to pull her out onto the street.

The docks were alive with motion, crates being hauled, gulls crying overhead, sailors calling orders that seemed half chaos, half command. Brenna hesitated at the edge of it, her gloved hand tightening around her reticule.

Julia, meanwhile, turned in a slow circle, taking it all in. "We are really doing this."

"We are really being sent," Brenna said under her breath.

Julia shot her a look. "You make it sound like exile."

"It feels rather like it," Brenna replied. "England. A husband I have never met. A future decided in ink long before I had any say in it."

Julia's expression softened, but her excitement did not dim. If anything, it sharpened. "Then all the more reason to make the journey our own."

Brenna laughed despite herself, then sobered again. Her gaze drifted to the dark water, restless and whispering secrets. "I don't like this," she murmured. "Not the journey. Not...him."

Julia's teasing of her best friend softened. "You only found out about the betrothal yesterday. Anyone would feel unsettled."

"Unsettled?" Brenna huffed. "I am being delivered like a parcel. 'Fragile, handle with care.'"

"And yet," Julia said, nudging her shoulder, "you are still going."

Brenna opened her reticule and unfolded the letter again, smoothing it carefully for Julia to see. "It instructs me to present myself in London."

Julia looked up. "In London? I thought Lord Ashcombe resided in Hampshire."

"He does," Brenna said. "Which is precisely why I find this… curious."

Julia leaned closer. "And it doesn't explain why?"

"No." Brenna's fingers tightened slightly on the page. "Only that I am to meet him there."

Julia frowned. "That seems unnecessarily inconvenient for a man of his standing."

Brenna gave a faint, thoughtful breath. "Yes."

"Which suggests," Julia added, "it is not inconvenience at all."

"The trustees insist it must remain quiet. Apparently, since certain… interests have taken notice of my family they fear word of my name traveling ahead of me."

Julia's brows knit. "So that is why they insisted you sail under escort."

"And why they insisted on secrecy," Brenna replied. "If anyone aboard recognizes my name, it could reach the wrong ears. I would rather not arrive in Portsmouth already hunted."

Julia was silent for a moment, then her lips curved into a slow, wicked smile. "Well. That is easily solved."

Brenna frowned. "I'm afraid nothing about this feels easy."

"We swap," Julia said simply. "Names at least. You become me. I will be you. No one watches a Julia. It is a perfectly unremarkable name."

Brenna stared. "I watch you."

That's because your my best friend in the world." Julia tapped her chin. "Besides, if anyone comes sniffing about Brenna Whitmore, they will find me instead. And I, dear friend, am exceedingly good at being uninteresting when required."

"You are incapable of being uninteresting," Brenna said. "It is a moral failing."

Julia laughed. Still, who would suspect a harmless companion? "We will tell the captain I am the one bound for England to meet a future husband, and you are merely along for the adventure."

Brenna's stomach fluttered. Adventure, yes, but also risk. Yet the thought of her name hidden, safe, brought quiet comfort. "You would do that for me?"

"Of course," Julia said, as though it were obvious. "You would do the same. And think of the entertainment, watching you pretend to be thrilled about a man you have never met."

"I am not thrilled."

"You will have to pretend better than that."

Brenna sighed, then smiled. "What if I forget and answer to my own name?"

"Then I shall cough loudly or step on your foot," Julia said cheerfully. "Repeatedly, if needed."

Brenna let out a soft laugh, "I am sure you would."

Behind them, trunks bearing the Whitmore crest were being loaded with care bordering on reverence. Julia, radiant, composed, every inch the heiress, spoke with the ship's captain while a power hovered attentively at her elbow.

The performance had begun.

"Miss Whitmore," the captain said warmly to Julia. "We shall see you safely to England."

Julia dipped her chin with effortless poise. "I have every confidence, Captain."

Brenna watched with something between pride and melancholy. Julia wore wealth easily. If anyone were observing, they would see precisely what they expected, the rich American bride traveling to secure a transatlantic alliance.

A hand brushed Brenna's sleeve. "You are staring," Julia whispered without turning.

"I am admiring your transformation," Brenna replied softly.

"Admire less. We must not look conspiratorial."

Brenna lowered her gaze obediently. And that is when she saw him.

Not close. Not brazen. But watching.

He stood half-shadowed near a stack of cargo crates, dressed plainly in a dark coat too fine to belong to a dock laborer and too worn to be entirely fashionable. His hat brim angled low, but not low enough to conceal the deliberate stillness of him.

He was not waiting for someone. He was studying. Specifically, Julia. His gaze tracked her movements with quiet intensity. Not admiration. Not curiosity.

A chill crept along Brenna's spine. "Do not turn suddenly," she said quietly. "There is a man near the west cargo stacks. Dark coat. Watching you."

"Or watching the trunks with our crest emblazoned across them," Julia replied.

"Perhaps."

Julia's fan fluttered open, an elegant, practiced motion that shielded her mouth as she angled her face slightly."Does he look like a creditor or a suitor?"

"Worse."

Julia's hand paused.

"Purposeful," Brenna finished quietly.

For a fleeting moment, Julia's composure faltered. Then it smoothed again, seamless. "That," she murmured, "is precisely why we are doing this."

Brenna dared another glance. The man had not moved. But now his eyes shifted. From Julia, to her.

The smallest thing. A flicker of recognition, or perhaps confusion. As though something in the arrangement did not sit properly.

Their conversation was interrupted just then. The ship's bell rang out across the harbor, sharp and commanding. Passengers stirred. Porters lifted the last crates. The swell of departure rose like a tide of sound and motion. Sailors shouted, lines were hauled in, and the great vessel groaned as if eager to be free of land.

When Brenna looked again, the man was gone. Simply gone, swallowed by crowd and cargo. "He has vanished."

"Good," Julia replied. "Now let us go watch the land fade away.

Brenna's heart lifted despite herself. The open sea. The promise of something beyond the narrow lanes of home. "At least the journey itself will be ours," she said. "No letters. No expectations."

"Just salt air, terrible food, and the thrill of not knowing what comes next," Julia agreed. "And a mysterious betrothed waiting on the other side."

Brenna groaned. "Please do not remind me."

Julia linked her arm through Brenna's. "Come on then, Miss Julia," she teased softly. "Let's go meet your destiny."

Taking a steadying breath, Brenna stepped forward under a borrowed name, her true one tucked safely away.

She now lay awake in the narrow berth, listening to the quiet creak of timbers and the soft rhythm of water moving against the hull. Above them the rigging whispered in the night wind as the vessel slipped farther and farther from the American coast.

Across the small cabin Julia had already drifted off, utterly content with the adventure she had so eagerly embraced.

But Brenna remained awake, not imagining a husband, but calculating risk. Which is why Julia's suggestion did not feel like mischief. It felt like strategy.

At the time it had seemed clever, even amusing. A small strategy to avoid unwanted attention on the long voyage and keep Brenna's identity quiet until they reached England.
Just until they arrived. Just until everything was settled.
Brenna turned onto her side, staring toward the small round porthole where moonlight shimmered faintly on the water outside. The sea stretched endlessly around them now. She exhaled slowly, finally letting her eyes close.

It had only been a precaution. A simple idea shared between friends... unaware that the sea, already restless, was listening.

Over the first few days at sea, the ship had developed a personality, and it was a loud one. She groaned and creaked, complained most bitterly at night, and seemed to take particular pleasure in lurching just as one grew accustomed to walking in a straight line. Brenna, *Julia*, to the world aboard, had learned to keep one hand free at all times, either for the closest sturdy item that was bolted down or for Julia herself, who had a habit of stopping short to gawk at anything remotely interesting. Which, as it turned out, was nearly everything.

Julia Fairchild had grown up beside Brenna, not as a servant, not quite as equal. Julia's father had once captained a

Whitmore vessel before losing his life at sea. The Whitmores had taken her in after, raising her with education and polish, though never with fortune. Julia had never been aboard a ship before now. She was young when her father passed and she had little desire to actually sail, until now. Although her education did expand to the knowledge of the family business and the workings of ships, Julia never wanted to set foot on a ship until the idea to be Brenna's escort across the ocean presented itself. England. She had longed to visit. How could she say no. They were sisters in everything but blood.

Brenna stood at the rail as the wind pressed strands of dark auburn hair loose from the careful twist at the nape of her neck, softening the otherwise composed figure she presented to the world. Her features were fine rather than bold, thoughtful eyes the color of deep moss, a mouth inclined more toward seriousness than laughter.

Beside her, Julia leaned forward without restraint, elbows braced boldly on the polished rail. Where Brenna carried quiet gravity, Julia carried light. Her hair a warm honey-blonde, refused discipline entirely, curling around her temples despite every effort to tame it beneath her bonnet. Her eyes were brighter, quick and curious, missing little.

Julia looked radiant in a pale blue traveling gown that had once been Brenna's. She accepted well wishes with practiced grace.

"You must not enjoy this too much," Brenna murmured beside her.

Julia's smile did not falter. "If I am to marry a lord, even temporary, I shall enjoy every second."

Brenna's laughter came easier than it had in weeks.

"Did you hear that?" Julia whispered excitedly as they slowly walked along the starboard rail. "Mr. Boyd says England smells different from America. Less pine. More...history."

Brenna smiled. "I imagine history smells like damp stone and poor decisions."

Julia laughed. "You are going to fit in splendidly."

Brenna's smile deepened just slightly, a rare transformation that altered her entirely when it came. When she smiled fully, it softened the thoughtful restraint in her expression and revealed warmth that many mistook for fragility.

It was not fragility. It was control.

The second morning at sea brought with it a noticeable change.

Passengers had begun to find their footing, literally and otherwise, and the deck, once sparse, now carried small clusters of conversation and cautious curiosity.

Brenna stood at the rail, her gaze fixed on the horizon, while Julia, far less inclined toward quiet observation, had already taken in nearly everything there was to see.

"Well," Julia said, turning slowly as though assessing the entire ship at once, "if this is to be our world for the next month, I intend to know all of it."

Brenna smiled faintly. "I had no doubt."

"And you," Julia added, glancing at her, "intend to stand there and pretend you don't wish to climb into the rigging and ask questions of every man on board."

"I do not."

"You do," Julia said lightly. "You simply have more restraint than I."

Brenna's lips pressed together, but the hint of amusement remained.

Before she could respond, a voice interrupted. "Forgive me, have I come at a poor moment?"

Both women turned.

Mrs. Abernathy stood a few steps away, composed and observant, her presence suggesting she had already noted far more than she would openly admit.

"Not at all," Julia said easily, stepping forward before Brenna could answer. "We were just deciding how much of the ship we might be allowed to explore without causing offense."

Mrs. Abernathy's brow lifted faintly. "I would advise… less than you are likely considering."

Julia smiled. "Sound counsel, though I suspect I shall ignore at least part of it."

Brenna inclined her head. "Mrs. Abernathy, I believe."

The woman returned the gesture. "And you are?"

"Miss Whitmore," Julia said smoothly, gesturing to herself before motioning to Brenna. "And Miss Fairchild."

The exchange was seamless. Confident.

Mrs. Abernathy noticed. "A pleasure," she said, though her gaze lingered just a moment longer than necessary. "Your first crossing?"

"Yes," Julia replied. "Though I intend to behave as though it is not."

Mrs. Abernathy allowed herself the smallest hint of a smile. "A bold strategy."

"I find it improves most situations."

Brenna glanced at Julia, amusement flickering.

Mrs. Abernathy turned her attention back to the sea briefly before speaking again. "You'll find that the first few days settle into a rhythm," she said. "After that, one either grows accustomed or grows restless."

Julia's eyes lit slightly. "Restless sounds far more appealing."

"It often is," the woman replied.

A brief pause followed before Julia leaned in just slightly, lowering her voice, not enough to seem secretive, but enough to invite confidence. "And what, Mrs. Abernathy," she asked, "have you found most interesting about this particular voyage?"

The woman studied her. Not surprised, but intrigued.

"You ask as though you expect there to be something worth noting."

Julia's smile didn't falter. "I always expect there to be something worth noting."

Mrs. Abernathy's gaze sharpened just slightly. "Then you may find yourself rewarded."

Brenna glanced between them. "And what should we be watching for?"

The woman's attention shifted to her now. "Not everything is as predictable as it appears," she said.

Julia's interest deepened. "Well," she said lightly, "that alone makes the journey worthwhile."

Mrs. Abernathy inclined her head. "I thought you might think so." Then, with quiet composure, "I'll leave you to your observations."

And just as smoothly as she had arrived, she moved on.

Julia watched her go, then let out a small breath. "Well," she said, "she knows something."

Brenna's gaze remained thoughtful. "Perhaps."

Julia turned back to her, a spark of excitement in her expression. "This is already far more interesting than I expected."

Brenna glanced toward the horizon again. "I had a feeling it might be."

Julia smiled. "Then perhaps," she said, "we should pay very close attention."

They walked the length of the deck a short while later. As the day softened toward evening, the deck grew quieter.

Brenna stood once more at the rail, her thoughts no longer as settled as they had been that morning.

Julia joined her after a moment. "You're thinking aboutit again."

"It would appear so."

"You shouldn't."

"I know."

Then Julia's voice lowered. "You handled that well."

Brenna glanced at her. "What?"

"The name."

Brenna's expression stilled. "Miss Fairchild." The words felt heavier now than they had earlier.

"You didn't hesitate," Julia continued.

Brenna looked back out at the water. "I couldn't."

"That doesn't make it easier."

"No," she said quietly. "It doesn't."

Silence stretched between them.

"We can still change it," Julia said.

Brenna turned sharply. "No."

"It's not too late."

"Yes, it is."

Julia frowned. "We agreed…"

"We agreed to keep me safe," Brenna said, her voice steady but firm. "And this is how we do it."

Julia hesitated. "And if something goes wrong?"

Brenna held her gaze. "Then we face it together."

The sun dipped lower, the sky softening into gold and shadow as the ship carried them steadily forward.

Chapter 3

The deck was lively despite the long passage. Trunks had been unpacked and repacked twice over, friendships struck up over shared meals and mutual complaints. There were families returning home, English accents softened by years abroad. They spoke of green hills and familiar lanes with a fondness that made Brenna ache for places she had never seen. Others were like them, wide-eyed and restless, bound for England for the first time. There was eagerness to glimpse grand cities, ancient houses, and a future that felt far larger than the horizon behind them.

A young couple practiced polite bows and curtsies as though England itself might be watching. A merchant boasted of contacts in London taverns. A quiet woman spent hours sketching the sea, convinced the color changed daily.

Brenna listened to all of it, storing away any pertinent information that might be useful in the future.

"You are awfully quiet today," Julia said, glancing sideways at her. "Thinking about *him*?"

Brenna grimaced. "I was enjoying not thinking about him, actually. Thank you for ruining that."

Julia leaned closer, lowering her voice. "If he turns out dreadful, we will simply leave him behind and take up respectable lives as mysterious widows."

"We are neither married or widowed."

"Details," Julia waved off. "England will never know."

Their conversation was interrupted by raised voices near the foredeck. A small group of passengers had gathered around a sailor who was clearly enjoying himself far too much.

"I'm telling you," he said, voice thick with drama, "these waters aren't as tame as the maps suggest. Ships gone missing. Cargo vanished. Whole crews, poof!"

"A storm could do that," someone argued.

The sailor shook his head solemnly. "Storms don't leave clean cuts on rigging."

"Pirates?" A young man asked eagerly, as if hoping for it.

"Rogue pirates," the sailor corrected. "No flag. No mercy."

Brenna held her tongue. She wanted to drag the two of them away from the crowd that had gathered before Julia got anymore silly ideas in her head. Around them, rumors blossomed. Some scoffed, others leaned in. A woman crossed herself. A boy begged for more details. England bound gentleman argued over whether pirates still plagued these routes or if such tales were meant only to keep passengers obedient and below deck.

They had seen nothing but open water and endless sky. Still, Brenna felt a shiver trace her spine, though she told herself it was foolish. The sea had a way of making even the sensible feel small.

Julia noticed at once. "Hey," she said softly. "We're fine. If pirates do appear, I will distract them with charm and wit while you escape."

"You will do no such thing."

"Then we will both escape. Together. Very heroic."

Brenna smiled, reassured despite herself. The ship was alive with stories, secrets and possibilities. England no longer seemed like a distant idea but a place steadily drawing closer with every mile beneath them.

Pausing only a moment to watch the sun sinking slowly toward the horizon, she turned back to Julia and said with a small smile, "We should probably start changing for supper."

The long dining table in the ship's main cabin was crowded with travelers who had slowly grown comfortable enough to speak freely with one another. Plates rattled gently with the motion of the ship as the lantern above swung with each roll of the waves.

Julia leaned closer to Brenna as a man across from them launched enthusiastically into another story. "I believe Mr. Carver has told this story three times already," she whispered.

Brenna hid a smile behind her glass. "Yes, but tonight he has added a cannon."

Across the table Mr. Carver gestured dramatically with his fork. "I'm telling you, the pirates came out of the fog like ghosts. Black sails. Not a lantern among them. More common than people like to admit," he said gravely.

Another passenger chuckled. "Oh nonsense, Carver. If there were that many pirates the navy would have half the Channel on fire."

Carver shook his head stubbornly. "You laugh now. But ships vanish every year."

Julia's eyes sparkled. "I think it sounds thrilling."

Brenna shot her a look. "You would."

Julia leaned back in her chair. "Well imagine it. Adventure at sea."

"I imagined a quiet voyage," Brenna replied.

From the far end of the table an older gentleman spoke up. "My niece sailed this route two years ago. Said a rogue vessel chased them for nearly half a day."

The table quieted slightly. "Did they escape?" someone asked.

"They outran her."

Julia looked delighted. "See? I knew the sea would be interesting."

Brenna sighed. "Interesting is rarely a comforting word."

Another passenger, a young woman returning to England for the first time, leaned forward curiously. "And you two are traveling alone?"

Julia answered cheerfully. "Quite independently."

The woman blinked. "No husbands?"

Brenna smiled politely. "No husbands."

"That's rather brave," the woman said.

Julia raised her glass. "We prefer the word adventurous."

Laughter rippled around the table.

Mr. Carver pointed his fork toward Brenna. "And what awaits you in England, Miss…?"

Brenna hesitated only briefly. "Fairchild," she said smoothly.

Julia nearly smiled into her wine.

"Well Miss Fairchild," Carver declared, "I hope England proves less dangerous than the sea."

Julia glanced toward Brenna. "Where would be the fun in that?"

Brenna shook her head softly, though she could not help smiling.

After dinner, the two decided on a quick stroll along the deck to enjoy the evening air.

Outside the lantern light, the dark ocean stretched endlessly around them. Brenna rested her hands on the rail, watching the sun dip low, unaware that storms were already beginning to gather.

That night, the sea found its voice.

It began as a subtle unease, a restless shifting beneath the hull that only the most seasoned sailors seemed to notice. The laughter that had drifted across the deck after supper faded early, replaced by whispers and watchful glances toward the horizon.

Julia stood beside Brenna near the stern rail, arms wrapped loosely around herself. "It's colder than I expected," she said, glancing toward the horizon.

Brenna followed her gaze. "Yes, and the wind has shifted."

Julia looked at her curiously. "You say that as though it means something."

Brenna rested her hands along the rail, watching the distant line where sea met sky. "The air feels heavier."

Julia squinted at the gathering clouds. "It looks like weather."

"More than weather," Brenna replied.

The shipped rolled slightly beneath them, the timbers groaning softly as the wind strengthened.

Julia now had to raise her voice some for Brenna to hear her. "I'm going below with the others."

Brenna nodded, "I'll be right behind you." She watched as Julia and the other passengers, that had remained on deck, go below to ride out the storm in their cabins.

The wind, once playful, now tugged sharply at her cloak. Far above, the rigging creaked. She had never known the ocean to feel alive this way. Not merely vast or powerful, but aware. Loose strands of hair from her bonnet were teased by the wind. The sea stretched endlessly around the vessel, dark now that the setting sun had been replaced by a menacing sky. Lantern light from the quarter deck cast golden ribbons across the planks, swaying gently with the ships rhythm.

Brenna glanced toward the rigging where sailors had begun moving quickly along the deck.

A sharp command rang out from somewhere forward. "Reef the topsails!"

Another gust tore across the deck, snapping the sails overhead with a loud crack. Brenna felt the first drops of rain against her face.

The wind rose suddenly, howling through the rigging as the ship pitched harder against the waves.

"Best get below, miss."

The voice came gently, yet carried the firmness of experience. She turned to find one of the older deckhands, his weathered face drawn tight with concern.

"Yes, straight away," she replied.

The storm arrived without ceremony.

The wind shrieked as it tore through rigging and sail. There was something about the salt air that wrapped around her. Each breath tasted of promise and places unseen.

Below, the passengers had surrendered to comfort and caution. But Brenna could not bring herself to follow. Brenna clutched the narrow railing that led below deck, her skirts soaked and heavy, every pitch of the ship threatening to send her tumbling. Somewhere below, Julia waited, Julia, wearing Brenna's name as carefully as she wore her borrowed gown, playing the part of betrothed heiress with a bravery that made Brenna's heart ache with gratitude.

It is only precaution, Brenna reminded herself, as she had a hundred times since they exchanged identities since boarding. *A simple deception to keep unwanted eyes away*. No one on board knew that the quiet companion was the true Miss Whitmore, nor that the lively, laughing "Brenna" was merely her dearest friend.

A violent lurch threw her against the bulkhead. A massive wave slammed against the side of the ship.

She cried out, fingers groping for something solid as the ship heaved again, harder this time. Brenna lost her footing and slammed against the mast, breath knocked from her lungs.

Thunder cracked somewhere out over the water. The deck tilted violently. Brenna stumbled, catching herself against a coil of rope as water rushed across the planks around her boots. The sea had begun to spill over the sides now, driven by the growing storm.

She pushed herself upright and moved agin. Another crash of thunder split the sky. Above her, rigging snapped. A sailor screamed a warning. A deafening crack of wood split the air.

The mainmast split with a sound that seemed to tear the night itself in two. Brenna had time to only gasp before the deck vanished beneath her.

The sea swallowed her whole.

The shock stole her breath from her lungs before she could even fight it, driving pain through her as icy water dragged her under. Brenna broke the surface with a gasp, water surging around her as the storm swallowed every sound she tried to make.

She fought wildly, skirts tangling around her legs, darkness pressing in from all sides. Panic clawed at her thoughts.

"Help…!" The word vanished into the wind.

A wave crashed over her, dragging her under again, down, spinning, disoriented.

No. Her arms flailed, then found purpose, forcing her upward until she broke through again, coughing, choking, clinging to air that felt just as violent as the sea.

"Stay up," she gasped. "Stay…"

A shattered length of mast bobbed in the raging water, rough and splintered, but solid. Brenna lunged, fingers slipping once, twice, then catching. Brenna wrapped herself around it, arms burning, knuckles white as waves battered her again and again. Salt stung her eyes.

She clung to it, pressing against the soaked timber as another wave slammed into her.

"Hold," she whispered, her voice raw. "Just hold..."

The ship that had carried her fate vanished into the storm, its lanterns swallowed by distance and darkness.

The sea stretched endlessly around her, rising and falling in dark, shifting walls.

"Don't let go," she said, though her grip already trembled. "Don't..."

Another wave tore at her, nearly wrenching the mast from her grip. Nails scraping, splinters bit into her palms. Her strength vanishing along with her clarity of thought.

Arms shaking with effort. Her breath came uneven now.

The cold had begun to settle deeper, seeping into her limbs, dulling them. "No," she murmured. "No, not yet."

Her fingers slipped again. This time, it took more effort to tighten them. More than it should have.

"Stay awake," she said, though her voice sounded distant now, even to herself. "Stay..."

The storm roared on, but it felt farther away.

The sharp edges of it softening into something... quieter.

Too quiet. Brenna's head dipped forward, her cheek scrapping the splintered wood. Darkness edged in at the corners of her vision.

A shape loomed through the rain, a ship, its lanterns swinging wildly, sails torn but intact, riding the waves with stubborn resolve.

Then, voices. Faint.

Shouting.

"...there!"

"...starboard!"

"Hold her!"

Brenna blinked, her vision blurring, struggling to focus on shapes that didn’t quite form.

Hands reached for her, someone was there. Strong arms

hauled her from the sea, pain flaring as her “Take her body left the water in!” A man’s voice, closer now. Urgent. Strong.

Brenna felt something grip her, firm, unyielding, pulling her from the water.

She tried to hold on to the mast, but her fingers no longer obeyed.

“Got her!”

The world lurched as she was dragged free, her body heavy, unresponsive as the sea released her.

For a moment, she was suspended between water and air, then hauled upward. Rough. Unsteady.

Voices, accented, all around her now.

“Careful!”

“Get her aboard!”

“She’s slipping!”

A stronger grip caught her under the arms, lifting, pulling, then…solid. Hard beneath her. A deck.

Brenna collapsed against it, the world spinning wildly as sound rushed back in all at once.

“Easy, easy.”

“She’s barely conscious.”

“Turn her!”

Hands moved her, turning her slightly as she coughed weakly, water leaving her lungs in shallow, broken breaths.

Brenna tried to open her eyes, but everything blurred.

A man’s voice, closer than the others now.

Steady.

“You’re safe,” he said.

The words barely reached her.

But something in them, cut through. Safe.

"Get her below, quickly!"

Her fingers twitched weakly against the deck. Then stilled. And the darkness, finally took her.

Chapter 4

The storm had been stalking them since dusk. Callum Hawthorne felt it in the deck beneath his boots long before the first shout came down from the rigging. The sea had gone unnaturally smooth. The wind, when it came, did so in sharp, testing breaths, like a predator deciding where to strike.

"She's turning," Elias Reed said. "Pressure dropped hard in the last half hour."

"How bad?" Hawthorne asked.

Reed glanced at the sails, already straining faintly. "Bad enough to swallow smaller ships whole."

"Reef the topsails," he ordered calmly, though his eyes never left the darkening horizon. "Double the lines. She'll hit us hard."

The *Hawthorne* looked, to any casual eye, like a respectable trades vessel. Her hull dark and unremarkable, her hold stacked with crates stamped with the seals of sugar, cloth and rum. Even her name was common enough to be forgettable.

That was the point.

Below deck, the true nature of the ship lay hidden beneath false panels and sealed bulkheads. Cannon ports were disguised as storage hatches, weapons wrapped in oilcloth, ledgers written in a cipher only six men aboard could read. They were pirates by rumor, rogues only by reputation.

In truth, they hunted pirates.

"Word travels faster than ships these days," muttered Reed, Hawthorne's first mate, bracing himself as the deck pitched. "Boston to Bristol all whispering about rogue vessels in these waters."

Hawthorne's mouth curved faintly. "And what do you think?"

"I think storms make excellent cover," Reed's gaze met Hawthorn's eyes directly. Silence passed between them, heavy, deliberate.

"There are whispers along the Bermudan lanes," Reed continued. "The *Black Mercy* was sighted two days ago.

Hawthorne's gaze sharpened. "Confirmed?"

"Two merchant captains described the same hull. Fast. Low. Flying no colors."

The wind rose in a sudden howl, ripping the words from Hawthorne's mouth. Rain followed, hard, stinging sheets that turned the deck slick and treacherous. A warning growl of thunder echoed overhead. "Close the gun deck and secure the powder. No unnecessary movement once the storm hits."

Reed's brow lifted slightly. "You're letting them slip?"

"We are traders tonight."

"And if the *Black Mercy* escapes again?"

Hawthorne's eyes returned to the darkening sea. "Then we decide," he said quietly, "whether we are merchants…"

Thunder cracked, closer now.

"…or something else." Hawthorne remained where he stood, braced easily against the tilt of the deck. Water plastered his dark coat to his frame, but he did not flinch.

Reed returned, voice lower now beneath the rising wind. "If they are out there," he said, "they'll be watching the trade lanes."

"Let them," Hawthorne replied.

"And if they mistake us for prey?"

A flicker, sharp and almost dangerous, crossed Hawthorne's expression. "Then they will learn differently."

Reed leaned closer, his voice barely audible over the roar. "You can't chase shadows forever, Hawthorne."

Hawthorne's gaze never left the blackening sea. "I don't hunt shadows," he replied. Lightning illuminated his face starkly. "I hunt men."

The wind shifted first. Subtle, then sharp.

Hawthorne felt it before he saw it, his gaze already fixed on the darkening horizon as the sea began to turn.

"That's not a passing squall," Reed said, stepping up beside him.

"No," Hawthorne replied. "It's building."

The wind tore harder through the rigging, snapping the sails with a force that made the mast groan in protest.

"Reef the topsails…now!" Hawthorne's voice cut sharply across the deck.

The men were already moving, hauling lines, fighting the canvas as it bucked violently above them.

"We're trying, Captain!" one of them shouted down. "The wind's against us!"

Another gust slammed into the ship, twisting the sail just as they pulled.

Hawthorne stepped forward, gripping the rail, his voice rising over the storm. "Then fight it! You've handled worse than this, move!"

"We are, sir!" came the strained reply. "She won't give!"

The sail snapped again, the line jerking hard in their hands.

Reed braced beside him, shaking his head. "She's not making it easy."

Hawthorne's gaze stayed fixed upward. "She doesn't need to," he said. "We do."

Another wave crashed over the bow, the ship pitching hard beneath them as the men in the rigging struggled to bring the sail under control.

"Keep at it!" Hawthorne called. "I want those topsails reefed before this storm takes them from us!"

Reed braced a hand against the rail, scanning the water. "We're losing light faster than we should."

Hawthorne didn't look away from the horizon. "We're losing more than that."

"The *Mercy* would use this," Reed said.

Hawthorne's jaw tightened. "Yes."

"Storm rolls in, visibility drops."

"And no one questions a ship that disappears inside it."

Reed glanced at him. "You still think they're close."

"I know they are."

The wind howled louder, driving spray across the deck as the first heavy swell struck the hull.

"Hard to track anything in this," Reed muttered. Hawthorne's gaze sharpened. "Not impossible." A sailor rushed past, hauling a line tight. "Wind's turning, Captain!" "I can see that," Hawthorne said. "Hold her steady, don't fight it!"

The ship pitched again, more violently this time.

Reed steadied himself. "If the Mercy's out there, she'll be running with it."

"Then we follow."

"In this?"

Hawthorne finally looked at him. "Yes."

Reed let out a breath. "You're either very certain... or very reckless."

Hawthorne's voice lowered. "Both."

Another wave crashed over the bow, sending water surging across the deck. This was no ordinary storm.

"Something's amiss," the lookout shouted from above. "Lights, off the port bow!" Hawthorne turned sharply. Through the curtain of rain, a larger ship reeled into view. Her lanterns swinging wildly, sails fighting wind they could not tame.

A passenger vessel.

"Confound it," Hawthorne breathed. "She's too close to the shoals."

"Man overboard!" The shout from the other ship was faint but the winds carried it over clearly.

Hawthorne's heart hammered once, hard. "To the rails! Now!"

Another wave struck, higher than the last, and the distant ship lurched violently. Even from here Hawthorne could hear the splintering wood. "Bring us about," he ordered. "Full sail. We can't leave her."

Reed's hesitation was brief, but not brief enough to escape the captain's eye.

Hawthorne felt the vessel surge forward, cutting through the chaos with practiced precision. This was what separated them from the monsters they hunted. They took orders, yes, but they chose their mercy.

A cry carried across the water, terrified, unmistakably human.

Cutting through the storm at an angle no merchant vessel would dare attempt. Lantern light swung high along its stern. The hull was darker than pitch. Its lines leaner. Faster.

The bell rang sharp over the wind.

"Hard to starboard!" A voice commanded from somewhere unseen. "She's off the port bow!"

Through sheets of rain he saw her, a dark shape tossed violently between waves, clinging desperately to a broken length of mast. She disappeared, reappeared, swallowed again by black water.

No hesitation.

Hawthorne shrugged off his coat and vaulted the rail.

The sea was ice and fury, dragging him like hands. He fought through it with grim focus, every muscle burning, every breath a battle. When he reached her she was barely conscious. "I've got you," she heard. Delicate fingers locked white-knuckled around the wood. Her lips starting to turn blue, eyes unfocused but stubbornly open. Her body shook uncontrollably now, not from fear, but from cold that bit into bone.

"Easy," he murmured, voice rough but steady. "Stay with me." His arm tightened around her as though defying the ocean itself.

"Hold steady!" A commanding voice cut through the storm. Controlled. Decisive. "Wait for the rise- now!"

A coil of rope arced through the rain.

She made a faint sound as he secured her and signaled the crew. Strong arms hauled them both from the sea, dumping them hard onto the deck of the *Hawthorne* as thunder split the sky.

Hawthorne coughed seawater and rolled to his knees, turning immediately to her.

She lay still for a terrifying moment, hair plastered to her face, clothes heavy with water, chest barely rising. She sputtered suddenly, gasping, drawing a shuddering breath as life rushed back into her lungs.

Hawthorne knelt over her assessing for injuries, consciousness, breathing, not with indifference, but with ruthless efficiency. "You're safe," he said quietly, for her alone. "I swear it."

Brenna's eyes fluttered open, dark and utterly arresting, even through exhaustion and fear. She looked at him, tried to speak, but darkness was claiming her as the storm pounded on.

As he rose, issuing quiet instructions to the first mate, "Keep us off the trade lanes. No lights once the storm breaks," Brenna drifted into unconsciousness. She did not see the way he lingered one heartbeat longer than necessary. She did not see his hand tighten at his side.

Chapter 5

Julia did not scream when the cry went up.

She did not rush the deck or demand answers. She stood frozen in the narrow passageway, one hand braced against the wall as the ship lurched violently beneath her, the words echoing again and again in her mind.

Man overboard.

No-*woman*

She knew before anyone said the name. Brenna.

The storm raged relentlessly. Rain pounded the deck above. Somewhere, sailors shouted orders, boots pounding, ropes whipping loose. Julia's breath became shallow, her chest tight as if something vital had been torn away.

They would not find her.

Julia knew the sea too well, not by experience, but by instinct. The Atlantic in a storm did not give back what it claimed.

Still, she climbed.

Her skirts tangled around her legs as she forced herself up onto the deck, salt and rain lashing her face. Lantern light swung wildly, illuminating terror and chaos. A sailor caught her arm, shouting something she could not hear, but she shook him off and stumbled toward the rail.

Only darkness greeted her.

The sea roared, swallowing every hope she flung into it. There was no sign of Brenna. No pale hand raised in defiance, no scrap of cloth, no miracle. Julia's knees buckled.

A crewman seized her about the waist just as another wave crashed across the deck. "Miss Whitmore!" The man cried. "You must go below, this is no place.."

Miss Whitmore.

The name struck like a blade.

Julia nodded mutely and allowed herself to be guided away, every step an act of betrayal. She wore Brenna's name still, even now.

Below deck, the air was thick with fear and damp wool. Someone pressed a blanket into Julia's hands. Someone else murmured prayers. None of it reached her. Her world had narrowed to a single, unbearable truth. I told her it would be safe, Julia thought, the guilt curling tight around her heart. I told her the storm would pass.

It was her idea, the exchange of identities. Her clever solution, her careful reasoning. No one would trouble the wealthy betrothed, she'd said. No one would notice the companion. Brenna had hesitated only a moment before agreeing, trusting Julia as she always had.

And now Brenna was gone.

Passengers crowded the narrow space, some weeping openly. Water seeped through seams in the hull.

"What's happened?" A woman cried, clutching a small child to her chest.

"The mast is gone!" A man answered. "We've lost the mainmast!"

"Are we sinking?"

"No, no, she'll hold."

"She's in the water!" Julia gasped. "She fell… the mast broke.. she…"

The captain burst down the companionway, hat gone, coat soaked. "Quiet!" He ordered. "All of you!"

The passengers fell silent instantly.

"Has she been sighted?" Julia demanded, stepping forward.

The captain's eyes found her, recognizing the woman he believed to be Miss Whitmore. "We're turning as best we can," he said tightly. "But we can not hold position long in this wind."

"You must!" She cried. "She's alive!"

"Miss, " he began.

The ship shuddered again, timbers groaning in protest.

A sailor rushed down from above. "Sir! The fore-rigging's gone loose! We'll lose more if we don't secure it."

The captain cursed under his breath.

"Throw lanterns!" Julia shouted suddenly. "Signal lights. She'll see them."

"We've thrown two already the sailor replied. "They're snuffed by the rain."

Another crash of thunder shook the hull. Water sloshed across the floorboards. The passengers began crying again.

Julia pressed both hands to her mouth, fighting for breath.

Above them, shouts continued. Ropes snapping. Orders shouted out against the wind.

"How long?" She demanded.

The captain hesitated. "Ten minutes," he said. "Perhaps less. We can not risk capsizing."

Ten minutes. The number hollowed her chest. "She cannot... she cannot simply vanish." Julia choked. "She is not gone. She is not."

But doubt had begun to creep in. Time stretched unbearably.

At last, the captain returned below, face grim.

"We've lost site," he said.

Julia stared at him. "No."

"We can not hold course in this storm."

A woman began sobbing. The ship lurched again, weaker now, crippled without its mast.

Julia pressed herself against the bulkhead, breath coming sharp and uneven.

Hours passed before the storm relented. Dawn crept in and revealed a battered ship and a crew hollow-eyed with loss. The captain spoke quietly with the officers. Julia did not need to hear the words to know their meaning.

No body was found.

When the captain finally approached her, his expression was grave, respectful. "Miss Whitmore," he said gently, "I am deeply sorry. We did all we could."

Julia inclined her head, because it was expected. Because grief, when witnessed, must be properly shaped. But inside her, something broke open.

That night, alone in the small cabin she and Brenna had shared, Julia pressed her face into Brenna's pillow and wept without restraint. She whispered apologies into the dark, confessions Brenna would never hear.

"I should have been the one," she said hoarsely. "It was my name they were watching. My risk, not yours."

England waited ahead, indifferent to her sorrow. A man awaited his bride, Brenna Whitmore, and Julia alone knew the cruel truth. She would arrive bearing another woman's name and carrying a grief so heavy it threatened to sink her just as surely as the sea had taken her dearest friend.

In the clear light of day, the ship looked… altered. Not broken, but no longer untouched.

Julia stepped onto the deck slowly, her gaze moving over it in silence. One section of the railing had been torn clean away, wood splintered outward where the sea had forced its way through. The gap opened directly to the water below, too close, too real.

She stopped there. Just for a moment. Then forced herself to move on.

What remained of the mainmast stood jagged where it had snapped, its upper length gone, the break rough and uneven. Men had already set to work around it, ropes looped and secured, voices rising as they hauled, measured, argued over what could be salvaged.

"Hold it there!"

"It won't take the weight…!"

"Then reinforce it!"

The sharp rhythm of hammer against wood carried across the deck, steady, relentless. Nearby, lengths of canvas had been stretched out and pinned, sailors bent over them, stitching through torn sail with thick thread, their hands moving quickly despite the damage.

Julia watched them. Watched how nothing stopped. Nothing paused. As though the storm had passed, and that was enough.

Movement at the far side of the deck drew her attention. Passengers. A small cluster of them.

Not gathered in conversation, but lingering, slower than before, careful in their steps.

One woman sat with her arm bound in a sling, her face pale but composed as another passenger adjusted the fabric at her shoulder.

"I told you not to brace against it."

"And I told you I didn't see it coming."

A strained laugh.

Nearby, an older gentleman was being guided carefully along the deck, his steps uneven. "Easy now, steady."

"I am steady," he insisted, though he leaned heavily on the man beside him. Another sat wrapped in a blanket despite the mild morning, her gaze distant, unfocused.

Julia watched them. A few injuries. That was what would be said. Manageable. Recoverable.

Her gaze shifted again. A coil of rope lay near the base of the mast, one of the sailors working it through his hands, looping, pulling, tightening with practiced ease despite the motion of the ship.

Julia stilled. Watched. He tied it once, quickly, then again, adjusting the tension with a small, precise movement before securing it. Clean. Efficient. Brenna would have noticed that.

Would have stepped closer, asking questions before the man had even finished. Show me that again. Julia could see it… the way Brenna's hands would have followed, determined, patient until she had mastered it.

"She would've liked that one," Julia murmured.

The words barely carried. The sailor glanced up, not quite catching it. "Miss?"

Julia shook her head slightly. "Nothing." He returned to his work without question.

Further along the deck, more damage revealed itself. A section of rigging hung loose where it had been cut free, lines coiled hastily to keep them from dragging. One of the smaller spars had splintered, now laid aside, already being measured for replacement.

Everywhere, evidence of what the ship had endured.

Julia moved carefully now, more aware of where she stepped, not out of fear, but because the ship itself demanded it.

"You should mind your footing."

She glanced up. An older sailor stood nearby, his tone practical rather than warning. "I am," she said.

He followed her gaze briefly toward the broken rail. "We were fortunate."

Julia's eyes remained fixed. "Yes."

The word came easily. Too easily. The sailor shifted his weight. "Passengers took a harder hit than most," he added. "Not used to moving with it."

Julia glanced back toward the cluster behind her. "I saw."

"Nothing they won't mend from," he said. "Given time."

Julia inclined her head faintly. "I'm sure they will."

The sound of more hammering echoed across the deck, sharp and constant. Julia watched it all. The work. The movement. The quiet determination in it.

And beneath it, the absence of what had been lost. Her gaze drifted once more to the rope. To the knot tied cleanly, holding fast against the strain. Brenna would have tested it. Pulled at it. Proven it.

Then smiled when it held. Julia exhaled slowly. The sea stretched out beyond the damaged rail, calm now, almost indifferent. As though it had taken what it wanted, and moved on.

Her hand rested lightly against the remaining wood. "They'll fix it," she said quietly. The mast. The sails. The ship. All of it.

Julia's gaze steadied, her shoulders drawing back just slightly. Because standing still, waiting, was not something she had ever done well. And she would not begin now. Her fingers curled once against the rail, then released.

"They move forward," she murmured. The crew. The ship. The journey.

Everything around her already continuing.

Julia turned from the broken edge at last. Not because it no longer mattered, but because she understood something she hadn't before. If she remained there, she would remain with it. And she refused to.

"Very well," she said under her breath, quieter now, but steadier. Then she stepped away, choosing, for the first time since the storm, to go forward with it.

Chapter 6

Brenna surfaced to consciousness as though rising through water once more, slowly, painfully, every sense dulled and aching. The first thing she felt was warmth. Not the sharp, unforgiving cold of the sea, but a steady heat that wrapped around her like a held breath finally released.

The second was motion. A gentle sway, nothing like the violent heaving that had cast her into the ocean.

She opened her eyes. Above her stretched a low wooden ceiling, dark beams cut with age and soot. A lantern burned nearby, its light soft and amber, rocking slightly. The air smelled of salt and something unfamiliar, tar perhaps, and spice.

Not her ship.

Panic surged, swiftly, and she tried to sit up at once. Pain flared through her limbs, a sharp protest that forced a cry from her throat.

"Easy now."

The voice was male, calm, measured, carrying an accent she could not immediately place. English, she realized distantly. Very English.

A man moved into her line of sight, his figure momentarily blurred as her vision swam. He set a steadying hand on her shoulder, firm but careful, as though she might shatter beneath his touch.

"You've been through quite enough," he said. "You are safe."

Safe.

The word did not belong in her mind. She had not allowed herself to imagine such a thing.

"I..." Her throat was raw, each syllable scraping. She swallowed and tried again. "Where am I?"

"Aboard the *Hawthorne*," he replied as he sat in the chair that had been placed near her. "Three days out from the storm."

"Three..." Her voice broke. "And you are?"

A pause, brief, deliberate. "Callum Hawthorne."

He saw the way she tested the name internally. "You pulled me from the water," she said.

"Yes."

Memory returned in fragments, the crack of wood, the cold, Julia. Her breath hitched as she grasped at the edges of the narrow bunk.

"My friend," she whispered. "The ship I was on..."

"Lost to the storm," he said gently. "Or scattered, at least. We sighted wreckage, but no other survivors."

The words struck harder than any wave. Julia.

Brenna turned her face away, tears burning hot against her eyes. Julia would believe her dead. Julia would arrive in England facing a future meant for someone else. When she finally gathered the strength to speak again, her voice was barely more than breath. "They will think I drowned."

The man hesitated. "They will," he said truthfully.

When her gaze met his, something sharpened in his expression, not surprise, not relief. Assessment.

She looked at him then, really looked. His eyes were steady and unblinking, as though nothing within this room escaped notice. He was perhaps a few years older than herself, dark haired, his expression open but sharp with intelligence. He was broad shouldered, the cut of his dark coat unmistakably fine beneath weathering and salt stains. His shirt collar had been loosened, revealing a strong throat marked by a pale scar that disappeared beneath linen. The mark was not recent, nor was it decorative.

This was not a man who merely commanded from distance. He acted.

"And who is it that they will think drowned?" Callum inquired.

Her pulse quickened. Name. The simplest answer in the world. "My name," Brenna paused. If she spoke *Brenna Whitmore*, she would carry with it wealth, betrothal, threat, everything that had forced her into secrecy in the first place.

He watched her closely now. Not impatient, not suspicious, but expectant.

"My name," she said carefully, "is Julia Fairchild."

Something in his gaze sharpened, as though he heard more in the pause than the words themselves. "Miss Fairchild," he repeated.

"You were traveling with family?" He asked.

"No." Brenna hesitated, then added, "Yes, my best friend who is like a sister to me."

"You were traveling to England, alone?" His gaze did not leave her face. "For what business would two young women travel all the way to England, unaccompanied by male escort?"

She hesitated only half a heartbeat, "Obligation."

For a moment, something almost like admiration flickered in his eyes. "You are stronger than you appear, Miss Fairchild."

He rose then and the cabin seemed smaller for it. "I will have food brought," he said. "You will need strength."

"Captain Hawthorne," she started, but he stopped her.

He paused at the door. "Hawthorne will do," then he left before she could finish.

Brenna lay back against the pillow, staring at the lantern's wavering flame. She had given him Julia's name and he had accepted it. But she had the distinct sense that Callum

Hawthorne was not a man who accepted anything without question.

A few minutes later, a young crewman arrived carrying a tray of simple broth, warm bread and a small cup of watered brandy. “Captain’s orders, miss,” the boy said shyly as he placed it in the now empty chair next to her.

When the door closed again, Brenna pushed herself upright carefully and lifted the cup. The broth was warm and inviting.

Brenna sat propped against the narrow pillows, the small tray balanced carefully across her lap. Her hands trembled slightly, not from cold now, but exhaustion that seemed woven into her bones.

The broth had cooled by the time she managed more than a few spoonfuls. A soft knock sounded before the door opened again.

A tall man stepped inside, ducking slightly beneath the low beam as he entered. His sharp gray eyes flicked first to Brenna, quickly assessing that she was awake. Then a faint grin tugged at the corner of his mouth. “Ah,” he said easily, “so the sea hasn’t managed to claim you after all.”

He stepped further into the cabin, bracing himself lightly against the sway of the ship. “Elias Reed,” he added with a small nod. “First mate of this particular vessel, and the unfortunate man tasked with keeping Captain Hawthorne from doing anything overly heroic.”

“You’ve eaten?” He asked bluntly.

“Some,” she replied.

“That will have to do for now.” He crossed the cabin and adjusted the lantern wick slightly lower. His manner was not unkind, simply efficient. “The captain said nothing heavy,” he added. “You’ll not argue with him, I expect.”

“Does anyone?” She asked.

Reed's mouth twitched faintly. "Not often."

She studied him carefully. "He remained three days?" She asked

Reed paused just long enough to make the answer deliberate. "Aye."

"Why?"

"He doesn't leave matters unfinished."

"That is not what I meant."

Reeds gaze sharpened briefly, but he did not answer further. Instead, he nodded once toward the tray. "Eat what you can. We sail steady now."

He turned toward the door. "Mr Reed," she called softly.

He paused. "If you sight…anything," she said carefully, "from my ship…"

He held her eyes. "You'll be told." The door closed quietly behind him.

The cabin fell still again. Brenna lifted another spoonful of broth, swallowing slowly. Julia would have made a joke by now. Julia would have complained about the lack of proper tea. Julia would have teased her relentlessly for nearly drowning before ever meeting her intended.

A faint laugh escaped her. "You would hate this cabin," she murmured into the quiet.

The lantern flame wavered as the ship shifted gently. Tears pricked her eyes before she could stop them. "We were sufficient to ourselves," she said softly to the empty room. "We did not need anyone."

The words felt hollow now. The ship creaked above her, steady and alive. Callum Hawthorne had turned his vessel in a storm for a stranger. He had not asked her wealth, not demanded explanation, he had simply chosen.

The thought unsettled her more than it should. She lay back slowly, the tray now on the floor beside her, drawing the blankets higher around her shoulders. Men like him did not stake ships on simple impulses. Her eyes grew heavy.

As sleep crept closer, memories blurred, the docks, Julia's laughter, the mast splitting, the sea swallowing everything.

And then, strong hands, a voice cutting through the storm. *Stay with me.*

She turned slightly in the bed, exhaustion claiming her at last. "Julia," she whispered, unsure whether she spoke to herself or to the dark.

Above deck, the wind hummed softly along the sails. Below, Brenna drifted into sleep, carrying grief in one hand, and something far more dangerous beginning to take root in the other.

The first time Brenna insisted upon climbing the ladder to the upper deck, the effort left her breathless. The ship no longer felt like an enemy beneath her feet, but it had not yet become steady ground. Each shift of weight sent a faint protest through her bruised ribs.

Brenna learned quickly that the *Hawthorne* was not like her previous vessel. The crew moved with purpose, disciplined but not cruel. They treated her with cautious respect, as though uncertain what to make of the lone survivor.

Hawthorne watched her from the quarterdeck, expression unreadable. He saw her the moment she stepped onto the deck. And for a fraction of a second, he forgot to breathe.

She wore what clothing the ship had to spare. What remained of her own had been mostly cut away the night she was brought aboard, salt-stiffened silk and ruined lace deemed useless against fever and cold.

A loose linen shirt, far too large, softened her frame. The sleeves had been rolled several times at her wrists. A woolen waistcoat sat slightly askew across her ribs, emphasizing the narrowness of her shoulders. Her skirts had been replaced by plain, mended trousers tied securely at the waist and tucked into thick wool socks. Her hair had been braided simply and tied back with a strip of cloth.

She looked…real. And that unsettled him.

Reed followed his gaze. "She's taken to ship wear quite nicely," the first mate observed

"She required something warm." His expression went still.

Below them, she moved carefully but with growing confidence, adjusting to the sway. When the wind caught her shirt, she pressed one palm to the fabric at her waist, laughing quietly at herself. The sound carried. It was not polished nor restrained, it was free.

A few crewmen pretended not to stare. One failed. The young deckhand, Thomas she had learned, flushed crimson when she caught his gaze. He quickly busied himself with coiling rope.

"You've my best shirt on, miss," he muttered, not quite meeting her eyes.

"It serves me well," she replied gently. "It's precisely what I require." A smile bloomed across her face, unguarded, transforming. It softened the faint hollowness beneath her eyes, brought color rushing into her cheeks, and lit her features from within.

The boy look absurdly pleased by that.

The crew went still. A coil of rope slipped unnoticed from one sailor's hand. Another stood mid-knot, staring as though he had witnessed something unnatural. They were men accustomed to weathered faces and hard expressions, to storms, to discipline, to silence broken only by command.

They were not accustomed to that.

Reed paused mid-stride, one brow lifting. "Would you look at that," he muttered under his breath.

Hawthorne did not move. He had seen her pale and half-drowned. Had watched her breathe between worlds. He had not seen this. That smile did something dangerous.

The wind tugged her braid loose again and she caught it, laughing softly as she tried to tame it.

One of the older sailors cleared his throat gruffly. "Best secure that knot miss" he called awkwardly. "Sea likes to steal what's loose."

"Then it will have to try harder," she replied.

A ripple of laughter moved through the crew. Hawthorne felt the shift immediately. Morale, subtle and invisible, lifting. The sea had taken much. But not this.

He realized with a clarity that unsettled him... She did not merely survive storms. She disrupted them. And the crew, gawking and grinning like boys, were already under her quiet command. He watched that exchange from the quarterdeck, expression unreadable.

Brenna moved toward the rail, aware of the odd sensation of trousers against her legs as the ship rolled beneath her. The practical clothing allowed for more free movement, steadier footing. She gripped the wood briefly, bracing herself, as the ship rolled gently. Her knuckles whitened for half a heartbeat, then relaxed.

She adjusted. Adapted. She did not retreat.

Reed followed Hawthorne's line of sight. "She's stubborn," the first mate observed.

"Yes."

"And you admire that."

Hawthorne's features sharpened slightly. "I respect survival."

He descended from his post without announcing his intent. He approached slowly, stopping within respectful distance.

"You've acquired new attire," he said.

She glanced down at herself. "I did not wish to waste another gown, " she replied.

His gaze lingered, not improperly, but thoughtfully. Taking in the borrowed sleeves, the rolled cuffs, the slight looseness at her shoulders. "It suits you," he said.

Her brow lifted. "I doubt that."

"You move more steadily."

"That is because I no longer risk tripping over propriety."

A faint shift at the corner of his mouth. "The boy appears honored."

"Thomas?" She asked lightly. "He believes I shall return it pressed."

"You intend to?"

"I intend to return it clean."

That answer pleased him more than it should have.

The wind shifted, stronger now. She swayed faintly, just enough that instinct pulled him half step closer.

Hawthorne's gaze moved briefly over her hands, then to the faint marks along her cheek "The worst of it seems to be healing," he said evenly. "The cuts were shallow, painful, but not lasting."

Brenna glanced down at her palms, the skin still tender where it had been torn. "They don't feel shallow."

"No," he replied. "They rarely do. The splinters that were embedded the deepest will take the longest to heal."

Brenna looked up at him. "You saw to that?"

Hawthorne held her gaze a moment. "Yes."

Another pause, the weight of it settling between them.

"I didn't intend to leave them there."

Their eyes held.

"Thank you," she said softly, her gaze slipping away as the realization settled.

His attention shifted to the loosened tie at her braid, the wind had again lifted it free. Without thinking, and then very aware that he had, he reached out and retied the knot more securely.

His fingers brushed her hair only once. "You'll catch cold if it loosens again," he said.

The gesture was practical. The air between them was not.

She swallowed faintly. "Thank you… Captain."

"Hawthorne," he corrected softly.

Her sleeve brushed lightly against his coat as the shipped rolled again. And for the first time since the storm, Brenna felt something steadier than the sea beneath her feet.

Chapter 7

Brenna found herself drawn to the deck more often than not, spending the better part of each day in the open air. The wind, the rhythm of the waves, and the endless stretch of sea gave her a sense of freedom she could not quite explain. It was the only place aboard the ship where she felt most like herself.

She saw him often. Always at a distance first, on deck at dawn, coat unbuttoned, dark hair tied back with careless precision. He moved with ease of someone utterly at home upon the sea. A gentleman's posture, yes, but his hands bore scars. Old ones. Earned. Pirate's hands, her mind whispered. Gentleman eyes, her heart replied. He spoke little, but when he did, men listened.

Brenna had begun to favor the quieter hours of the afternoon, the crew less hurried than in the morning, their work settling into something more routine.

It made watching easier. Safer. She stood near the rail, her fingers resting lightly against the wood as she looked out over the water. It stretched endlessly, unchanged, and yet never the same twice.

"You spend a great deal of time looking at it."

She didn't turn. "It gives the impression it might tell me something eventually."

Hawthorne stepped beside her. "It won't."

"That's unfortunate."

"It's not meant to be understood."

Brenna glanced at him. "And yet you navigate it."

"That's not the same thing."

"Then what is it?" she asked. "If not something to be understood?"

Hawthorne's gaze remained on the horizon. "It's something to be respected."

Brenna's lips curved faintly. "That sounds like something learned the hard way."

"It usually is."

Reed joined them a moment later, leaning casually against the rail. "What are we respecting today?"

"The ocean," Brenna said.

Reed nodded. "A worthy subject."

"Do you ever tire of it?" she asked.

Reed glanced out over the water. "No."

"Why not?"

He shrugged slightly. "It's never the same long enough to grow dull."

Brenna considered that. "And what about what's in it?"

That caught his attention. Reed turned slightly. "What do you mean?"

"The water isn't empty," she said. "There's something beneath it. Always."

Hawthorne's gaze shifted, just slightly. "There is."

Brenna looked between them. "And you're content not knowing exactly what?"

Reed's mouth curved faintly. "I prefer not to know everything that could drag me under."

Brenna smiled faintly. "That seems practical."

A brief silence followed as the ship cut forward.

"Do you ever fish?" Brenna asked.

Hawthorne let out a quiet breath. "What?" then added, "That question tells me you've been thinking about this longer than you've admitted."

Brenna lifted a brow. "Is it so unusual?"

"From most passengers?" he said. "Yes."

She tilted her head slightly. “Then I suppose I’m continuing to be unusual.”

Reed glanced at Hawthorne. “She is, isn’t she.”

Hawthorne didn’t respond immediately. “No,” he said at last. “She’s consistent.”

“Yes,” Reed said, answering her at last. “We fish.”

Brenna’s attention sharpened, just slightly. “How?”

“A line,” he said. “Sometimes nets, if we’ve the time and patience.”

“And you trust what you pull from the water?”

Reed laughed quietly. “Trust is a strong word.”

Hawthorne added, “You learn what to keep, and what not to.”

Brenna looked back out at the sea. “And what have you learned?”

Reed folded his arms lightly. “That most of it isn’t worth the trouble.”

“That is rather disappointing.”

“It’s practical.”

A shout came from further down the deck. “Line’s ready!”

Reed glanced over his shoulder. “Well,” he said, pushing off the rail, “that’s fortunate timing.”

Brenna’s gaze followed. “You’re fishing now?”

“Yes.” Her interest sharpened further, though she tried to temper it. “I’d like to see.”

Reed paused, glancing at Hawthorne. “She’s not supposed to be over there.”

“I’m allowed on deck,” Brenna said.

“That’s not the same as being in the way,” Hawthorne replied.

“I won’t be.”

Hawthorne studied her a moment. “Stay behind the line.”

A hint of a smile formed on Brenna's lips. "I've been warned."

"Be warned again."

They moved toward the activity. A small group of sailors had gathered, a line cast out beyond the side of the ship, tension already pulling against it.

"Feels like something decent," one of them muttered.

"Or something that'll snap it clean…"

"Don't say that!"

Brenna stopped just where she had been told. Watching. Always watching.

The line jerked suddenly. "Easy!"

"Hold it, don't fight it too fast.!"

Reed stepped closer, taking hold to steady it. "Let it run, then bring it in."

Brenna's gaze fixed on the movement. The timing. The control. It wasn't so different from handling lines in a storm.

Hawthorne's voice came low beside her. "You're following it."

Brenna didn't look at him. "I'm watching."

"That's not the same."

She exhaled softly. "No," she admitted. "It isn't."

The line pulled again, harder this time. "Now, bring it!"

The sailors hauled together, drawing something up through the water, the surface breaking. A flash of silver. Movement. Life.

"There!"

"Not bad!"

The fish thrashed as it was pulled aboard, landing hard against the deck.

Brenna watched it, fascinated.

"Still think it's empty?" Reed asked, glancing back at her.

"No," she said quietly. "I never did."

The fish stilled. The moment passed. The crew returned to their work. As though it had been nothing at all.

The wind had gentled with sunset, no longer sharp but cool and thoughtful. Lanterns glowed low along the rail. The sea stretched endless and dark, its surface broken only by faint silver where moonlight caught the swell.

Brenna joined Hawthorne at the rail. For a moment, neither spoke. The ship moved beneath them in long, patient breaths.

He showed her constellations, she told him about Boston markets and how her friend once convinced a baker she was royalty simply to get a better tart. Brenna smiled then.

"She sounds dangerous," he said dryly.

"She is," Brenna replied softly, her smile dimming.

He noticed. "You cared for her."

"She was my better half."

"You believe the ship is gone," he said quietly.

She did not pretend to misunderstand. "Yes," she replied as her fingers curled around the wood.

"We searched debris fields," he continued "Broken spars, crates. Nothing intact."

She nodded once. "There would not be," she said. "The mast split before I went overboard."

He glanced at her. "You remember that?"

"I remember the sound," she answered.

"You think no one survived," he said.

"I know the Atlantic."

"She might have," he offered carefully.

She looked at him then. "No," she said softly. "If she had, she would be here.

"Storms scatter ships."

"Not for long."

The certainty in her tone surprised him. “You speak of one accustomed to loss.”

“My father taught me numbers,” she replied. “Tonnage. Crew ratios. Distance from the shore. Survival probabilities.”

“That is a cold education.”

“It was practical.”

The sea rolled dark beneath them. “If she lived,” Brenna continued, voice quieter now, “she would not let me believe her dead.”

“You blame yourself,” he said.

Her fingers tightened faintly. “I suggested we remain above deck for a little while longer,” she admitted. “I wanted the air, but she went ahead and went below with the others.”

“You were not responsible for the storm.”

“I was responsible for being there.”

He turned toward her fully now. “Listen to me.”

The firmness in his tone made her look up. “You survived because you held on, you fought. Because you did not surrender when others might have.”

“But you did not see anyone else?”

“I’m afraid not.”

“But you saw me.”

“Yes.”

“And you pulled me out.”

“I did,” he said. “You would have done the same.”

She shook her head faintly. “No.”

That startled him. “No?” He repeated.

“I would have hesitated,” she said honestly. “I would have calculated weight, distance, probability."

“And then?”

“And then I would have pulled you out,” she admitted.

The corner of his mouth shifted slightly.

The wind tugged at her hair, and without thinking, he reached to steady the loose strand whipping across her face. His fingers brushed her temple, brief, electric.

They both froze. The moment lingered, too close, too aware.

"Forgive me," he said, stepping back as though distance could restore order.

"You should get some sleep," he said, voice steadier now. "You have pushed yourself enough for one day."

The authority had returned, not cold, but deliberate.

Brenna did not move. "I am not fragile," she replied softly.

"I know."

"Then why send me below?"

His gaze held hers, longer than necessary. "Because exhaustion makes the sea careless," he said. "And I have no intention of pulling you from it twice."

The words were practical. But something beneath them was not.

"Rest," he added more quietly. "Tomorrow will require more of you."

She studied him one last moment before turning toward the companionway.

Behind her, he did not immediately move. His pulse did not slow until she reached the ladder.

Reed waited near the helm. "You're lingering," the first mate said without preamble.

"I am not."

"You are."

Hawthorne's gaze drifted briefly toward the cabin below deck.

"She believes her ship lost."

Reed studied him. "And you believe?

"I believe storms rarely take only what they appear to."

Reed watched him another moment. "You're stepping into dangerous waters."

Hawthorne turned toward the horizon. "I am accustomed to dangerous waters."

"But this one…"

This one had eyes the color of grief and a name that did not quite fit her. And for the first time in years, Callum Hawthorne felt something dangerously close to distraction.

Chapter 8

The next morning the Sails were full. Wind consistent. The deck alive with movement that no longer felt chaotic, only deliberate.

Brenna stood near the rail, watching. There was something hypnotic about it now. The way each man moved with intention, as though the ship itself spoke and they simply answered.

"Still observing?"

Hawthorne's voice came from behind her.

She didn't turn immediately. "I am deciding whether I've learned anything at all."

"That depends," he said, stepping closer, "on whether you've been paying attention."

Brenna glanced over her shoulder. "I've been paying attention."

"Then you should know what that is." He nodded toward a length of rope coiled near the mast, one of the sailors working it quickly through practiced hands.

Brenna followed his gaze. "A knot," she said.

Hawthorne's mouth shifted slightly. "A specific one."

She turned fully now. "You expect me to know the difference?"

"I expect you to learn it."

There was something in his tone, not dismissive, not challenging exactly, but certain.

Brenna stepped past him without waiting. "Then show me."

Hawthorne watched her for a moment, then followed.

The sailor stepped aside immediately at the captain's approach, leaving the rope behind.

Brenna picked it up, weighing it slightly in her hands. It was heavier than she expected. “Go on,” she said.

Hawthorne reached for the rope, his movements efficient. “This is used to secure a line under strain,” he said. “It needs to hold fast, but release when necessary.”

He tied it quickly. Too quickly.

Brenna frowned. “That was not helpful.”

Hawthorne glanced at her. “It was clear.”

“It was not repeatable, show me again.”

Something in her tone made him hesitate, just slightly.

Then he stepped closer. “Watch carefully.”

He untied it, slower this time. Brenna leaned in, her attention fixed on his hands.

“Over, then under,” he said. “Back through…here.”

She nodded once. “I see.”

Hawthorne stepped back. “Try it.”

Brenna set to work immediately. Her fingers moved with purpose, but not precision. The rope twisted wrong Too tight in one place, too loose in another.

Hawthorne watched for a moment. “Not like that.”

“I am aware,” she said.

“You’re pulling too much tension through the wrong point.”

Brenna didn’t look up. “I am adjusting.”

“You’re undoing it.”

She exhaled. “Then perhaps you should explain it better.”

Hawthorne stepped forward again. “Or perhaps,” he said quietly, “you should listen more closely.”

That…that made her pause. She looked up at him. “I am listening.”

“Then let me show you.”

Before she could respond, his hands closed over hers. Firm. Guiding. Brenna stilled. Not because she needed to. Because she felt it. The shift. The closeness.

His voice lowered slightly. "Here," he said, adjusting her grip. "You're forcing it."

"I thought it needed to hold."

"It does," he said. "But not by brute force."

His hands moved with hers, slower now. More deliberate.

"Let it settle," he added. "The rope will do part of the work if you allow it."

Brenna's breath caught, just slightly. Not from the instruction. From the proximity. She became suddenly, acutely aware of everything. The warmth of his hands. The steadiness of his voice.

The fact that he had not stepped away. "You're not letting go," she said quietly.

His hands stilled. "No." The word came softer than before.

Brenna swallowed lightly. "Is that part of the lesson?"

Hawthorne's grip shifted, loosening, but not entirely releasing. "It depends," he said.

"On what?"

His gaze lifted to hers. "On whether you're learning."

The world around them seemed to fade for a moment. The sound of the ship. The crew. The sea. All of it distant.

Brenna held his gaze. "I think," she said carefully, "I am beginning to understand."

Hawthorne's expression didn't change.

But something in it… shifted. "Good," he said.

Still not stepping back. Still not letting go. The knot formed beneath their hands, properly this time. Secure. Balanced. Finished.

Neither of them moved. Not immediately.

A voice called from across the deck. "Captain!"

The moment broke. Hawthorne stepped back at once. Too quickly. His hands falling away from hers as though the contact had been unintentional.

It hadn't.

Brenna looked down at the rope. The knot held. Perfect. She flexed her fingers slightly, as though they still remembered his touch.

Hawthorne cleared his throat. "That will hold," he said.

Brenna didn't look up. "Yes," she said quietly. "I believe it will."

The afternoon had settled into a steadier rhythm than the morning.

The wind held firm, the ship cutting cleanly through the water as the crew moved with practiced ease.

Brenna stood near the mid-deck, watching again, though this time, there was less distance in it.

"You're in the way."

She turned. A sailor stood behind her, not unkind, but direct. Brenna stepped aside immediately "I'm beginning to understand that seems to be a recurring issue."

The man gave a short grin. "You'll learn where not to stand soon enough."

"I'd prefer to learn where I *should* stand."

"That's easier," he said. "Anywhere we're not about to send something flying."

Brenna glanced at the coiled rope nearby.

"That seems like a narrow margin."

"It is."

She smiled faintly. "Then I'll do my best to stay out of your way."

The sailor nodded once before moving past her.

"You're improving."

Brenna didn't need to turn this time. "Hawthorne," she said, still watching the deck.

His presence settled beside her. "You didn't argue."

"I'm learning that arguing here serves little purpose."

"That's a useful lesson."

Brenna glanced at him. "I suspect most of your lessons are."

"You suspect correctly."

She folded her arms lightly. "And yet, you've only shown me one knot."

"So far."

"That seems a limited education."

Hawthorne's gaze shifted toward the rigging. "You've managed to occupy yourself regardless."

Brenna's expression stilled, just slightly. "I've been observing."

"Yes," he said. "You have."

There was something in his tone. Not accusatory. But not entirely neutral either.

Brenna met his gaze. "Is that a problem?"

"No," he said. "It's interesting."

A shout carried across the deck. "Line…coming through!"

Brenna stepped back instinctively as a length of rope snapped past where she had been standing moments before.

She exhaled softly. "That would have been unpleasant."

Hawthorne's mouth shifted faintly. "You're beginning to anticipate."

"I'm beginning to listen."

"That's the same thing."

Reed approached from the opposite side, his expression far too relaxed for the motion of the ship. "She hasn't been knocked over yet," he said. "I'm impressed."

Brenna lifted a brow. "I intend to remain upright."

"A worthy goal."

Reed leaned casually against the rail. "You've been out here most of the day."

"I have."

"And you're not tired of it?"

Brenna glanced around. "No."

Reed studied her. "Most would be."

"I'm not most."

"No," he said lightly. "You're not."

A brief silence settled between them, broken only by the steady sounds of the ship.

"Tell me something," Brenna said, turning slightly toward Hawthorne.

"What?"

"You trust them," she said, nodding toward the crew.

"Yes."

"Completely?"

"Without question."

Brenna considered that. "And they trust you."

"They do."

She tilted her head slightly. "That seems… unusual."

Hawthorne's gaze shifted to her. "How so?"

"I've seen men follow orders," she said. "That's not the same thing."

Reed's mouth curved faintly. "No," he said. "It isn't."

Brenna's eyes returned to Hawthorne. "They don't just follow you."

"No," he said quietly. "They don't."

"Why?"

Hawthorne held her gaze. "Because I don't ask them to do anything I wouldn't do myself."

Brenna's expression softened, just slightly. "That matters."

"Yes."

The ship tilted gently as the wind shifted again, the movement familiar now.

Brenna adjusted her stance without thinking.

Reed noticed. “That was quicker.”

“What was?”

“You didn’t stumble.”

Brenna glanced down briefly, then back up. “I told you, I’m learning.”

Reed exchanged a look with Hawthorne. “Yes,” he said. “You are.”

A younger sailor approached hesitantly, holding a length of rope. “Captain, this line’s caught wrong.”

Hawthorne stepped forward at once, taking it from him. “Where?”

“Forward rigging, won’t hold properly.”

Hawthorne examined it quickly, then gestured. “Show me.”

The sailor nodded and hurried off.

Hawthorne followed, then paused, glancing back at Brenna. “Stay clear of the lines.”

Brenna looked at him with faint amusement, “I’ve been warned before.”

“Be warned again.”

Then he was gone.

Reed remained. Watching her. “You don’t behave like someone unfamiliar with this,” he said after a moment.

Brenna didn’t look at him. “I’ve been told that today.”

“And before today?”

“Not often.”

Reed studied her. “And yet here you are.”

Brenna finally turned. “And yet here I am.”

Reed’s expression shifted slightly. “Interesting.”

They watched as Hawthorne moved easily through the crew, correcting the line with quick precision, his movements efficient, controlled.

Brenna's gaze lingered. "He's different out here," she said quietly.

Reed glanced at her. "Yes."

"How?"

Reed considered the question. "Clearer."

Brenna's eyes didn't leave Hawthorne. "Yes," she said. "That's it."

Hawthorne returned a few minutes later, his attention immediately finding her again. "You stayed where you were told."

"I can follow instruction."

"So it would seem."

Brenna tilted her head slightly. "You sound surprised."

"I'm not," he said. "Just confirming."

Brenna looked out at the water again. "It's calmer now."

"For the moment."

"It won't last," Reed added.

"No," Hawthorne agreed.

She nodded slightly. "I'm beginning to understand that as well."

Hawthorne's voice lowered. "You're understanding more than that."

Brenna glanced at him. "And what else do you think I understand?"

He held her gaze. "That remains to be seen."

Reed pushed off the rail. "Well," he said lightly, "I'll leave you to your observations."

Brenna's brow lifted. "Running off so soon?"

"I've learned when I'm no longer needed."

Hawthorne didn't react.

Reed smiled faintly. "Enjoy the afternoon."

Then he was gone.

A crewman passed between them, carrying a crate, forcing Brenna to step slightly closer to Hawthorne to avoid being struck.

"Apologies, miss," the man muttered.

"No harm done," she replied.

Hawthorne waited until the path cleared before speaking again. "You don't need to stay here."

Brenna lifted a brow. "No?"

He shook his head slightly. "You're free to move about the ship."

Her gaze sharpened. "That sounds like a privilege."

"It's a practical allowance."

"And the difference?"

Hawthorne's voice remained even. "You'll learn more by seeing than standing in one place."

Brenna glanced toward the length of the deck, then back at him. "And where am I not permitted to go?"

"The crew's quarters," he said. "Below deck, forward."

"Of course, anywhere else?"

Hawthorne studied her a moment. "No."

That, was unexpected. Brenna tilted her head slightly. "You trust me not to get in the way."

"I trust you to pay attention."

A faint smile touched her lips. "That's not the same thing."

"No," he said. "It isn't."

Brenna glanced toward the length of the deck, the open space now hers to explore.

"You're certain?" she asked.

Hawthorne followed her gaze. "Yes."

She looked back at him. "And if I end up somewhere I shouldn't be?"

His voice lowered slightly. "You won't."

The certainty of it settled between them. Brenna held his gaze a moment longer.

"Very well," she said.

And for the first time since boarding, she turned away not because she was uncertain, but because she had been given the freedom to choose where to go next.

The deck had quieted as the afternoon wore on.

Most of the crew were occupied forward, leaving the midship lines momentarily unattended.

Hawthorne noticed her before she noticed him. Brenna stood near the coil of rope, her movements deliberate, focused. Not experimenting. Not guessing. Working.

His gaze narrowed slightly. She looped the line once, twice, then drew it back through with practiced precision, tightening it cleanly into place.

Not the knot he had shown her. Something else. Something better.

Hawthorne stepped closer, silent enough that she didn't hear him until, "That's not what I taught you."

Brenna's hands stilled. Just for a moment. Then she finished the knot anyway, pulling it snug before letting the rope fall. "I didn't realize there was only one way to tie them," she said, without turning.

Hawthorne's voice lowered."There isn't. But that isn't a beginner's knot."

Now she turned. Her expression calm. Too calm. "I've had time to observe."

Hawthorne studied her. "That's more than observation."

Brenna tilted her head slightly. "You underestimate how quickly I learn."

"I don't," he said. "I question where you learned it."

A flicker passed through her expression. Gone just as quickly. "I pay attention," she said.

Hawthorne stepped closer. "Not like that."

His gaze dropped briefly to the rope, then back to her. "You tied that cleanly. Without hesitation."

Brenna's fingers brushed lightly against the line, as though it meant nothing. "Perhaps I am more capable than you assumed."

Hawthorne's mouth shifted slightly. "That's becoming increasingly clear."

The air between them shifted.

"What else are you not telling me?" he asked.

The question landed quietly. But not lightly.

Brenna held his gaze. "Must there be something?"

"Yes." The certainty in his voice made her breath catch, just slightly.

"You seem very convinced."

"I am. People don't acquire skill like that overnight."

Brenna's voice softened. "And yet you expected me to learn from you."

"I expected you to struggle."

Her lips curved faintly. "Perhaps I prefer not to."

Hawthorne didn't smile. "You prefer control."

Brenna's expression stilled. "That's not a fault."

"No," he said. "But it is revealing."

Silence stretched between them. Not comfortable. Not entirely tense. But something in between.

Hawthorne stepped closer again, his voice quieter now. "You don't move like someone unfamiliar with ships."

Brenna's breath slowed. "You're drawing conclusions."

"I'm asking questions."

"Then ask them plainly."

Hawthorne held her gaze. "Who are you?"

The words lingered. Heavy. Too close to the truth.

Brenna didn't answer immediately. Couldn't. "Someone who doesn't intend to be underestimated," she said.

Hawthorne watched her carefully. "That's not an answer."

"No," she said softly. "It isn't."

Then she stepped past him, brushing just close enough to be deliberate. "Perhaps," she added, without looking back, "you'll have to decide what you believe."

Hawthorne didn't move. His gaze followed her as she walked away. The rope still hung between them.

The knot she had tied, precise. Controlled. Not accidental.

He reached out, testing it briefly. It held. Of course it did.

Hawthorne exhaled slowly. Then, under his breath, "Interesting."

Because whatever she was hiding, it was more than a name.

Chapter 9

Brenna Whitmore had been raised on the sea. Not literally, her childhood had been in a tall brick house near the Boston harbor, but the ocean had shaped every corner of her life. Shipping ledgers had lined her father's study. Route maps had decorated the walls more frequently than landscapes. She could read a trade chart as easily as a novel.

She had crossed the Atlantic before. She knew the difference between a merchant brig and a naval sloop. Between a vessel armed for appearance and one armed for purpose.

And she knew the *Hawthorne* was not what it claimed.

The first clue had been the speed.

The second was the silence when certain compartments were accessed.

The third came when the wind caught her shawl.

The shawl had been left folded at the foot of her bunk, soft wool, charcoal gray, far finer than anything a common sailor would own. "Captain's orders," the boy had said. She had not asked why a man like Hawthorne carried something so gentle.

The wind tore across the deck in sharp gusts, whipping the shawl loose from her shoulders before she could grab it. The dark fabric lifted into the air and spiraled across the deck before vanishing neatly through the forward hatch. She followed without hesitation.

The moment she descended she knew. The air was different below. Dry. Prepared.

Not the cluttered hold of a trader stuffed with crates and barrels, but ordered space, measured weight.

Her shawl lay forgotten as her eyes adjusted to lantern light.

Twelve guns. Six to port. Six to starboard.

Nine-pounders by the look of them, not massive naval cannons, but swift efficient. Carriages reinforced. Wheels freshly greased. Powder sealed tight in waxed casts. Shot stacked in tight formations.

Two swivel guns mounted forward. Boarding deterrents. Not decorative. Not defensive alone.

This ship was built to chase. A slow breathe left her. "Brig-rigged," she murmured almost to herself. "Fast in crosswind. Maneuverable. Armed enough to outmatch raiders."

"You assess accurately."

Hawthorne's voice came from behind her.

She did not startle. She turned instead, hands loosely clasped behind her back as though inspecting cargo on one of her father's vessels.

"You are no merchant captain," she said calmly.

"Not exactly."

"You trimmed your sails tighter than trade brigs typically risk in storm."

"That's right."

"You corrected course north instead of east once the wind broke."

His brow lifted faintly. "You were watching."

"I was raised to." She stepped closer to one of the cannons, resting her palm lightly against the cool iron.

"My father owned twelve ships," she said "Three were armed. Only two carried more than eight guns."

Hawthorne studied her different now. Not as a rescued woman. As an equal.

"You miss the sea," he observed.

Her fingers tightened slightly against the cannon barrel. "It is the only place I do not feel… arranged."

The confession slipped out quietly. Above deck, the world expected her to marry, to merge fortunes, to perform alliances.

At sea, she was breath and wind and horizon.

"You feel alive here," he said.

"More than in any other place," she said evenly.

Their eyes held. The lantern flame flickered between them, casting shifting shadows across iron and wood.

"You should not," he replied. "The sea takes without asking."

"It gives without asking as well."

He stepped closer, boots silent on planks. "You are not afraid of it."

"I respect it."

"And men like me?"

The question carried weight. She considered him fully now, the lean strength in his stance, the scar along his throat, the tension coiled beneath composure.

"You are not the sea," she said.

"No?"

"You choose."

He reached down, retrieving her shawl where it had slipped near powder crates. "And what do you believe I have chosen?" he asked.

She stepped into the space between two cannons, closing the distance enough to feel the warmth radiating from him.

"You sail under false colors," she said. "You hunt. Not for plunder."

"No."

"For justice?" she ventured

His jaw shifted slightly. "For balance."

There it was. Not vengeance. Not glory. Balance.

"You believe the sea should answer to law," she said.

"Perhaps."

"And if the law fails?"

He did not look away. "Then I do not."

The words settled between them like a drawn blade. She felt the danger of him fully now. Not pirate. Not merchant. Something sharper.

"And you turned this ship for me," she said softly. "In that storm."

Her pulse quickened, not from fear. From recognition.

"You understand ships," he said.

"That's right."

"You understand what this vessel is."

"Yes."

"And you are not frightened."

"Hardly."

A faint shift touched his expression, something between admiration and caution. "You are dangerous, Miss Fairchild," he murmured.

She tilted her head slightly. "Because I understand?"

"Because you do not shrink."

Above them a distant shout carried across deck, routine, steady. She extended her hand for the shawl.

He did not release it immediately. Instead he draped it around her shoulders himself, fingers brushing the nape of her neck, the contact brief but unmistakably aware.

"You feel alive at sea," he said quietly, confirming what she had admitted earlier.

"Yes."

His voice lowered. "So do I."

And that…

That was the most dangerous thing he had said yet.

The fleeting storm that had went through that morning had long since passed, leaving the sea rolling in long, steady swells beneath the Hawthorne's hull. Lanterns swung gently along the deck, casting shifting light across the rigging where sailors moved about their evening duties.

Below, Reed leaned casually against a barrel while Hawthorne stood near the ladder, arms folded.

"She saw them," Hawthorne said quietly.

Reed lifted a brow. "Hard to miss an entire gun deck."

"She knew exactly what they were."

Reed chuckled. "You expected otherwise?"

Hawthorne shot him a look. "She noticed too quickly."

Reed shrugged. "You said yourself you suspect she's a Whitmore."

"We don't know for sure."

Reed pushed off the barrel and crossed his arms. "She knows ships. She noticed the armament. She doesn't scare easily." He grinned slightly. "Sounds like a Whitmore to me."

Hawthorne didn't answer.

Reed tilted his head toward the ladder leading up to the deck. "Besides, you didn't exactly hide them well."

Hawthorne exhaled slowly. "That wasn't the problem."

Reed's grin widened. "Oh?"

Gesturing upward Hawthorne replied, "That is."

Reed climbed the ladder and stopped just long enough to take in the scene.

Brenna stood near the rail, the borrowed shawl wrapped around her shoulders. The lantern light caught in her hair as the wind lifted it slightly around her face.

More than one sailor nearby had slowed his work.

A coil of rope was suddenly being tied far more carefully than necessary.

Another man had stopped mid-task entirely.

Reed smirked. "Well."

Hawthorne stepped up beside him. From here the lantern light outlined Brenna clearly. The oversized sailor's shirt she'd been given hung loosely at the shoulders, but the fabric moved with the wind just enough to reveal the fine lines beneath it when she turned.

Hawthorne's expression hardened.

The sailors were noticing.

Reed noticed something else. "You're glowering."

"I'm observing."

Reed laughed quietly. "You're smitten."

Hawthorne shot him a cold look. "Don't be ridiculous."

Reed leaned closer. "You're watching her like a man guarding a treasure chest."

"I'm watching my crew forget their duties."

Reed chuckled. "Same difference."

Hawthorne stepped forward across the deck. "Miss… Fairchild."

Brenna turned. "Yes, Captain?"

He gestured toward the hatch. "You should go below."

Her brows lifted slightly. "Why?"

"Because this deck is not meant for passengers."

She glanced around at the crew. "I'm not in anyone's way."

"That isn't the point."

Brenna folded her arms. "Then perhaps you should explain the point."

Hawthorne's voice cooled. "You're attracting attention."

Brenna blinked. "I beg your pardon?"

Several nearby sailors suddenly found their work extremely interesting again.

Hawthorne lowered his voice slightly. "My crew has duties to perform."

"And my presence prevents that?"

"Apparently."

Brenna's eyes flashed. "That sounds like their problem."

Hawthorne took another step closer. "It becomes my problem when discipline slips."

"And your solution is to send me below like a child?"

"My solution is to keep order on my ship."

Brenna lifted her chin slightly. "I survived a storm and the open sea. I think I can manage standing on a deck."

Reed watched the exchange from the ladder with growing amusement.

Hawthorne's patience thinned. "You may find that refusing a captain's instruction aboard his ship is unwise."

Brenna met his gaze without flinching. "And you may find that ordering people around without explanation makes them far less inclined to listen."

The wind stirred the lantern light between them.

Brenna adjusted the shawl around her shoulders. "Speaking of explanations…"

Hawthorne frowned slightly. "Yes?"

She held the edge of the shawl between her fingers. "Where exactly did you acquire this?"

Hawthorne blinked. "The shawl?"

"Yes." She gestured lightly to the fabric. "Woman's clothing on a ship full of sailors seems… unusual."

Reed snorted softly behind them.

Hawthorne shot him a warning look before answering.

"It was left behind."

"By whom?"

"A passenger."

Brenna's eyes narrowed. "You carry passengers?"

"Occasionally."

"And they abandon their clothing?"

Hawthorne shrugged slightly. "Sometimes."

Brenna stepped closer. "You're lying."

Hawthorne's brow lifted. "That's a bold accusation."

"You have a ship armed like a war vessel and a mysterious lady's shawl conveniently waiting for me." She tilted her head. "You expect me not to question that?"

Hawthorne studied her for a moment. "You ask dangerous questions."

Brenna smiled faintly. "I'm beginning to think they're the right ones."

Silence stretched between them.

Finally Hawthorne nodded toward the hatch again. "Below."

Brenna held his gaze another moment. Then she adjusted the shawl. "Eventually."

She walked calmly past him toward the stairs.

Reed waited until she was out of earshot before leaning toward Hawthorne. "You are absolutely smitten."

Hawthorne stared out at the dark sea. "I am absolutely not."

Reed laughed. "Oh, this is going to be fun."

Chapter 10

In the days that followed her rescue, the motion of the ship steadied, but nothing between them did. Callum found himself watching her more often than he intended, drawn by something he neither trusted nor permitted. More than once, standing too close in the quiet moments between duties, he felt the impulse, to close the distance, to forget the rest of the world, but each time he forced it back, a sharp reminder that she was promised elsewhere.

Brenna felt it too. The shift. The unspoken pull that lingered in every glance and unfinished sentence. It unsettled her more than the storm ever had. She told herself it was gratitude, nothing more, but that explanation grew weaker with each passing day. Because whatever this was… it did not feel like something she could simply set aside.

Those days turned to weeks.

The sea had been unusually calm that afternoon, long silver swells beneath a pale sky. The wind steady, sails trimmed tight. The *Hawthorne* cut cleanly through water, lean and swift.

Brenna spotted her first. She stood near the bow, one hand braced against the rail, eyes narrowed toward the southern horizon.

There. A speck.

Not merchant heavy. Too low in the water. Too fast for her size.

She shifted slightly, adjusting her angle. The hull rode sharp. Lean. No bright paint. No company markings visible even at a distance.

No colors flying. Her breath slowed.

Behind her, Hawthorne's voice carried quietly, "What do you see?"

She did not turn. "Brig," she answered. "Fast-rigged. Running north by northwest."

His boots approached. Stopped beside her. "Are you certain?"

"She carries herself too lightly for cargo."

He followed her line of sight. The speck resolved slowly into shape.

Reed appeared at his other side. "I've had word of a brig in these waters," he muttered. "No flag. No mercy."

The name slid into place. The *Black Mercy*.

As if summoned by thought alone. The approaching vessel altered course slightly, subtle, almost imperceptible.

Not fleeing. Testing.

Brenna felt the shift before she saw it fully. "She's measuring us," she said.

Hawthorne did not look at her. "Yes."

The crew began noticing. Sailors moved with more intention, glancing toward the quarterdeck.

She's too bold for trader," Brenna continued. "And too confident for privateer."

Hawthorne's voice dropped. "She's hunted before."

The *Black Mercy* came nearer now, still distant, but distinct enough to make out the dark hull, stripped of ornament. Her sails were patched but strong. She moved like something accustomed to pursuit.

No signal. No greeting. No flag.

"She could break off," Reed said.

"Yes," Hawthorne replied. "But she won't."

Because the *Hawthorne* flew neutral trade colors. Because they looked profitable. Because predators prefer easy prey.

Hawthorn'e jaw set. "Maintain course," he ordered calmly. "Do not alter speed."

The crew obeyed instantly, though tension rippled through them like drawn wire.

Brenna glanced at him. "You intend to let her close."

"Yes."

"That is reckless."

"That is necessary."

The distance between ships narrowed further. The *Mercy's* sails angled deliberately.

"She's adjusting for wind advantage," Brenna murmured.

Hawthorne's gaze flicked towards her briefly. "You truly do understand ships."

"I believe you've discovered that already."

"And you remain."

The question beneath the statement hung heavy. She did not look away from the approaching vessel. "If she is the one who took one of my father's ships," Brenna said quietly, "I would rather see her face than imagine it."

Something sharp moved through him at that.

Below deck, unseen, the gun ports had already been loosened. The *Hawthorne* still appeared merchant-soft from the outside. But beneath the hull, twelve cannons waited.

The *Mercy* drew close enough now that figures were visible along her rail. Rough men. Weapons slung carelessly. Watching.

Hawthorne's voice lowered further. "Reed."

"Aye"

"Signal below."

Reed gave the smallest nod and moved off without flourish.

From above, nothing changed. From below, iron shifted softly in its braces. Powder prepared. Shot rolled into ready reach.

Brenna felt it, the subtle hum beneath deck. The tension of men about to become something else. “You enjoy this,” she said suddenly.

His gaze did not leave the horizon. “I do not enjoy injustice.”

“That is not what I meant.”

Now he looked at her. Truly looked. “There are men,” he said, “who believe the sea erases consequences.”

“And you disagree.”

“Yes.”

The *Black Mercy* angled further. Now there could be no doubt. She was closing. Testing distance of cannon range. Or boarding.

A shout carried faintly from the enemy deck, mocking.

Hawthorne stepped half a pace forward, posture changing almost imperceptibly. He was no longer merchant. He was commander. “Stand ready,” he said calmly, not loud, but enough.

The crew straightened as one.

Brenna’s heart pounded, not with fear. With something fierce. She stood her ground beside him.

“You should go below,” he said without turning.

“No.”

His eye flicker to her. “This is not spectacle.”

“I know.”

“Then go.”

“If they took my ship,” she said steadily, “I will not hide from them.”

Silence hung between them for one charged breath. Then…

Signal flag snapped upward from the *Black Mercy*. Not greeting. Not trade. Black.

Hawthorne's expression hardened into something carved from steel. "Open gun ports."

Wood panels dropped in unison along the *Hawthorne's* hull. Six dark mouths, on either side, revealed themselves in a single devastating line.

The effect was immediate. Shouts erupted from the *Mercy*. Too late.

Hawthorne's voice cut clean and cold through wind. "Run out the guns."

Iron rolled forward. Cannon mouths extended. The *Hawthorne* shed her disguise in a single breath.

Beside him, Brenna did not flinch. The sea wind tore at her borrowed sleeve.

The enemy ship loomed closer.

Hawthorne leaned slightly towards her, just enough for his voice to reach her ear without being carried off. "Whatever happens," he said quietly, "stay behind me."

She met his gaze. "I have no intention of drowning twice."

And for one impossible heartbeat, in the space between loaded cannon and closing enemy, he almost smiled.

"Hard to port," he commanded."

Then the first shot thundered, the boom splitting the air. *Black Mercy's* shot splashed short.

Hawthorne did not flinch. "Now," he ordered.

The *Hawthorne's* broadside answered. The cannons roared in unison. The deck shook violently beneath them. Smoke exploded outward, thick and choking, swallowing wind and sky in white fury.

Across the water, splintered wood burst from the *Mercy's* side.

Chaos followed. Men shouting. Rigging snapping. Return fire scrambling.

Hawthorne stepped forward into smoke like he had been born in it. His expression did not change. He did not shout wildly. He watched. Calculated.

"Reload," he said calmly. "She'll try to swing starboard. He was right.

The *Black Mercy* attempted to angle away, but the *Hawthorne* matched her with predatory grace.

"You knew they would engage," Brenna said, voice nearly swallowed by cannon thunder.

"Yes."

"You wanted them to."

"You're very perceptive."

The honesty should have terrified her. Instead, something fierce ignited in her chest.

His gaze flicked toward her, eyes dark, intense. "We end them."

Another cannon volley thundered. Smoke wrapped around them both, thick and acrid. For a moment the world narrowed to iron, fire and the violent rhythm of war. Brenna stood beside him, breath sharp, heart racing. She should have recoiled from this version of him. Instead, she understood it. The sea had taken from her. He took back.

When the smoke thinned briefly, she saw it, the unmistakable satisfaction in his posture as the *Black Mercy's* mast splintered under the second volley. Not joy. Not cruelty. Completion.

He turned slightly toward her, wind and gunpowder cutting across his features. "This," he said "is who I am at sea. The man who saved you is not the man who fights. I don't soften in battle." There was no apology in it. No excuse. Only truth.

Brenna held his gaze. "And I," she replied steadily, "am not frightened."

That, more than cannon fire, made something shift between his eyes. Because most woman would have stepped back. She stepped closer.

And Callum Hawthorne, hunter of wolves, realized the most dangerous thing aboard his ship was not the *Mercy*. It was the woman standing beside him who did not flinch from his darkness.

The sea had settled into uneasy calm. Debris drifted where the *Black Mercy* had once cut through water, splintered rail, torn sailcloth, a broken spar turning slowly in the swell. The pirate brig had fled under crippled mast rather than risk a third broadside.

The *Hawthorne* bore scorch marks along her hull but stood steady.

Brenna remained on deck long after the last cannon cooled.

Hawthorne stood near the stern rail, issuing final orders.

Reed approached him with a ledger tucked beneath one arm, expression unreadable. "She won't chase," Reed said quietly. "Not in that state.

"No." he replied.

Reeds's gaze flicked toward Brenna. "She saw enough."

Hawthorne followed the glance. "Yes."

Then perhaps," Reed said dryly, "she deserves explanation."

Hawthorne did not immediately answer. Instead, he crossed the deck toward Brenna.

She did not flinch at the faint scent of gun powder still clinging to him.

"You wished to see her face," he said quietly.

"I did." "And?" "She was not as large as I imagined," Brenna replied.

"Only crueler."

Reed joined them, folding his arms. "You're not frightened," he observed.

"I am thinking," she answered.

Hawthorne inclined his head slightly. "Ask it."

She did not hesitate.

"You sail under false colors," Brenna said. "You provoke engagement. You destroy without boarding for plunder."

"That is correct."

"You do not behave like pirates."

"That is one way to put it."

"You do not behave like navy."

Reed gave a short breath of amusement. "We're neither."

"Then what are you?" She asked evenly.

Silence stretched for a moment, broken only by the low creak of timber.

Hawthorne spoke first. "We operate with sanction."

"From whom?"

"The Crown."

The word did not echo loudly. But it landed.

Her breath caught. "The Crown sanctions this? You are privateers?"

"No," Reed corrected calmly. "Privateers profit."

"We do not," Hawthorne added.

"You take no prize cargo?" She asked.

"Only what is needed to fund the voyage," Reed said. "And even that is recorded."

"Recorded for whom?" She pressed.

Hawthorne's gaze held hers. "For London."

Understanding dawned slowly. "You hunt pirates under royal authority," she said.

"That's one way of putting it."

"And the world believes you merchant traders."

Reed answered. "Yes. Officially we transport sugar and textiles."

"And if the world knew?"

Reed gave a faint shrug. "It would complicate matters.

"Our authority is deliberate but discreet. We remove vessels the navy can not publicly pursue."

"Because?"

"Because diplomacy prefers plausible ignorance," Reed answered plainly.

Brenna absorbed that. "You operate in shadow," she said.

Hawthorne's voice lowered. "We remove threats before they grow bold enough to attack vessels like the one you sailed on."

"And if you are captured?"

Reed's expression hardened faintly. "Then we were traders."

The implication was clear. No public acknowledgement. No rescue. No recognition. "You risk much," she said.

"You could have boarded," she added.

"And risk losing men to deck fight?" Hawthorne countered. "Not worth it. We break the hull, we break her ability to prey. We do not duel for spectacle."

Her eyes moved between them. "You are efficient," she said.

Hawthorne met her gaze. "I told you I would be."

Silence settled.

She drew a slow breath. "Then why tell me?"

Reed's eyes flickered toward Hawthorne.

He did not look away from her. "Because you are not foolish," he said. "And because you already understood enough to be dangerous."

A faint curve touched her mouth. "And now?"

"Now," Reed said evenly, "you must decide whether to remain on board knowing who we are."

"And if I choose not to?"

Hawthorne's voice softened, but did not weaken. "I would see you safely to port."

Reed studied him at that but said nothing.

Brenna looked out over the darkening sea. "You hunt men who believe themselves untouchable. And you do so quietly." She turned back to them.

"Then perhaps," she said calmly, "you are precisely what these waters require."

Reed blinked once.

Hawthorne did not move. "You approve?" He asked.

"I understand."

"And you are not afraid?" Reed pressed.

She met his gaze steadily. "No."

Brenna glanced at Hawthorne. For the first time since cannon fire split the sky, something almost like surprise crossed his face.

He did not smile but his eyes warmed.

"You are either very brave," Reed muttered, "or very dangerous."

Brenna's lips curved faintly. "I suspect the sea requires both."

The wind shifted gently around them. And though the smokehad cleared, something deeper had just been revealed.

Chapter 11

The sea had quieted into something almost unreal. No wind worth naming. No sharp movement beneath the hull. Only a slow, steady glide through dark water that reflected the sky so clearly it was difficult to tell where one ended and the other began.

Brenna stood near the rail, her gaze lifted. The stars were brighter here. Sharper. Endless.

"You'll strain your eyes if you try to take them all in at once." Hawthorne's voice came from beside her.

She didn't look away. "I don't think I could, even if I tried."

Hawthorne followed her gaze upward. "You're not meant to."

"Then what am I meant to see?"

He stepped closer, not touching, but near enough that his presence settled beside her. "Patterns," he said. "Points that don't move. The rest you ignore."

Brenna glanced at him briefly. "That seems… selective."

"It is."

He lifted a hand, gesturing upward. "Do you see that cluster there?"

She narrowed her eyes slightly. "Yes."

"Follow the line," he said. "Those three, there. They'll always guide you north."

Brenna studied it more carefully now, tracing the path as he spoke. "And you trust that?"

"I trust what doesn't change."

The words settled between them.

Brenna looked back at him. "And what does?"

Hawthorne's gaze remained on the sky. "People," he said.

Something in his tone shifted, quiet, but unmistakable.

Brenna turned back to the stars. "That sounds like experience." "It is." A silence followed, softer now. The kind that didn't need

to be filled.

"This is where you're truly yourself," Brenna said at last.

He glanced at her. "More than anywhere else."

She nodded slightly, her eyes still lifted. "I think I understand that."

Hawthorne studied her profile. "You do?"

"It's… different," she said. "Out here, everything feels uncertain, and yet somehow clearer."

Hawthorne's mouth curved faintly. "That's not how most would describe it."

"Most are looking for something solid," she said.

"And you're not?"

Brenna's gaze shifted, just slightly. "I thought I was. Now I'm not so certain."

The admission hung between them.

Hawthorne didn't look away.

"And when this ends?" she asked.

His expression stilled. The sea moved quietly beneath them.

"It doesn't," he said.

Brenna studied him then. "That sounds like something you tell yourself."

Hawthorne exhaled faintly. "Perhaps." He paused before adding quietly, "Out here, you don't answer to anyone."

Brenna tilted her head. "You're the captain."

"That's different."

"How?"

His gaze drifted back to the horizon. "I chose this."

The words carried more weight than he intended.

Brenna caught it. "And the rest?"

Hawthorne's jaw tightened slightly. "The rest was chosen for me."

Too close. He shifted, his voice steadier again.

"Watch the stars," he said. "You'll lose your position if you don't keep your focus."

Brenna didn't move. "You almost said something."

Hawthorne's eyes flicked to hers. "I didn't."

"You were going to."

He held her gaze a moment.

"Then you must have imagined it," Hawthorne said.

The moment stretched. Balanced on something neither of them named.

Hawthorne looked away first. "Find north again," he said.

Brenna followed his earlier instruction, her eyes returning to the sky. "The three stars," she said quietly. "They don't move."

"No."

"And everything else does."

"That's correct."

Brenna's voice softened. "That seems like a dangerous way to live."

Hawthorne's expression shifted. "It's the only way I know."

Brenna turned to him again. "And when you reach land?"

Hawthorne met her gaze. Something unguarded flickered there. "Then I wait until I can leave it again."

The honesty of it caught her. "You don't belong anywhere else."

Hawthorne didn't answer. Because the truth was, he didn't know if that was still true. Not anymore.

Brenna looked back to the stars, her fingers resting lightly against the rail. "Show me again," she said quietly.

He stepped closer once more.

"North is there," he said, guiding her line of sight, not touching, but near enough that she felt it anyway.

Brenna followed it. Steady. Certain.

For a moment, everything felt aligned. The stars. The sea. The space between them. And neither of them spoke, because neither trusted what might follow if they did.

Hawthorne stood just beyond the main deck, half in shadow, where he could see without being seen.

Brenna stood among a small group of the crew, something one of them had said drawing a rare, unguarded laugh from her.

It caught him off guard. Not the sound, but how easily it came.

One of the sailors handed her a length of rope, demonstrating something with exaggerated seriousness. She tried to mimic it, failing the first time, then succeeding just enough to earn another round of quiet amusement.

"You've tied it wrong," the man said.

"I have not," Brenna replied, lifting her chin slightly. "It's holding, isn't it?"

"For now."

"That seems sufficient."

Another laugh.

Hawthorne's features grew stern.

Reed stepped beside him, unnoticed at first.

"You could join them," Reed said under his breath.

Hawthorne didn't look away. "No."

"She doesn't appear to mind their company."

Hawthorne's gaze remained fixed. "She shouldn't."

Reed glanced at him. "That's not what I meant."

Hawthorne exhaled slowly. "I know what you meant."

"She's promised to another," he added.

The words were steady. Practiced.

Reed studied him. "And that has never stopped men before."

"It should."

"Does it stop you?"

Hawthorne didn't answer. Below, Brenna turned slightly, brushing a stray piece of hair back from her face as she listened to something else being explained. At ease. Unaware.

Reed followed his gaze. "She's not behaving like a woman concerned with her future husband."

Hawthorne's voice lowered. "She doesn't know him."

"No," Reed said. "But she knows you."

Hawthorne finally looked away. "That changes nothing."

Reed's mouth curved faintly. "It changes everything."

Hawthorne's jaw tightened again. "She's under my protection."

"And that is all?"

"Yes."

Reed let the silence sit. "Of course."

Hawthorne didn't miss the tone. But he didn't respond to it either.

Instead, his gaze drifted back to her, just for a moment longer than necessary. Then he turned away. Because he knew better. He had no right to want what was already spoken for.

And yet, he did.

Hawthorne joined her quietly on deck. "You've been staring out there for some time."

Brenna didn't look at him right away. "We should reach Portsmouth soon."

"A few days, if the wind holds," he said.

Brenna nodded. "And then?"

Hawthorne rested his hands along the rail beside her. "Then you'll go ashore."

She glanced at him. "That sounds very certain."

"It is."

Brenna turned slightly, studying him. "I was meant to arrive in London," she said. "That was always the plan."

Hawthorne's gaze shifted briefly to her. "Yes."

"Everything was arranged for it." A faint pause. "Before the storm."

Hawthorne didn't interrupt.

Brenna looked back out at the sea. "I suppose I simply continue on as intended."

"It would make sense." She glanced at him again. "You don't sound convinced." "I think," he said carefully, "you should not travel alone." Brenna's brow lifted slightly. "That seems to concern you more than it should."

"You nearly died."

"And you saved me, that doesn't make me incapable."

"No," Hawthorne said. "It makes you a target."

The words settled between them.

Brenna turned more fully toward him. "For what?"

Hawthorne held her gaze. "For something we don't yet understand."

"What would you have me do?" she asked.

His jaw set slightly. "I would see you safely to London."

Brenna tilted her head. "That sounds very much like another arrangement."

"I suppose that's true."

"And one I'm expected to accept without question?"

"No." Hawthorne continued, "But I would recommend it."

Brenna studied him. "You are very determined."

"I am."

A faint smile touched her lips. “That is becoming increasingly inconvenient.”

Hawthorne’s mouth curved slightly. “I’ve been told that.”

Brenna looked out at the water again, her thoughts clearly turning. “London,” she said quietly. “After I’ve made myself presentable again.”

“That would be advisable.”

Another brief silence passed. Then she added, “I will continue on as planned.”

Hawthorne nodded once. “Then I’ll make the arrangements.”

She nodded, though her expression remained distant.

He studied her a moment before speaking again. “You’re thinking about the other ship.

Brenna exhaled softly. “Yes.” Her eyes moved slowly across the endless stretch of water “I can not help but wonder what became of her.”

Hawthorne rested his arms along the rail beside her. “The storm was severe.”

“That’s what troubles me.”

She turned toward him now. “I still remember the sound of the mast snapping.

Hawthorne’s gaze shifted briefly toward the sails above. “A ship can survive worse.”

“But can everyone aboard?”

The question hung heavily between them.

Brenna looked back toward the horizon.

His voice softened slightly. “Ships limp into port more often than people expect.”

Brenna shook her head gently. “I don’t know if that comforts me.”

The wind lifted the edge of her shawl as the *Hawthorne* cut through another long swell.

Julia's laugh echoed faintly in her memory. "She was so excited about the journey," Brenna said quietly. "London. The adventure of it all."

Hawthorne glanced at her. "She sounds formidable."

Brenna almost smiled. "She is."

Another silence passed. "If the ship survived," Brenna said at last, "she'll be in England already."

He nodded slowly. "Then we'll find out soon enough."

Brenna looked back toward the horizon. For a moment, the only sound between them was the sea.

"Do you ever regret it?" She asked softly.

"Regret what?"

"This life. The secrecy. The danger."

He was quiet a long time. "We do what must be done," he said. "There are men who deserve no mercy. If we stop them before they take another ship…" His jaw tightened. "Then its worth the cost."

"And the cost?"

He met her eyes fully. "Attachment," he said.

The word hung between them.

"You believe caring for someone is a weakness?" She asked.

"I believe it gives the sea something to take."

Her breathe caught. "Not everything is meant to be taken," she whispered.

For a moment, the hardened captain, the rogue gentlemen of whispered rumor, looked almost uncertain. "You should rest," he said quietly.

"So should you."

Neither moved.

Later, alone in his cabin, Hawthorne stared at the map spread before him, though he no longer saw routes or patrol lines.

A survivor with borrowed sorrow. Eyes to brave for someone who had lost everything.

He had told himself it was coincidence. That saving her had been duty. That the Crown's mission left no room for distractions.

But when he pictured England's coast rising ahead, he felt something dangerously like reluctance.

On the other side of the door, Brenna stood beneath unfamiliar stars, hand resting over the place where her true named lived, hidden, guarded.

She did not yet know that the man she was beginning to trust carried secrets as carefully as she did. Nor that England woulddemand truths from them both.

Chapter 12

The ship did not arrive with dignity. It crawled.

Her mainmast had been crudely reinforced at sea, canvas patched unevenly, rigging mismatched and strained. Salt scars streaked her hull. One rail remained splintered where the mast had torn free.

Julia stood at the rail, dressed now in Brenna's traveling cloak. The weight of it felt wrong. Her gaze fixed ahead as the outline of the harbor came into view.

Portsmouth revealed itself slowly, through mist and movement, through the gradual shift from open sea to something structured, crowded, and unmistakably human.

Ships. So many ships. Masts rising in uneven clusters, rigging cutting sharp lines against the pale morning sky. Smaller vessels darted between them, purposeful and quick, while larger ships sat anchored, heavy and immovable, their presence commanding the water around them.

The smell reached them next. Salt, but mixed now with smoke, tar, and something distinctly alive. Busy. Loud. A port that did not pause.

"We've made it," someone said nearby.

A woman stepped up beside her, clutching her shawl tightly around her shoulders despite the mild air.

"I didn't think we would," she said quietly

Julia turned slightly. "You doubted the ship?"

The woman shook her head. "No," she said. "I doubted the sea, it felt as though it meant to keep us."

Julia's gaze returned forward. "It tried."

The woman swallowed. "And yet here we are."

"Yes," Julia said.

Further down the deck, a small cluster of passengers had gathered, their voices rising in uneven conversation.

"…never seen weather like it."

"…thought the mast would take us all down…"

"…captain handled it well."

"That's not what I heard."

"Well, you heard wrong…"

Julia watched them. Some relieved. Some unsettled. None untouched.

A gentleman approached the rail, exhaling deeply as he took in the sight of the harbor "Well," he said, "I, for one, am quite pleased to see land again."

Another man beside him nodded quickly. "Agreed. I've had my fill of the sea."

The ship slowed as it entered the harbor proper, the sounds of the port growing louder with every passing moment.

Calls from the dock. Orders shouted across water. The creak of ropes and wood as ships adjusted to their moorings.

"They'll have us disembarked within the hour," someone said.

"I'll not set foot on another vessel for the rest of my life."

"That's what you said before we left…"

"And I meant it then too…"

Julia's gaze shifted again. Not everyone agreed.

A younger woman stood apart from the others, her expression thoughtful rather than relieved. "It wasn't all terrible," she said softly.

The older man beside her turned sharply. "Not terrible?"

"Miss."

Julia turned.

A crewman stood nearby. "We'll be tying off shortly. Best be ready to move once the gangway's set."

Julia inclined her head. "Thank you."

He hesitated, then added, "You handled yourself well."
Julia blinked slightly. "I stood still."
"Not everyone managed that," he said.
Julia turned back to the harbor. Closer now. Details sharpening. Men moving along the docks. Crates stacked high. Carriages waiting.

Everything in motion. Everything continuing. As though storms happened, and were simply absorbed into what came next.

The ship gave a final slow turn, aligning with the dock as lines were thrown and caught, secured with practiced ease.

"Stand clear!"

"Hold her there!"

"Easy…!"

Passengers began to gather their things, the energy shifting from observation to movement, from reflection to action.

Julia didn't move immediately. Not because she couldn't. But because something in her resisted the ease of it.

The idea that one simply stepped off, and continued. As though nothing had been left behind.

The gangway was lowered. Julia drew a slow breath.

The harbor at Portsmouth was cold and efficient. Dockworkers moved briskly. Naval vessels loomed larger than anything she had seen in America. Bells rang. Orders carried crisply.

England did not care that the Atlantic had nearly swallowed them.

A carriage waited on the quay. A man stood beside it. Tall. Impeccably dressed. Expression politely expectant.

He removed his hat as she descended the gangplank. "Miss Whitmore," he said smoothly. "I trust your voyage was… instructive."

Julia's stomach turned. "You are Lord Edmund Ashcombe?" She asked carefully.

A faint bow. "At your service." His smile did not reach his eyes. They were assessing. Calculating.

"I regret the loss of your companion," he continued lightly. "I was informed there was an incident on board."

Julia swallowed. "Yes."

"How unfortunate." There was no warmth in the words. Only curiosity.

He extended his arm. "My carriage awaits. You must be exhausted after the long journey. I shall have your trunks seen to. "

She hesitated only a moment before allowing the footman to assist her into the carriage. The interior was elegant, though dim after the brightness of the quay.

The gentleman followed, settling opposite her. The door shut with a solid click.

They had barely left the harbor when his tone shifted. "Your father's trustees have confirmed the final transfer," he said conversationally.

"Transfer?" She asked.

"Of assets of course. The marriage will consolidate your holdings cleanly."

The air inside the carriage tightened. "You speak of this as though it is business," Julia said carefully.

"It is," he replied.

"And marriage?"

"An arrangement." He studied her. "You are quieter than described.

Julia forced a polite smile. "The storm was, sobering."

"Yes. So I imagine." He leaned back comfortably. "One never knows what the sea will take."

Soon the carriage turned down a narrow lane flanked by tall hedges and stone walls.

It was not London. It was not even near the proper road.

"This is not the Ashcombe estate," Julia stated.

"A temporary residence," he replied.

The gates opened quickly for them. Two men stood waiting. Not servants.

Guards. Julia's spine went rigid.

"You were expected," one of them muttered.

Expected. Her pulse spiked. The man beside her turned, smile thinning. "The marriage requires certain formalities," he said smoothly. "Until then, it is prudent that you remain, private."

Private. The word rang wrong. "I was told London," she said.

"You were told what was necessary."

He stepped out first, offering his hand. Julia was escorted inside.

The room she was escorted to was comfortable. That was the cruelty of it. Clean linens. Fireplace. Lock on the outside.

The door shut with a heavy, final sound. Julia stood in the center of the small room, listening as the bolt slid into place. She crossed quickly to the door. "Hello?"

Silence. She pressed her hand against the wood. "This is unnecessary," she called, keeping her voice steady. "If there has been some mistake…"

The first night she told herself it was precaution.

The second night she began listening. Voices in the hall. Men not speaking with noble cadence. Boot steps too heavy. Laughter too coarse.

The morning of the third day she pressed her ear to the door. "You're certain she's the one?" A voice asked.

"That's what the trustees confirmed," another replied.

"And the other girl?"

"Lost. Convenient."

Convenient. Julia's blood ran cold. She sat slowly on the edge of the bed. The man who claimed to be Edmund...spoke like someone awaiting inheritance. Not marriage.

A commotion coming from the guards got her attention. "You're not Ashcombe," one man snapped.

"Name's good as any," came the reply.

Julia froze.

"Does the real lord know your using it?"

"He knows what he needs to know."

Silence. The voices came lower then. "He wants her signature. That's all."

Julia's breathe caught. Signature. Transfer. They did not need a wedding. They needed documents.

She stepped back from the door slowly. The man who had met her at the docks was not Edmund Ashcombe. He was using the name. Which meant, the real lord Ashcombe was elsewhere.

And if Brenna arrived under her own name, she would be delivered into this trap. Julia's heart pounded so violently she felt dizzy. She had to get out. Now.

The opportunity came later that morning.

One guard left his post. The other lingered too near the stairwell.

A tray was delivered. The door opened briefly. Julia moved before she could think.

The metal candlestick from the bedside struck fast and clean against the guard's temple.

He collapsed and she did not wait around to see if he would rise.

She ran. Down the corridor. Through the back kitchen. Out into the cold English air. Shouts erupted behind her.

She did not turn. She ran until her lungs burned. Untilthe hedges gave way to road. Until the road gave way to town.

Chapter 13

By late afternoon the *Hawthorne* had settled into harbor order. Cargo manifests inspected. Dock fees negotiated. Repairs assessed. Sailcloth furled tight against the damp English air.

Callum did not seek her immediately. He made himself finish what required finishing. Only when the ship no longer demanded him did he climb back to the upper deck. He knew where he would find her.

She stood at the stern rail, exactly where the sea widened beyond the harbor's clutter. The tide moved slowly now, obedient to land. Fishing boats bobbed near the quay. The open channel lay beyond.

She had not removed the shawl. "You favor that view," he said.

She did not startle. "It is the only direction that does not ask something of me."

He stepped beside her. "Land asks much."

"Yes."

Silence settled, but not uncomfortable.

"You have not stepped ashore," he observed.

"No."

"And why is that?"

"Because once I do, I must become someone that I have yet to figure out who that someone is exactly supposed to be."

"And here?" He asked quietly.

She gave the faintest smile.

"Here I am only myself."

The words stirred something in him. Only herself.

He watched her profile, the steadiness, the intelligence in her gaze. The way she held herself like someone accustomed to command yet forced into concealment.

The more time he spent near her, the less "Julia Fairchild" fit. "You told me," he said carefully, "that your marriage was arranged."

"Yes, by my father before he passed. The trustees had agreed to act upon it with circumstances as they are."

"Trustees of what?"

She hesitated, barely. "My father's estate."

"And that estate is…?"

"Considerable."

He studied her closely. He had suspected. Now he was nearly certain. "Shipping," he said. "I believe you told me twelve ships."

"Yes."

"And you traveled unescorted across the Atlantic to meet a man you have never met."

"Yes. And what is your point in all this?"

"You do not find that usual?"

"I find it necessary," she replied.

"Tell me his name."

The wind shifted faintly. She stilled. "Why?"

"I would know the sort of man who expects you."

Her gaze searched his face. "Lord Edmund Ashcombe," she said quietly.

Everything in him went still. Outwardly, he did not move. Inwardly, the world tilted.

"Do you know him?" She asked.

He forced an even voice. "That is impossible."

Her brow furrowed. "Impossible?"

He stepped back slightly. "Yes."

"But why? Who is he?"

He opened his mouth… Boot steps thundered up the gangway.

"Captain!" One of the crew called. "Carriage has arrived. From the estate. A matter of urgency."

Brenna watched Callum's composure harden. "Estate?"

He did not answer that. "Who sent it," he demanded of the crewman.

"I don't know, Captain. Though the driver was insistent."

Her eyes searched his face, searching for something honest. "Why does his name disturb you?"

Because she was not sailing towards another man. Because she was sailing toward… him. Because someone had sent for her in his name without his knowledge. Because he had spent weeks convincing himself she was beyond reach.

He stepped closer before he meant to. "You crossed an ocean to meet him," he said.

"Yes."

"You intend to marry him."

"I intend to fulfill what was arranged."

"And if he is not what you expect?"

She gave a faint, defiant lift of her chin. "I have endured worse."

The words struck him harder than they should have. "You should not have to endure anything."

"That is not how arrangements work."

The wind caught her hair loose and brushed against her cheek. He had told himself she was promised. Told himself she was not his concern beyond safety. Told himself the distance was necessary.

But she had just spoken his name. And something inside him shifted irrevocably. "You do not even know him, and yet you would give yourself to him."

Her pulse flickered at her throat. “That is how these things are done.”

His restraint frayed.

The crewman called again from below. “Captain!”

Callum ignored him. “You should not walk blindly into a man’s house,” he said, voice low. “Not without knowing who stands inside it.”

“And you do?” She challenged.

“Yes.”

“How?”

He stepped into her space fully now. “Because I know the sort of men who arrange such crossings. The kind who believe a woman is currency.”

She did not step back. “Why does it matter so much to you?’

There it was. The truth neither of them had named. He could continue pretending she was another man’s future, or, he could stop pretending. “I do not like the thought of you stepping into a man’s arms that you have never met,” he confessed in a low voice as not to carry on the wind.

Her breathe caught. The air went very still. “That is not your concern.”

“No,” he agreed. “But it is.”

She stared at him. “Why?”

He did not speak any of his thoughts aloud, instead, he reached for her. Not gently. Not cautiously. His hand closed around her waist and pulled her towards him in one decisive movement.

She gasped. And he kissed her. It was not tentative. It was not polite. It was weeks of restraint breaking at once. Salt and wind and something dangerously close to hunger.

For a heartbeat she went rigid in shock. Then her fingers twisted in his coat. The harbor disappeared. The world narrowed toheat and breath and the undeniable fact that this was not indifference.

When he pulled back, it was abrupt, as though he had nearly done something unforgivable.

Her eyes were wide.

His voice was rougher than before. "You are not stepping off this ship until I understand what waits for you," he said.

"You cannot..."

"I can." His jaw tightened. He stepped back, regaining control. "I don't trust this situation. I do not have time to explain."

The crewman cleared his throat loudly below. "Should I send the carriage on its way?"

Callum released her fully. He straightened his coat. "I will return before nightfall," he said. "Do not leave this ship."

"You do not get to do that and then leave," she said breathlessly.

"I do."

"You have no right."

"No," he agreed. "But I will not apologize."

He turned before she could respond further and defended the gangway.

She watched from the rail, breath uneven and lips still warm from his, he descended the gangway and crossed the quay toward the waiting carriage. No crest marked it. No herald announced it. Just a plain dark vehicle waiting with impatient stillness.

Brenna felt something colder than sea and wind. Lord Edmund Ashcombe. Impossible, he had said.

Not because he did not know the name. But because he knew it too well.

Callum did not look back at the ship. If he did, he might hesitate.

Instead, he spoke quietly to the first mate of the watch before stepping off the quay. "Keep two men aboard tonight," he instructed. "Rotate them. No one unfamiliar comes near her without my approval."

"Aye, Captain," the sailor hesitated, "and if she attempts to leave?"

"Delay her," Callum said evenly. "Without force."

By the time Callum reached the waiting carriage, his expression had settled into controlled stillness.

Reed had gone ashore earlier that afternoon, not to the markets yet, but to inspect his own modest estate on the outskirts of town. He would roam the markets in the morning. Reed always did. If there was gossip, debt, dock rumor, or whispered conspiracy to be heard, it would be found there among the fishmongers and dock clerks.

The door shut behind him. Callum let the motion of the carriage carry him while he reviewed it all.

Shipping magnate in Boston. Trustees. A daughter crossing alone. And the name she had spoken… Lord Edmund Ashcombe.

Years ago, her father had stood in his very study and made a proposal. Not a romantic one. A practical one. An alliance of shipping and landed title.

Callum had been younger then, not reckless, but not yet tempered by the sea. He remembered the conversation clearly.

"You would secure her future," her father had said. "And our lines would merge."

Callum had declined. Not cruelly. Not dismissively. He had paid the final outstanding investment between their houses in full, an old investment from his father's time, and made himself clear. "I will not bind a woman I have never met," he had said then.

Her father had pressed.

Callum had refused. The account had been settled. The agreement dissolved.

Or so he believed. After her father's passing, he had never given it another thought. He had assumed the man had made other arraignments. The trustees would have amended matters. That the world had moved forward.

He had never called for her. He had never sent a letter. He had never expected her to cross the Atlantic in his name. And yet, she had.

The carriage rocked over uneven stone. Something colder settled in his chest. If he had refused, and if her father had died, who revived the arrangement? And why?

The carriage rolled through iron gates as dusk bled across the sky. The Ashcombe estate stood quiet and dignified above the Channel cliffs. Lamps burned in the lower windows.

Nothing appeared disturbed. That, perhaps, unsettled him more. He stepped down before the footman could open the door. "Who sent the carriage?" He asked abruptly.

"Message came from inside, my lord," the footman replied. "Said you were required."

Required.

Callum mounted the steps without slowing.

The butler, Mr Carrington, opened before he knocked. "My lord," the man said evenly.

"Who summoned me?"

"A letter arrived not an hour past," Carrington replied. "Delivered by hand. Insisted upon speaking with you privately."

"From whom?"

"He declined to give a name."

Callum's features grew stern. "Where is he?"

"He departed ten minutes before your arrival. The letter was left in your study."

Callum went still. "He departed?"

"Yes, my lord. Said he would not wait."

"Did you allow him in the house?"

"He presented knowledge only a familiar party would possess."

Cold moved through Callum's veins.

He did not remove his coat. He moved directly down the corridor, boots echoing sharply against stone.

The study door stood closed. He paused only a moment before opening it. The fire burned low. The room appeared undisturbed.

The desk remained orderly. Then he saw it. A single folded paper lay at its center. No seal. No crest. Just his name written in confident hand.

The message inside was short.

You were wise torefuse once.

You will not refuse again.

The girl has already crossed.

This time, the sea will not save her.

The fire cracked softly behind him. Callum read it twice. His expression did not change. But something behind his eyes hardened into iron.

He lowered the paper slowly. No mention of marriage. No mention of estates. Just possession. The girl. Crossed. And a threat.

The sea will not save her. That meant they already knew. Knew she had sailed. Knew she had been at risk. Knew she had survived.

Which meant someone had been watching far longer than he had realized. He turned toward the butler, who hovered near the door. "Describe him."

"Mid-thirties perhaps, my lord. Dark coat. Carried himself confidently. He carried an accent that is difficult to place. Spoke as an educated gentleman." Carrington paused as he seemed to be trying to recall any other details he could give. "I did not let him alone in your study, my lord."

Callum returned his attention to the single sheet of paper. The girl has already crossed. This time, the sea will not save her.

Not if he had anything to say about it. He slipped the paper into his coat pocket. "Double the watch at the gates tonight," he ordered calmly.

"Yes, my lord."

"And if that man returns," Callum added.

The butler swallowed. "Yes?"

"Do not admit him." He stepped to the window overlooking the cliffs. Below, the Channel moved dark and restless.

They had lured her once. They had nearly succeeded. They believed he would be forced into compliance. They believed invoking her would corner him. They did not understand him at all.

Years ago, he had refused to bind her to an arrangement made without her consent. He had paid the debt to her father in full and dissolved the understanding. He had assumed the matter buried with the older man.

Instead, someone had dug it up. And sharpened it. The sea will not save her. His gaze shifted toward the distant harbor where the Hawthorne lay moored. She remained aboard. Unaware. Still believing she was walking toward a future. Not a trap.

He turned sharply from the window. "Prepare the carriage," he said.

"But you only just arrived, my lord."

"I am returning to the harbor."

And this time, the hunt would not be at sea.

By the time Callum returned, the harbor had gone dim and silvered by moonlight. Most of Portsmouth had settled. Only taverns near the quay still murmured with laughter and argument. The tide had shifted, pulling gently at mooring lines.

The *Hawthorne* lay steady. Two lanterns burned low along her deck, exactly as he had ordered.

Callum stepped from the carriage without waiting for assistance and crossed the dock at once. One of the watch straightened.

"Captain."

"What's the report?"

"No one boarded, sir. No inquiries. Quiet night."

"Any sign of surveillance?"

"None we saw, Captain."

He gave a brief nod. "And our guest?"

"She has remained onboard. Retired not long ago."

Relief did not show on his face. But it registered. He mounted the gangway without another word.

The ship felt different at night. Quieter. Breathing wood and rope. The low creak of timbers expanding and settling with the tide.

He did not knock at first. He paused outside her temporary cabin, listening. Silence.

He lifted his hand and rapped softly. No answer.

After a moment, he opened the door. The lantern inside had burned low. She had clearly tried to stay awake.

A book lay open across her lap, fingers still loosely curled around its edge. The shawl he had given her was draped over her shoulders, but one corner had slipped to the floor.

Her head rested against the wall, chin tilted slightly down. Exhaustion had claimed her despite her effort. He stood there longer than he should have. She looked beautiful even in her sleep. Less guarded. Less deliberate. The storm, the secrecy, the crossing, all of it softened in stillness.

He stepped inside quietly and closed the door behind him. The letter burned in his coat pocket.

This time, the sea will not save her. His jaw tightened. He crossed the room carefully and lifted the fallen edge of the shawl, settling it back over her shoulders.

She stirred faintly. "Callum?" She murmured, not fully waking.

He hadn't expected to hear his name from her, and the quiet way she said it lingered longer than it should have. "Yes."

"You returned."

A corner of his mouth tilted in the way she sounded doubtful of his return. "I said I would."

Her eyes fluttered open briefly, unfocused in the lantern light. "Did you learn anything?"

"Enough."

That seemed to satisfy her half-conscious mind.

"I tried to wait," she said half asleep.

"I know."

"I thought…if I slept…you might not…"

"I am here."

Her breathing slowed again. For a moment he considered waking her fully. Telling her everything. Telling her nothing.

Instead, he crouched slightly so his voice would not carry beyond the cabin. "You are not stepping off this ship tomorrow," he said quietly, more to himself than to her.

Her fingers shifted faintly against the fabric of the book.

"You are safe here," he added. That word, safe, felt insufficient now. Because the threat was not random. It was deliberate. Someone had entered his house. Left a message and named her.

He studied her face again, the strength in it even at rest.

He rose slowly. Before leaving, he extinguished the lantern to dimmer glow and ensured the latch rested quietly into place.

Outside her cabin, the deck lay still under moonlight. Callum stood at the rail, eyes on the dark harbor. The sea had nearly taken her. Now the land will try.

He had refused to bind her years ago because it was the right thing. Now someone sought to force his hand by placing her in danger.

They miscalculated. Because there was one thing they had not considered. He would protect her whether bound or not. And this time, he would not wait.

Chapter 14

Brenna would soon wake, and Callum would have to decide how much to tell her. The harbor stirred slowly, ropes groaning as tide shifted. The *Hawthorne* rocked gently against her berth, outwardly calm. Reed had just left.

Callum had not slept.

By the time Brenna stepped onto the deck, he was already there. He stood near the foremast, speaking to two of the remaining crew. When he saw her, he dismissed them with a nod.

Callum walked over to her, his face unreadable. "Come below," he said quietly.

"Why?"

"We must leave tonight under the cover of darkness."

Her brow furrowed. "You said we were safe here."

The wind shifted, carrying the distant murmur of dockside voices.

"Below," he said, with more force than he intended.

Once below and Callum was certain their voices wouldn't travel he briefly explained that they will travel by carriage to his estate. In darkness. No witnesses.

He led her toward a small storage chest near the companionway. He opened it and rummaged through and began pulling out items left behind by crewmen.

She watched as he pulled out a rough wool coat. "What are you doing?"

"Ensuring no one recognizes you." He approached her and held out the cloak. "It's not elegant, it will serve."

"You believe I am in danger," she stated as she looked at the cloak he offered.

"I do."

Her breath caught faintly. "You know something," she said.

"I will not tell you here. Stay below today. Tonight we will travel."

"And what will I be at your estate?" She asked.

"You will be there as my guest."

She did not move immediately. "You kissed me yesterday," she said suddenly.

His expression did not shift, but something behind it tightened.

"Yes."

"And now you expect me to follow you."

"I expect you to follow me cautiously. I do not have time to explain," he said

Her expression shifted, hurt flickering there. "You ask me to trust you, yet offer no explanation."

He draped the plain cloak gently over her shoulders. "Put this on and pull the hood when we depart."

"Very well," she said.

Relief did not show, but it settled in him none the less. The harbor was growing busier now. Men shouting. Cargo shifting. Eyes turning.

He could see the hurt the moment he withheld information from her. He expects her to trust him when he is guarding his words so closely. It flickered through her composure before she could disguise it, a small tightening around her eyes, a quiet withdrawal of trust.

Someone had arranged this long before the sea intervened. And he, Lord Edmund Callum Ashcombe, would uncover who stood behind this, hunt them through shadow and silence alike, if it took his last breath to do so.

"Now," Callum said quietly. "We should go now."

Brenna pulled the rough cloak tighter around her shoulders. The gangplank had been lifted. The dock quiet. Only a single lantern burned near the far post.

"Keep your head down," he murmured.

"You make it sound as though I am a fugitive."

"Tonight you are unseen."

They moved quickly down the quay, slipping past stacked crates and coiled rope.

"Was my ship here?" She asked softly.

"It was," he said.

Her breath caught. "Was?"

"Gone for repairs."

Hope faltered.

"It matched your description perfectly. They sent the passengers inland."

She swallowed. "And my friend?"

"I do not know. Now quiet, no more talking."

The carriage waited in the shadow. They stepped inside the dark interior without further word. Behind them, the *Hawthorne* rocked gently as though nothing had changed.

The carriage rolled over uneven stone. Outside, Portsmouth had gone quiet, shutters drawn, tavern laughter distant. Brenna stared out at dark hedgerows as the carriage rolled. "If she survived," she whispered, "she would come for me."

"Yes," Callum said. He truly believed that. "But she also may believe you drowned."

And yet the dock clerk's words echoed. Sent inland quick as they could walk. Inland to where?

"You told me the ship was safe," she said at last.

"It was," Callum replied evenly.

"And now?"

"It no longer suffices."

She tried to study him but was impossible with the dim moonlight shining in. "What changed in the span of a few hours?"

He did not answer immediately. "Reed overheard talk this morning," he said.

"What sort of talk?"

"That a man stood near the quay last night. Watching."

"Watching what?"

"Our ship," he said. "For you."

Her pulse quickened. Silence filled the carriage.

"How could he know I was aboard?"

"He did not know," Callum answered. "He suspected."

"That is hardly reason to flee in the dark."

"It is reason enough to adjust position."

She gave a faint, sharp exhale. "I am not a shipment."

"No," he said quietly. "You are the objective."

The word hung between them. "Objective?" She repeated. She shifted slightly, the carriage rocking beneath them. "And you determined that remaining aboard was too obvious?"

"Yes."

"You said the *Hawthorne* could not be touched."

"She cannot," he agreed. "But the harbor can."

"You really think this person would have waited, to follow me the moment I stepped ashore?"

"I believe that was the intention, yes."

"Then why not let them?" She challenged "Why not see who approaches?"

His gaze met hers in the moonlight, steady, unflinching. "Because I will not use you as bait."

The words were quiet, but iron. "I did not realize that was the alternative."

"It was."

The carriage turned, gravel crunching as the left the main road.

"You could have told me," she said more softly now.

"I am telling you."

"And if I refused?"

The corner of his mouth tilted upward. "I would have carried you."

Her breath caught, half indignation, half awareness that he meant it. "You are insufferable."

"I am practical. And cautious."

They rode in silence a moment longer. "Why your estate?" She asked finally.

"Because it is private. And I control who enters it."

"And if this man follows?"

"He will not."

"How are you so certain?"

Callum leaned closer. He could feel her breath on his cheek as he whispered, "Because I will see him before he sees you."

Her breath slowed at his nearness. "You speak as though you have done this before."

"I have."

"Protected women from unseen men?"

"No."

"Then what?"

"Hunted unseen men."

Brenna's fingers tightened slightly in her lap. The carriagerolled steadily forward.

And for the first time since leaving the ship, Brenna did not feellike she was being removed from safety.

Earlier that same morning, Reed had made his way to the bustling area that served well for fresh goods, a vast array of supplies, and information.

By the time the sun burned thin gold through the mist, the lower market already hummed. Fishmongers shouted prices. Dockhands argued over crates. Women haggled over flour and salt porks. Sailors, half-rested and half-drunk, drifted between stalls.

Reed moved through it like a man without a purpose. Which meant he heard everything.

He stopped at a fish stall first. "Storm a fortnight ago pull in any wreckage?" He asked casually, flipping a coin between his fingers.

The old fisherman squinted at him. "Bits. Broken spar. Some crates."

Reeds pulse ticked once. He nodded, not revealing disappointment.

He moved on. A short while later he neared the rope seller, two dockhands spoke low.

"… stood there near midnight."

"Who?" the other asked.

"Tall one. Dark coat. Didn't look like dock labor. Near stood by that brig the entire time."

Reed slowed his pace without appearing to. "Which brig do you say?" He asked mildly, as though curious.

"The sleek one. Dark hull. Came in but yesterday." The dockhand seemed more than pleased to share this tidbit of secret information.

The *Hawthorne*.

Reed leaned casually against the stall. "Men watch ships all the time."

"Not like this one," the dockhand said. "He wasn't waiting for cargo."

Looking curious, Reed asked, "What was he waiting for then?"

The man shrugged uneasily. "For someone I 'spos."

Reed's coin stilled. "What someone?"

"Woman, I think. Asked if a lady had disembarked."

Reed's expression did not change.

"And I'm tellin' you," he went on, enjoying how the others hung on his words. "I told him I didn't know. Didn't like the way he asked."

The fisherman behind them snorted. "He stood there long enough. Near an hour after dusk."

Reed's thoughts sharpened. Callum had returned late. If someone had been watching... They were checking whether she stepped ashore.

"You see where he went?" Reed asked lightly.

"Up towards the cliff road."

Towards the estates. Reed dropped two coins onto the stall. "Much obliged." He walked away without haste. But his mind moved quickly.

A man entered Ashcombe's estate the night before. A man watched the *Hawthorne* from the quay. A man asking if a woman disembarked. The same man? Or part of the same design.

Reed turned down a quieter lane and paused beneath the shadow of a stone archway. If the watcher expected her to leave the ship, then the letter to Callum was not merely a threat. It was surveillance. They did not know she had remained aboard. Which meant, they would check again.

Reed glanced toward the harbor. The *Hawthorne* gleamed dark against the morning light. Too visible, Too predictable. He adjusted his coat and began walking back toward the quay.

If someone had watched last night, he would watch again today. And this time, Reed intended to see him first.

Chapter 15

The carriage moved swiftly through the last stretch of darkness, the rhythmic clatter of hooves muffled by the early morning mist that clung low to the ground.

Inside, Brenna sat opposite Callum, her hands folded tightly in her lap as the events of the night settled uneasily around her. "You said someone would be making inquiries," she said at last.

"Reed," Callum replied. "He went ashore earlier this morning."

"So quickly?"

"He knows where to look."

Brenna studied him. "The markets."

Callum's brow lifted slightly. "Yes, that is where news travels first and the fastest."

She gave a nod of agreement. "If my friend reached port, someone will have seen her."

Callum watched her closely. "You've spoken of your friend more than once," he said. "Yet you've never given me her name."

Brenna stilled.

The carriage rocked gently as it moved along the narrow road, the soft rhythm of the wheels filling the silence between them.

For just a moment, her fingers tightened slightly in her lap as she held his gaze. "She…" she began, then hesitated.

Callum noticed. "Yes?"

Brenna looked away briefly toward the window before answering. "Brenna." The name felt strange on her tongue.

Callum studied her carefully. She held his gaze.

A quiet moment passed between them.

Callum shifted slightly as the carriage turned onto a narrower road. "We'll know any information soon enough."

"That's not particularly comforting."

"No."

The carriage rolled on.

Outside, the faint gray light of dawn began to reveal the landscape, wide stretches of land bordered by low stone walls and tall hedgerows that seemed to run endlessly alongside the road.

Brenna leaned slightly toward the window, peering out. "This road is well kept," she observed.

"It is."

"Not a common route then."

"No."

She glanced back at him. "We've not passed another carriage."

Callum didn't answer.

Brenna looked out again, her eyes tracing the length of the road ahead as it curved gently between open fields and clusters of ancient trees. "Is this leading to a larger estate?"

Callum's mouth curved slightly. "It is."

"How much farther?"

"We've been on it for some time," Callum replied.

Brenna turned back toward him, catching something in his tone. "What does that mean?"

Callum met her gaze evenly. "It means you've been on my land for the past several minutes."

Brenna blinked. She turned quickly back to the window. The realization settled in slowly. The fields stretched farther than she could see, broken only by distant tree lines and carefully maintained boundaries that spoke of wealth and control.

"This is all yours?"

"It is."

Brenna let out a quiet breath.

Callum almost smiled.

The carriage rounded a final bend. And then the estate came into view. It rose from the landscape with quiet authority, a sprawling stone manor set back from the road, its façade catching the first light of dawn. Tall windows reflected the pale sky, and ivy climbed along portions of the walls, softening the strength of its structure without diminishing its presence.

Wide steps led to a grand entrance, flanked by columns and lanterns still faintly glowing from the night. Beyond it, the grounds stretched outward in carefully designed order, gardens, hedges, and distant outbuildings just visible through the morning haze.

Brenna studied him. "You are more than a sea captain."

"I never said I was not."

"You said you only stayed here occasionally."

"I do."

"This is not a place one visits occasionally."

The carriage slowed as it approached the front of the house.

"You would be surprised."

Brenna leaned back slightly, still taking it in. "I'm not easily surprised."

Callum glanced at her. "I've noticed."

The carriage came to a smooth stop. Callum stepped down first, turning to offer his hand "Careful."

Brenna accepted it, stepping onto the gravel drive as the cool dawn air settled around them. Before they reached the door, it opened.

A tall man stood waiting, composed and precise, as though he had been aware of their arrival well before they came into view. "Welcome home, my lord."

Callum inclined his head. "Carrington."

Brenna's attention was on the staircase beyond the foyer and did not linger on the title that Callum was given.

"Prepare a guest chamber," Callum instructed evenly.

"Yes, my lord."

The word slipped past her again in the quiet movement of arrival. Callum turned to her. "You will be comfortable here."

"That remains to be seen."

"You are safer here than the harbor."

"You repeat that often," Brenna pointed out.

"Because it is true."

She held his gaze a moment longer, searching for something he had not yet given.

"When will you explain?" She asked.

"Soon."

That word again. Soon. She exhaled, then allowed the butler to lead her upstairs.

Callum did not watch her go. He listened. The faint rhythm of her steps along the corridor. A door closing. Silence.

The study felt smaller than it had the night before.

He closed the door behind him and removed his coat, laying it carefully across the back of the chair. He unfolded the letter again, though he did not need to reread it.

His mind replayed her words from the deck of his ship. She had spoken without hesitation. As someone who had grown up reading manifests.

He had suspected then.

But when she said the name, Lord Edmund Ashcombe, there had been no more doubt.

She was not simply the companion. She was the heiress. His once betrothed. And someone had maneuvered her.

A sharp knock interrupted his thoughts. He stilled.

"Enter."

Carrington stepped inside. “My lord, a message has arrived from the harbor.”

Callum’s expression did not change. “From whom?”

“Mr. Reed has sent word he will call upon you before evening.”

Callum nodded once. “Very well.”

The butler hesitated. “He mentioned he may not come alone.”

Callum’s gaze sharpened slightly. “Did he say more?”

“No, my lord.”

“Very well. Has Miss…” he caught himself. “Has our guest been shown to her chamber?”

“Yes, my lord. The housekeeper took it upon herself to see her settled in.”

“See that she has hot bath water at once. And something proper to eat. She’s had little rest these past weeks.”

“And her things?”

“She has none,” he said quietly. “Send word to the dressmaker in town. Discreetly. A few gowns suitable for the season.”

Carrington nodded and withdrew.

Callum had grown accustomed to seeing her in borrowed wool and salt stiff linen. The thought of her dressed again in silk, in colors chosen for her rather than necessity, struck him unexpectedly. Not because she required finery, she carried herself in elegance even in rough cloth, but because she deserved to feel restored to herself.

And he found, against his better judgement, that he wanted to be there when she did.

Julia stepped into the narrow street just as the first light began to stretch across the rooftops, pale and uncertain. The air carried that heavy stillness that lingered after too many hours of noise, of drink, of voices, of things better left unspoken.

She didn't stop. Didn't look back. Her pace was steady, though her heart refused to follow suit. Each step felt louder than it should, the scrape of her shoes against the uneven ground echoing far too clearly in her ears.

Keep moving.

The street opened gradually, widening as it gave way to the early stirrings of the market. Vendors were only just beginning to set their stalls, crates dragged into place, cloths shaken out, the low murmur of voices still rough with sleep.

It was not yet busy. But it would be. And that was what she needed. People. Noise. Witnesses.

Julia lowed her head just enough to avoid attention without appearing as though she was hiding. She could not afford to look afraid. Even if she was.

A man staggered past her, the smell of drink clinging heavily to him. He glanced at her once, then again, slower this time.

"Well now," he muttered, his voice thick. "Bit early for a stroll, isn't it?"

Julia didn't answer. Didn't break her stride.

His hand caught her arm before she had taken two more steps. "Didn't say you could go," he added, his grip tightening.

Julia's breath hitched, but only for a moment. She turned, her expression sharper than she felt. "Then it's fortunate I didn't ask."

The words surprised even her.

The man blinked, thrown off just enough. "Careful," he said, though his grip loosened slightly. "You don't look like you belong down here."

Julia met his gaze evenly. "Then perhaps you should let me pass."

Then, with a low chuckle, he released her. “Go on, then,” he said. “Before someone else decides otherwise.”

Julia didn’t wait. She pulled free and continued forward, her pace just a fraction faster now.

The market grew busier with every step. Voices rose. Movement increased. The world began to fill in around her.

And with it, her chances.

Julia moved between the stalls, her eyes scanning without appearing to. Faces blurred together, vendors, laborers, early buyers, none of them looking closely enough to see what she was. Or where she had come from. That was good. That was what she needed.

Still, she could feel it. The awareness. The possibility that someone had noticed her absence. That someone might already be looking.

She forced herself to slow. To breathe.

Not running. Not yet.

A cart rolled past, its wheels creaking loudly as it cut across the narrow path. Julia stepped aside, letting it pass, using the moment to steady herself.

Portsmouth’s lower market swallowed her. She had escaped. And she had nothing. Julia left too quickly to think about grabbing anything. She did find coin sewn into a hidden pocket of her… what was left of her gown.

She moved through Portsmouth with her sleeves rolled and hair hastily pinned back, trying to look less like a lady and more like someone who belonged on the streets. She had found a quiet, dark place to hide for the night. The cold had crept through the boards beneath her.

For the first time since striking the guard, the full weight of it pressed in. A little over a fortnight ago they had stood together at the rail of a ship, laughing at rumors of pirates.

Now she lay on straw in a foreign country, hunted by men who wore titles like masks.

Sleep came in fragments. Every creak of wood startled her awake.

When dawn finally thinned the darkness, she rose stiff and sore. With one purpose in mind, to find the real Lord Edmund Ashcombe, she set off for the market.

"You look lost." The voice came from her left.

Julia turned slightly. A woman stood behind a small stall, arranging bundles of herbs with practiced hands.

"I'm not," Julia said.

The woman glanced up briefly, her gaze assessing, but not unkind. "Mm," she said. "Then you're in a hurry for no reason."

Julia's lips pressed together faintly. "Perhaps I am."

The woman shrugged. "Market's no place for hurry. Makes you noticeable."

That was true.

Julia inclined her head slightly. "Thank you."

The woman returned her attention to her work. "Don't thank me. Just slow down."

Julia did. Just enough. But not enough to quiet the tension coiling tighter in her chest.

Every sound felt sharper now. Every voice louder. Every movement, too close.

A shout carried from somewhere behind her. Not directed. But enough to send a flicker of urgency through her.

Julia didn't turn. Didn't run. But she moved. More deliberate.

Her eyes scanned the crowd again, searching for something.

Julia quickly pulled a shawl from a vendor's stall and left coins, without counting, and hurried away. Her cloak was gone. Her hair in disarray. She forced her breathing steady.

She had to find the real Edmund Ashcombe. She approached a fishmonger first. "Pardon," she asked quietly. "Would you know where Lord Edmund Ashcombe resides?"

"Ashecombe? Keeps property near the western cliffs. But he's rarely there."

"Does he live here?" She pressed.

"Mostly London when he's not out on one of his ships."

A woman beside her leaned closer. "Why would you be seeking him?" She asked.

Julia forced calm. She provided an answer without having to divulge too much. "I was expected."

The woman shrugged. "Best ask near the harbor office."

Julia turned, and collided lightly with someone solid.

"Careful," a calm male voice said. His hand caught her elbow before she stumbled.

She looked up. And forgot, briefly, why she had been running at all. A stranger, a very handsome stranger. Broad-shouldered. Weathered. Eyes sharp and assessing beneath a low brimmed hat. He was not dressed as a gentleman, yet he carried himself like one accustomed to command.

"My apologies," she managed.

"No harm done." He did not release her immediately. His gaze lingered a fraction too long, assessing, not admiring.

"You're not from Portsmouth," he observed.

"And I assume you are?" She countered.

The corner of his mouth shifted faintly. "Often enough."

She realized she was still starring. At the line of his mouth. The steadiness of his posture. The way he seemed both relaxed and entirely aware. She forced her eyes upward. "I am looking for Lord Edmund Ashcombe," she said, hoping to sound composed.

His expression did not change, but something sharpened in his gaze.

She swallowed. "You can release me now. I'm quit steady."

"For what purpose do you have with Ashcombe?" He said casually as he released her.

"That is none of your concern."

His gaze did not leave her face. "Humor me."

She hesitated. Then made a decision. "My name is Julia Fairchild," she said firmly. "I must locate…"

The name hit him like cannon fire. His eyes sharpened. He did not let her finish her sentence. "Julia," he repeated slowly.

"Yes."

"You need to come with me."

She stiffened. "I will not be taken again."

He paused. "Again?" He said calmly, looking at her. "There is a man who needs to hear what you have just said."

Julia's pulse raced. "Who?"

"Captain Callum Hawthorne."

The name meant nothing to her. But something in his tone suggested urgency, not threat.

"Speaking of names sir, just who are you?" She questioned.

"His first mate, Elias Reed."

Chapter 16

This is Lord Ashcombe's residence?" Julia asked.

"This is where Captain Hawthorne is currently residing." Reed answered, trying to hide a smile at what was about to unfold.

The estate rose from the cliffs in pale stone severity, overlooking the restless gray sweep of the channel.

As the carriage rolled to a stop, Reed exited first to assist Julia down. He then mounted the steps and knocked firmly.

Moments later, the door opened. A butler stood framed in polished wood and restraint.

Callum could hear raised voices carried faintly from the front hall. Reed must have came straight away.

Carrington appeared at the door of the study. "My lord, Mr. Reed has arrived, and he brings, a lady."

That made him look up. Callum's brow lifted slightly. "Has he." Reed does not bring ladies. "Show them in."

Moments later Reed entered the study with infuriating calm.

Behind him stood a woman Callum had never seen. Blonde, Eyes bright and anxious. Movements quick and expressive.

Not Brenna.

Reed moved his hat slowly, half grinning. "Afternoon, Captain," he said deliberately.

Callum's eyes flicked toward him in warning. Reed's grin widened. "I found this lady looking for you." Julia stepped forward. "Captain Hawthorne?" She began. Callum went still. "Yes," he said smoothly.

My name is Julia Fairchild. I traveled with Miss Brenna Whitmore from America. I was seeing you regarding her arrival…"

Upstairs, Brenna had just reached the middle of the corridor on her way to bathe when she heard Reed's voice. Forgoing the bath for the moment, she hurried toward the study, hoping he had news.

The study door opened abruptly. Brenna, still wearing her garments from aboard ship, entered and came to a stop.

Her breath stopped. "Julia?"

Julia turned. Neither moved.

Then chaos.

"Brenna!"

They collided into each other, hands gripping shoulders, faces disbelieving and tears streaming.

"You're alive!"

"I thought you drowned!"

"You were swept…"

"You were lost…"

They laughed and cried at once, clinging as though the Atlantic still separated them.

Brenna pulled back first, hands still gripping Julia's arms. "You're here," she breathed.

Reed leaned casually against the wall, watching.

Callum did not move. He watched Brenna.

His gaze moved from Brenna, to Julia, and back to Brenna. Calm. Measured. "Is there something I should know?" He asked quietly.

Julia looked between them. "You didn't tell him?" She whispered.

Brenna swallowed.

"Tell me what?" Callum asked. His tone was even. Too even.

Reed watched the exchange with undisguised interest, enjoying the tension.

Julia straightened. “My friend,” she said carefully, “is Brenna Whitmore.”

Silence.

Brenna’s breath left her slowly.

Callum did not blink. “I know,” he said

Both women froze. “You…what?” Brenna whispered.

“I suspected the moment you spoke of shipping routes,” he replied calmly. “The moment you corrected my sail trim. The moment you told me your father owned twelve vessels.”

His gaze softened slightly, though something sharper remained beneath it.

“No merchant’s daughter speaks of tonnage with that precision.”

Brenna stared at him. “You let me lie,” She said. “Why?”

He stepped around the desk slowly. “Because you had reason.”

Julia looked between them in dawning disbelief. “You knew she wasn’t me, and you said nothing?”

His eyes returned to Brenna. “I was waiting.”

“For what,” Brenna asked.

“For you to trust me.”

Brenna held his gaze a fraction longer, something wounded and resolute flickering there.

“Trust is not summoned at command,” she said evenly, her voice steady despite the storm beneath it.

Brenna turned her attention back to Julia. She caught her friend by the shoulders, pulling her back just enough to study her properly.

“When did your ship dock?” She asked quickly. “We were told it limped in before ours.”

Julia hesitated.

"And why," Brenna continued softly, her brow furrowing now, "do you look as though you've crossed the Channel by foot?"

Her gaze moved over the rumpled, torn dress, the loose hair, the faint bruise near Julia's wrist.

"We left America with trunks," Brenna said. "What happened to you?"

"I escaped," Julia started to explain. "I was searching for Lord Ashcombe…"

"Julia," Brenna cut in sharply.

Julia blinked.

"I had to find Lord Ashcombe before you arrived because the man at the docks was not him and I thought if he tried to…"

"Julia."

The second interruption was firmer. Julia froze.

Brenna pulled back first, scanning Julia's face urgently. "You escaped?"

"Yes. I escaped and ran as fast as I could. I ended up in the market. That is where Mr. Reed found me."

"From what?" She had Callum's full attention now.

"I was taken by a man claiming to be Lord Edmund Ashcombe."

Silence dropped like a blade. Callum's gaze sharpened. "Tell me everything."

Julia did. The false Edmund at the docks. The isolated house. The mention of signatures. The conversation overheard.

Brenna's eyes flicked toward Callum. Silence fell heavy into the room.

"He said the trustees confirmed the transfer," Julia added. "That once the marriage was complete, the holdings would consolidate cleanly."

"My trustees," Brenna said slowly, "would not release holdings without formal correspondence."

"They might," Reed added, "if presented with convincing seals."

Brenna's hand flew suddenly to her side. "My reticule."

"It is somewhere in the trunks that were packed up," Julia told her.

"The letter." Brenna looked up sharply. "The letter is in my reticule."

Callum's gaze sharpened. "What letter?"

"The one arranging the meeting," she said. "The letter from Lord Ashcombe."

Callum stepped closer. "This letter. Describe it."

"Cream paper. Formal hand. Signed Edmund Ashcombe. It instructed me to sail under discretion. It said the marriage should be expedited upon arrival. It detailed the estate. The arrangement."

Callum's jaw tightened.

"It had a seal I did not recognize."

"What seal?" Reed asked.

"A crest," she said. "A falcon."

Reed swore under his breath.

Callum's eyes darkened. "My family crest is a stag."

The air shifted violently. "Your family crest?" Brenna repeated.

"Yes," Callum said.

Reed pushed himself off the bookcase and moved to the sideboard, pouring himself a drink with deliberate leisure.

"My crest is a stag," he repeated calmly. "A falcon belongs to another house."

Brenna's pulse became visible at her throat. "Which house?"

Callum's eyes went distant. "House Hawthorne."

The name hung between them.

"You wished to know why the name unsettled me." He held Brenna's gaze steadily. "It unsettled me because it is mine."

Julia's eyes widened first.

Brenna did not move.

"You are…" Julia breathed.

"Yes."

"The man I was to meet," Brenna began faintly.

"No."

Reed lifted his glass, watching the storm unfold with open amusement.

"I have never written to you," Callum said evenly. "I sent no such instruction."

"It instructed me to travel quietly," Brenna said slowly. "To come without escort."

"To make you vulnerable," Reed added.

Callum's voice dropped lower. "The letter was bait."

Brenna's thoughts reeled backward. The suspicious figure at the docks in America. The insistence on secrecy. The convenient timing.

"You were meant to sail," Callum continued, voice steady but edged now. "Under the belief you were expected."

"And intercepted," Reed finished.

Julia looked between them. "The man at the docks knew about the transfer," she said.

"Yes," Callum replied. "Because he sent the letter."

The pieces slid into place with brutal clarity.

"You were lured," Julia whispered to Brenna.

Callum's gaze remained fixed on Brenna. "You were meant to arrive here alone. With your wealth in transit and your name secured."

"And sign it away," she breathed.

"Or disappear."

Julia paled. "You think he would have…"

"Yes," Callum said simply. "Miss Fairchild, I need you to think carefully. The man who claimed my name, what did he look like?"

Julia frowned slightly, concentrating.

"He was tall," she said. "He dressed well enough. Fine coat, polished boots. The sort of man who wished to appear important. There was something slightly forced about it. The way he spoke, the way he carried himself. Not refined enough to be noble, but he knew enough to play one."

"Age?"

"Near your own, perhaps a little older. Dark hair. A trimmed beard. And a ring he turned constantly while he spoke."

"Then he is connected," Reed said.

"To whom?" Julia asked.

"To someone who knows my affairs," Callum answered. "And yours," he added, looking at Brenna.

Her thoughts raced. "The shipping routes," she said slowly. "The Atlantic crossings. My departure date."

"Your wealth is not secret," Reed said. "But your betrothal was."

"And the letter demanded secrecy," Brenna whispered.

Callum stepped closer, not touching, but near enough that his presence steadied rather than crowded. "You were never meant to marry me," he said quietly.

The truth rang between them.

"You were meant to vanish."

Reed cleared his throat. "If someone used the falcon," he said, "they meant to frame House Hawthorne."

Callum's gaze sharpened. "And stir trouble between houses."

Julia blinked. "Why?"

Callum's voice was quiet. "Because if I am drawn into scandal, and Brenna's wealth vanishes, the sea grows quieter for certain men."

Silence filled the study.

Brenna looked back at Callum. "You did not summon me?"

"No."

"You did not revive the agreement?"

"No."

"Then why…"

"Because someone believes I can be forced into it."

"You refused the arrangement," Brenna said, looking at Callum. "Years ago. And you never expected me."

"No."

The truth settled between them.

Brenna's voice lowered. "And yet you kissed me."

Reed nearly choked on his drink.

Callum did not look away. "Yes."

Julia's head snapped toward Brenna. "You what?"

"That is not the pressing matter," Callum said evenly.

"Oh, I believe it is," Reed muttered, deeply entertained.

Brenna's eye burned now, not with tears, but with something fiercer. "You ask for my trust," she said. "While withholding your name."

"I withheld it until I understood the threat."

"And now?"

"Now you know."

Silence stretched.

Julia reached for Brenna's hand. "We were lured," she said softly. "Both of us."

Brenna inhaled slowly, steadying herself. "And what do you intend to do about it, Lord Ashcombe?"

Callum's expression shifted, steel beneath composure. "I intend to find the man who used my name."

"And then?"

His. Gaze did not waiver. "And then I will end it."

Reed set his glass down, satisfaction plain. "Well," he said lightly, "this promises to be interesting."

Chapter 17

The study remained quiet for a moment after the truth settled between them. Brenna stood near the desk. Julia's hand clasp tightly in hers as though she feared letting go might make her vanish.

At last Julia leaned back, squinting at Brenna more carefully. "Good heavens," she said slowly.

Brenna blinked. "What?"

"You look dreadful."

Reed let out a quiet laugh into his glass.

Brenna frowned. "I beg your pardon?"

Julia gestured vaguely toward her. "Your hair is full of salt, that shirt belongs to a cabin boy, and you smell faintly of bilge water."

Brenna glanced down at the rough sailor's trousers and borrowed linen she still wore. "That is because," she said dryly, "I was rescued from the Atlantic."

Julia wrinkled her nose. "And you've remained dressed like a dockhand ever since?"

Brenna looked Julia over in return now, her expression shifting from indignation to disbelief.

"And you," she said, "look as though you fought your way here through a chimney."

Julia's hair hung loose and tangled, her torn dress creased and stained from her escape.

She lifted a hand to her head self-consciously. "Yes... well...circumstances were not ideal."

Callum cleared his throat lightly. "Ladies," he said, with a calm that suggested he had weathered far worse chaos.

Both women turned toward him.

"I believe the first order of business," he continued, "is that you remove yourselves upstairs."

Brenna crossed her arms. "That sounds suspiciously like dismissal."

"It is a recommendation," Callum replied. "You have both survived storms, kidnappers, and questionable lodging. You deserve hot water before further interrogation."

Julia nodded immediately. "I agree with the captain."

Brenna gave her a betrayed look.

Julia leaned closer and whispered, "You truly do smell of the sea."

Reed chuckled outright now.

Callum rang the small bell on his desk. A moment later the housekeeper appeared.

"Mrs. Dalton," he said, "prepare baths for our guests immediately."

"Yes, my lord."

"And see that whatever garments can be spared are sent to their chambers."

Mrs. Dalton inclined her head.

Julia was already guiding Brenna toward the door. "Come along," she said. "If I must explain everything that has happened to me, I intend to it while soaking in the hottest water in England.

Brenna allowed herself to be pulled away, though she cast one last look back at Callum. "This conversation is not finished," she warned.

"I would be disappointed if it were," he replied.

The door closed behind them and silence settled again in the study.

Reed leaned back against the bookcase, folding his arms. "Well, that went better than expected."

Callum exhaled slowly. "They will need clothing," he said. "Their trunks should have arrived with the other ship."

Reed nodded. "The one currently in dry dock."

"And in possession of whoever attempted to intercept them." Callum's jaw tightened as he continued, "until we recover those trunks, we assume anything in them has been examined."

"Which means whoever orchestrated this knows precisely who Brenna Whitmore is," Reed added.

"Yes."

Reed pushed himself away from the wall and stepped toward the desk. "So," he said, "what is our next move?"

Callum looked toward the door the women had just disappeared through. "First," he said quietly, "we make certain they remain safe."

"And then?"

His gaze hardened. "Then we find the man who used my name."

Reed smiled faintly. "Good," he said. "Because I've already started looking."

Steam curled softly through the bathing chamber, fogging the tall window as the hot water filled the copper tubs. The servants had long since withdrawn, leaving only the quiet sound of water lapping and the faint crackle of the small hearth.

Julia sank deeper into the warmth with a long sigh of relief. "I may never leave this tub again," she said.

Brenna sat in an adjacent tub scrubbing stubborn salt from the ends of her hair. "You might reconsider when it cools," she said dryly.

Julia studied her friend carefully now that the shock had settled. "I truly believed you were gone," she said quietly.

"When the mast snapped and they shouted you had gone over…"

Brenna's hands slowed. "I remember the railing giving away," she said. "Then the water. After that…very little."

"You clung to the wreckage?"

"A portion of the mast," Brenna answered. "By sheer stubbornness, I believe."

Julia gave a weak laugh. "That sounds precisely like you."

"The *Hawthorne* found me what seemed like hours later. I was barely conscious."

Julia's brows lifted. "And that man downstairs pulled you from the sea?"

"Yes."

"Julia shook her head slightly, amazed. "And you have been sailing beside your own betrothed all this time."

Brenna groaned softly. "Do not remind me."

Julia grinned faintly. "He is pleasing on the eyes. You kissed him."

Brenna splashed water towards her. "That was not the point of the story."

"It absolutely is."

Brenna tried to hide a smile before returning to seriousness. "But enough about me," she said. "What happened to you?"

Julia's expression sobered immediately. "Our ship reached England first," she began. "Damaged but afloat. They rushed passengers ashore before sending the vessel to dry dock for repairs."

"And then?'

"A carriage was waiting," Julia said. "With a gentleman claiming to be Lord Ashcombe. He already knew about losing you at sea. That is what stuck with me the most. You heard most of it in the study earlier."

Julia dipped her hands into the water, watching the ripples. "I had no reason not to believe him," she continued. "He knew we would be on that vessel, he was the one that made the arrangements."

Silence settled heavily between them.

"Exactly how did you escape?" Brenna asked.

Julia's lip curved slightly. "Poor planning on their part."

"You hit someone."

"Yes."

Brenna laughed despite herself. "I knew it."

"I ran through half of Portsmouth afterward," Julia continued. "Until I was certain no one followed."

"You had no coin, no escort, where did you stay?"

Julia let out a slow breath. "I found a quiet, secluded area near the docks. Some sort of shed I believe. It was safe enough. No one saw me, and by morning I could reach the market. I found a few coin sewn into a hidden pocket of the gown."

Brenna looked over at Julia. "I had forgotten about the hidden coins. Most of my gowns have them sewn in, for situations that may arise."

Julia looked at her gratefully. "I will be forever grateful for that. I purchased a shawl the next morning at the market. And then soon after I ran into Mr. Reed, literally."

Brenna sat quietly after that. Remembering another shawl. The one Callum placed around her shoulders aboard the *Hawthorne*. She remembered how warm it had been. How the scent of salt and cedar clung faintly to the fabric. And how strangely, steady, she had felt afterward.

Julia's voice pulled her back. "You haven't told me where you found yours. I saw it in your room."

Brenna blinked, returning to the present. "I didn't find it," she replied.

Julia raised an eyebrow. "Then where did it come from?"

Brenna allowed the faintest smile. "The captain."

Julia expression brightened instantly, studying Brenna again. "So," she said slowly, "what do you truly think of him?"
Brenna frowned. "Of who?"
Julia looked over at Brenna, "The man who rescued you, argued with you for two weeks, hid his name, and then admitted he is the very man you crossed an ocean to meet."

Brenna sank deeper into the cooling bath water, staring at the ceiling beams. "He is infuriating."

Julia smiled knowingly. "That is not what I asked."

Brenna hesitated. Then she said quietly, "He makes me feel as though the ground is never quite where I expect it to be."

Julia's smiled widened. "Yes," she said. "That sounds like trouble."

And Brenna had the distinct feeling she was right.

Steam still lingered faintly in the corridor as Brenna and Julia stepped from their chambers, hair damp and loosely pinned, the borrowed dresses falling a little differently on each of them.

The gowns had clearly been drawn from whatever could be found in the house, simple muslin, serviceable rather than elegant. But after weeks of salt, storm, and survival, even plain linen felt luxurious.

Julia smoothed the sleeve of her dress and turned slowly in the hallway. "I had nearly forgotten what it felt like to be clean," she said.

Brenna smiled faintly. "You should thank Callum for that. I suspect the entire household has been set into motion on our account."

Julia raised a brow. “Callum, is it?” She said with a smile tugging at her lips.

Just then the housekeeper appeared at the end of the corridor carrying a folded cloth. “My lady,” she said to Brenna with a small nod. “Lord Ashcombe asked that I tell you he and Mr. Reed have gone out on business.”

Brenna’s brows lifted. “So soon?”

“Yes miss. He said they would return before supper,” she continued, “and in the meantime he asked that you both eat and rest.”

Julia glanced sideways at Brenna. “Rest,” she repeated with quiet amusement.

The housekeeper gestured toward the stairs. “Lunch has been laid in the small dining room should you wish it.”

“Thank you,” Brenna said.

The woman inclined her head and disappeared down the hall.

The moment she was gone, Julia leaned closer. “Well,” she said.

“Well what?” Brenna asked.

“You heard the man. We are to eat and rest.”

“And?”

Julia’s eyes sparkled. “And I have no intention of doing either until I know where we have landed.”

Brenna laughed softly. “You mean to explore.”

“Of course.”

Julia moved toward the stairs, pausing halfway down to peer at the tall windows that overlooked the grounds. “Honestly Brenna,” she said, lowering her voice, “you crossed an ocean to meet this man and somehow ended up living in his house without knowing his name.”

“That was not precisely my plan.”

"No," Julia agreed, grinning slightly. "But it is undeniably entertaining."

Brenna followed her down the stairs, curiosity stirring despite everything. The house was quiet, the sort of quiet that belonged to old walls and well run households. Portraits lined the corridor. Tall windows spilled light across polished floors. Somehow deeper in the house a clock chimed the hour.

Brenna slowed near a portrait in the hall, studying the brass nameplate beneath it. "Strange," she murmured.

"What is?" Julia asked.

"The house staff call him *my lord*," Brenna said, "yet every sailor on that ship calls him Hawthorne."

Julia frowned slightly. "Perhaps both are true."

Brenna glanced toward the distant study door, where Callum stood earlier that morning, then back toward the sunlit grounds beyond the glass. "Not many men move between two worlds like that," she said thoughtfully. "One name for land, and another for the sea."

Julia considered it.

"A clever arrangement," Brenna continued. "A nobleman hunting pirates might prefer not to announce himself."

Julia nodded in agreement then paused at a doorway leading toward the back garden. "Shall we?" she asked.

"For a short walk," she said.

"Of course." Julia pushed the door open. Warm afternoon air drifted inside, carrying the scent of clipped hedges and sea wind from the cliffs beyond.

They stepped out together. And for the first time since Englandhad come into view, neither storm or conspirator stood immediately over them. But both women knew the calm would not lastlong.

Chapter 18

The Portsmouth market swelled with the usual chaos of morning, fishmongers shouting prices, carts rattling over cobbles, the smell of salt, tar, and fresh bread mingling in the air.

Callum and Reed moved through it with practiced ease, neither drawing attention nor appearing idle.

Reed paused beside a stall stacked with secondhand goods, coats, hats, belts, and travel cases piled in uneven rows. "Convenient sort of business," Reed muttered quietly. "Goods that arrive without questions."

Callum's gaze had already settled on two familiar shapes behind the stall.

Leather trunks. American make. He stepped closer.

The vendor, a narrow man with restless eyes, straightened. "Morning gentlemen. Looking for something particular?"

Callum rested a hand on the edge of the nearest trunk. "Perhaps."

The man smiled thinly. "Fine pieces. Just came in."

"From where?" Callum asked evenly.

The vendor shrugged. "A traveler down on his luck."

Reed chuckled softly beside him. "Funny thing about travelers," he said. "They rarely abandon their trunks."

The vendor's smile stiffened. "Well…circumstances change."

Callum opened one of the trunks slowly. Inside lay folded dresses, gloves and linens.

Julia's. Brenna's

Reed gave a low whistle. "Remarkable luck."

The vendor shifted his weight. "Quality goods fetch quality coin."

Callum closed the lid. "How much?"

The man named a price that made Reed laugh outright. "You're robbing us in daylight," Reed said.

The vendor shrugged again. "Fine ladies' things don't come cheap."

Callum met his gaze calmly. "You came by these this morning."

The man hesitated just long enough. "Perhaps."

"Who brought them?"

"A man."

Reed leaned closer to the stall. "Very helpful. You will have to do better than that."

"I don't keep records."

Callum placed a few coins on the table, far more than the trunks deserved.

The vendor's eyes lit immediately.

Callum pushed the money forward slowly. "You'll take this," he said, "and you'll tell me everything you remember about the man who sold them."

The vendor studied the coins, then scooped them up. "Tall fellow," he said. "Dark coat. Gloves. Didn't speak much."

"Accent?" Callum asked.

"Educated. Not local."

"Alone?"

The vendor scratched his chin. "Think so."

Reed tilted his head. "Think?"

The man hesitated. "There might've been someone waiting down the street. Didn't see him clear."
Callum exchanged a glance with Reed. "Which way did they go?" Reed asked.

The vendor pointed toward the harbor road. "Back that way."

"Have these delivered to Ashcombe estate," Callum said, nodding toward the trunks.

The vendor's eyes widened. "Yes, sir."

Reed picked up the smaller of the two cases, inspecting the clasp. "Outrageous price," he murmured once they stepped away.

Callum didn't slow his stride. "If it gives us a lead," he said quietly, "it's worth twice that."

Reed glanced back toward the vendor. "You think he told us everything?"

"No."

"Then what did we buy?"

Callum looked toward the harbor where ships rocked against their moorings. "A trail."

And for the first time since arriving in Portsmouth, it pointed somewhere.

The dining room felt unusually warm after the cool evening outside. Candles burned low along the table, their light catching the polished silver and the quiet tension between the four occupants.

Julia had just begun recounting the grounds she and Brenna had explored when the door opened and Callum and Reed entered.

"You've returned," Brenna said, setting down her glass.

"As promised," Callum replied, removing his gloves and taking his seat. "And not empty handed."

Julia leaned forward immediately. "That sounds promising."

Reed dropped into the chair opposite her with a faint grin. "That depends on your definition of promising."

The servant finished placing the last dish before withdrawing, leaving the room to them.

"Well?" Brenna asked.

Callum glanced briefly at Reed. "You spoke with the vendor," he said.

Reed nodded, reaching for the bread. "A trader near the south end of the market. Deals in secondhand goods mostly, cargo that 'changes hands' before anyone asks too many questions."

Julia stiffened slightly. "And?"

He had two trunks appear in his possession this morning," Reed continued. "American make. Fine leather. Brass fittings."

Brenna's heart skipped. "Our trunks."

"Very likely," Callum said.

Julia leaned forward. "Were they opened?"

Reed gave a dry laugh. "Madam, a man who buys trunks without asking questions does not leave them closed."

Julia grimaced. "I suspected as much."

Callum continued calmly. "The content had been disturbed. Some items missing surely."

"What sort of items tend to go missing?" Brenna asked.

"Jewelry mostly," Reed said. "Anything easily sold. Gloves. Smaller personal things."

Julia sighed. "Of course."

"But the dresses remain," Reed added.

Brenna blinked. "They didn't take them?"

"Too distinctive," Reed said. "Fine gowns are harder to move quietly unless one has the right clientele."

Julia leaned back in her chair. "So our clothing is now sitting in a merchant's stall?"

"Locked in his storeroom," Reed corrected.

Callum folded his hands on the table. "I purchased the trunks."

Both women looked up at once. "You what?" Julia said.

"They will arrive here tomorrow," he said simply.

Julia smiled in relief. "I should like to see my own wardrobe again before winter."

Brenna, however, was watching Callum more carefully.

"If they were in the market," she said slowly, "then the man who took them did not intend to keep them."

"No," Callum agreed. "He intended to empty them."

Julia frowned. "Meaning he has what he wanted already."

Reed nodded. "Likely searching for documents."

Brenna's pulse tightened. "Letters. Titles. Anything proving identity."

Callum met her eyes. "Exactly."

A quiet moment passed as that realization settled.

Julia broke the silence. "Well," she said, lifting her glass slightly, "at least we know where our dresses are."

Reed chuckled, "And tomorrow Portsmouth will wonder why a sea captain suddenly purchased half a lady's wardrobe."

Callum allowed the faintest hint of amusement. "It would not be the strangest rumor to circulate the docks."

Brenna studied him across the candlelight. "And the man who sold them?" She asked.

Reed shrugged. "He knows nothing useful. Claims the trunks were delivered before dawn by someone he had never seen before."

"Convenient," Julia murmured.

Callum's voice lowered slightly. "But it confirms one thing."

"And what is that?" Brenna asked.

He looked around the table at the three of them. "The man using my name is still here in Portsmouth."

The candles flickered softly as that truth settled over dinner. And suddenly the room felt a great deal smaller.

After dinner the four of them lingered in the study, the fire burning low while the last of the wine was poured. The evening had settled comfortably around them after the long day.

At length Callum rose. "There are a few matters I must see to before morning," he said, setting his glass aside. "I trust you can all manage perfectly well without me tonight."

"We shall try our best," Julia said, lifting her glass.

Callum chuckled softly. "Reed will be staying over this evening," he added, nodding toward his friend. "There are a few matters we need to see to early in the morning."

Reed raised his brows. "See? I am here under official orders."

Brenna smiled. Callum stepped away from the desk and paused at the door. "Try not to uncover too many secrets in my study in my absence."

"No promises," Julia replied.

Callum shook his head with quiet amusement. "Goodnight ladies."

"Goodnight," Brenna replied.

He lingered a brief moment longer, his eyes meeting hers, before stepping out into the hall and closing the door behind him.

Julia wandered about the study while Reed remained near the fire, looking entirely at ease. The room clearly belonged to Callum, maps of the Channel lined one wall, shelves of ledgers and navigation charts filled another.

Julia stopped in front of the mantle. "Oh."

Brenna looked up.

Julia leaned closer to the large portrait mounted above the fireplace. It was unmistakably Callum, though dressed in the formal attire of a nobleman rather than the sea worn captain they knew.

Below the frame was a small brass nameplate that Julia read aloud. "Lord Edmund Callum Ashcombe."

Brenna stepped beside her, studying the portrait with interest.

"Yes."

Brenna turned slowly toward Reed. "But everyone on the ship calls him Hawthorne."

Reed gave a small smile, clearly expecting the question to arise sooner or later. "That would also be correct."

Julia folded her arms. "So which one is he?"

Reed lifted his glass thoughtfully before answering. "Both."

Julia raised a brow. "That seems unnecessarily complicated."

Reed chuckled. "Perhaps. But there is a reason for it."

Brenna turned toward Reed. "The Crown?"

Reed nodded. "Years ago the Crown took notice of Ashcombe's shipping empire. His routes, his knowledge of the Channel, the ports…the business side of the sea."

Julia glanced again at the portrait. "That sounds rather respectable."

"Oh it was," Reed said dry. "But they also noticed something else."

Brenna smiled faintly. "His fondness for adventure."

Reed returned the smile. "Exactly."

He leaned forward slightly. "They knew Ascombe understood ships better than most naval officers. And they knew he had, certain talents when trouble appeared on the water."

Both ladies were intrigued now. "So what did they do?" Brenna asked.

They made him a proposal," Reed said. "If he would quietly assist in dealing with certain, pirate problems along the Channel, they would allow him a great deal of freedom in how it was done."

"And the name?" Brenna asked

"The Crown gave him one."

"Hawthorne."

Reed nodded to Brenna in response. "And it keeps Lord Ashcombe out of the gossip columns," Reed added. "A titled lord sailing about the Channel hunting pirates would be a very easy man to identify, and a very easy man to ambush."

Brenna looked thoughtfully at the portrait. "So Hawthorne belongs to the sea."

"And Ashcombe belongs to England," Reed said. "A captain without title attracts far less attention than a nobleman with one."

"And the crew?" Brenna asked.

"Most know him only as Hawthorne," Reed said. "A few of us know both names. But that isn't the whole of it."

Julia leaned forward. "Then what is it?"

Reed exhaled slowly and reached for the glass on the desk, though he didn't drink. "Years ago," he said, "an Ashcombe merchant brig vanished in the Channel."

Brenna's attention sharpened. "Vanished?"

"Completely," Reed said. "Cargo gone. Crew gone. Not a trace left behind."

Julia shook her head. "And no one questioned it?"

"Oh, it was questioned," Reed replied. "But the official answer was simple. The sea claimed it."

Brenna crossed her arms slightly. "And the unofficial answer?"

Reed's gaze flicked toward the door Callum had just exited through. "Pirates."

The word settled heavily in the room.

"They stripped her," Reed continued. "Took everything of value. Then burned what remained."

Julia's expression softened. "And Callum knows this?"

Reed let out a quiet breath. "He learned it himself."

Brenna's voice was quieter now. "It affected him."

Reed gave a short laugh. "That's one way to put it."

Julia tilted her head. "You said what he does is sanctioned by the Crown?"

"It is."

"But," Brenna pressed, "that isn't why he does it."

Reed met her gaze directly. "No."

Silence lingered for a moment.

"It started as duty," Reed continued. "The Crown saw his ships, his routes, his knowledge of the water. They offered him an arrangement."

Julia frowned. "And he accepted."

"Yes."

"But that isn't what drives him now."

Reed shook his head. "No."

He set the untouched glass back down. "What drives him," Reed said quietly, "is balance."

Brenna's brows drew together slightly. "Balance."

"He doesn't hunt pirates for glory," Reed continued. "Or even for the Crown."

Julia's voice softened. "Then why?"

Reed glanced once more toward the door. "Because the sea took something from him."

Brenna's expression shifted. "And he intends to take something back."

Reed gave a faint nod. "Yes."

The room fell quiet again.

Julia leaned back slowly. "That sounds less like duty…"

Reed's mouth curved slightly. "And more like obsession?"

Julia nodded.

Reed didn't deny it.

"He doesn't seem like a man easily consumed by something," Brenna said.

Reed huffed a quiet laugh. "No."

His gaze sharpened slightly. "But you haven't seen him in a storm."

Brenna glanced toward the door Callum had exited through. "Well," she said lightly, "that explains why the man seems so comfortable commanding both a ballroom and a warship."

Reed nodded. "You're beginning to understand him."

Chapter 19

The trunks arrived shortly after noon the following day, carried in by two stable hands and set carefully in the entry hall. Though the leather bore fresh scuffs and the brass corners had clearly been handled more than once, Brenna recognized them immediately.

"Our trunks," Julia breathed, hurrying forward.

Brenna knelt beside the nearest one and lifted the lid.

Inside, the contents were not quite as she remembered. Dresses remained, though fewer than before. Gloves and ribbons had been disturbed. Several velvet cases that once held jewelry were gone entirely.

Julia sighed softly as she lifted one of her gowns."Well," she said, holding it up to the light,
"it appears our mysterious impostor had a discerning taste for valuables."

"And less patience for muslin," Brenna replied.

Still, the sight of familiar belongings brought unexpected relief.

"Though more trunks came with us from Boston," Brenna said quietly, "I am grateful to have even these returned."

Julia nodded. "It is a small victory."

Later that evening the four of them gathered again in the study. Brenna sat perched on the arm of a chair, Julia pacing slowly near the window while Callum and Reed reviewed a small stack of notes from their investigations.

Julia stopped suddenly. "Well," she said, "if we are to count this as our first triumph, I think it deserves proper celebration."

Reed looked up warily. "That sounds expensive."

"I was thinking London."

The room fell quiet.

Brenna's eyes brightened instantly. "Oh, Julia…"

Reed groaned. "No."

Callum leaned back slightly in his chair, studying them both.

"The trunks are recovered," Julia continued. "We are alive, mostly respectable again, and there are far better dressmakers in London than in Portsmouth."

Brenna clasped her hands. "And the Season must still be underway."

Julia grinned. "The *ton*, Brenna."

Reed pinched the bridge of his nose. "Absolutely not."

Callum's mouth twitched faintly.

Julia turned toward him with hopeful determination.

"Captain Hawthorne…" Julia started.

"Lord Ashcombe," Reed muttered.

Julia waved a dismissive hand. "Surely you maintain some sort of respectable presence in the city?"

Callum sighed. "I have a townhouse."

Brenna's eyes lit. "You do?"

"Only for business trips."

Julia clasped her hands together. "Perfect."

Reed leaned toward Callum. "You are not considering this."

Callum folded his arms. "I might."

Reed stared at him. "You would willingly march into the center of London society while someone is actively attempting to steal the lady's fortune?"

Callum shrugged slightly. "I would agree under one condition."

Reed narrowed his eyes. "I don't like where this is going."

Callum looked directly at him. "You come with us."

Reed groaned loudly. "You want me miserable as well."

"Exactly."

Julia laughed. "Oh, Mr. Reed, imagine the stories you will gather."

"I prefer stories that don't involve chandeliers and aristocrats," Reed muttered.

Brenna leaned forward eagerly. "Oh come now, surely you can endure a few evenings of polite society."

Reed looked from Brenna to Julia, then back to Callum. "You're serious."

Callum nodded. "Entirely."

Reed sighed dramatically and dropped back into his chair. "I hope you both understand," he said to the women, "that this is the worst idea anyone in this room has ever had."

Julia beamed. "Then it will be marvelous."

Callum glanced toward Brenna, amused despite himself.

For the first time since the entire ordeal began, the tension in the room had eased. And though danger still lingered somewhere beyond their walls, the prospect of London, lights, and society suddenly felt like something worth looking forward to.

The journey to London proved far less dramatic than the weeks that had preceded it. The carriage rolled steadily along the road north, wheels humming over packed earth as hedgerows and open fields slipped quietly past. After storms, kidnappers, and hidden identities, the calm almost felt unnatural.

Julia and Brenna filled the silence easily. They spoke of the voyage from America, of the strange assortment of passengers who had shared the crossing. Julia described a nervous gentleman who had refused to leave his cabin whenever the sea so much as lifted.

"Do you remember the clergyman from Boston?" Julia asked suddenly.

"The one who believed the ocean punished vanity?" Brenna replied.

Julia laughed. "Yes! He blamed every rough wave on the ladies wearing ribbons."

Reed smirked from across the carriage. "A dangerous theory on a ship full of fashionable passengers."

"And yet," Brenna added, smiling faintly, "he spent half the journey lecturing anyone who would listen about pirates."

Julia nodded enthusiastically. "He insisted the waters were crawling with them."

"That's because sailors encouraged him," Brenna said.

"They did," Julia agreed. "One of the deckhands swore he'd seen black sails on the horizon the night before."

Reed exchanged a glance with Callum but said nothing.

"And then there was the widow from Charleston," Brenna continued. "The one who carried pistols."

Julia groaned softly. "She kept them under her pillow."

"Loaded?" Reed asked.

"Always," Julia said.

Reed laughed outright. "I like her already."

"She said if pirates boarded," Brenna continued, "she intended to shoot the first one herself."

Callum's mouth twitched faintly. "A bold strategy."

Julia leaned back in the seat. "She spent the entire crossing telling us dreadful stories. Ships disappearing. Crews vanishing."

Reed nodded slowly. "Some of those stories have truth in them."

Julia waved a hand. “Well, none of them actually happened to us.”

Callum glanced out the carriage window. “Not exactly.”

Julia frowned slightly. “What does that mean?”

Reed scratched his jaw thoughtfully. “Well,” he said mildly, “there was the small matter of the *Mercy*.”

Julia blinked. “The what?”

Brenna looked at Reed sharply.

Reed ignored her. “A brig that decided to test the *Hawthorne's* patience,” he said.

Julia leaned forward. “Test it how?”

Reed shrugged. “With cannon fire, mostly.”

Julia stared at him. “You're joking.”

Callum spoke calmly. “The ship approached under false colors.”

“And then?” Julia asked.

“And then we disagreed,” Reed said.

Julia's gaze snapped to Brenna. “You knew about this?”

Brenna hesitated. “Well…”

Julia's eyes widened. “You did know!”

Brenna tried to sound casual. “It was rather brief.”

Reed laughed. “That depends on your definition of brief.”

Julia sat upright now, incredulous. “There was a battle at sea and no one thought to tell me?”

“You weren't there,” Brenna said carefully.

Julia blinked. “Exactly. Which means someone should explain why you're speaking about it so calmly.”

Reed leaned back in the seat, clearly enjoying himself. “Well, Miss Fairchild, since you insist.”

Callum shot him a warning look, but Reed continued anyway.

“The *Mercy* appeared without warning,” he said. “Closed fast and under colors that didn't quite suit her.”

Julia leaned forward, captivated despite herself. "And then?"

"And then," Reed said, "our captain here decided he'd had enough of her games."

Callum sighed quietly. "She fired first."

"Twice," Reed added helpfully.

Julia's eyes widened. "And Brenna?" she asked.

Reed grinned. "Oh, Brenna was already on deck."

Julia turned slowly toward her friend. "You were where?"

Brenna lifted a shoulder. "I had no intention of hiding below while history unfolded."

Callum's voice cut in calmly. "I told her to go below."

Julia pointed at Brenna. "And you listened?"

Brenna smiled faintly. "Not particularly."

Reed chuckled. "She stood at the rail like she'd purchased a ticket to the spectacle."

Julia stared. "You watched a cannon battle."

"It was rather impressive," Brenna said.

Callum shook his head slightly. "She insisted the sea air was invigorating."

Julia's disbelief only deepened. "You could have been killed!"

"Unlikely," Brenna replied.

Reed lifted a brow. "The *Mercy's* aim suggested otherwise."

Julia turned back to Callum. "And you allowed this?"

"I did not," he said evenly. "She simply ignored every order given."

Reed leaned forward. "I'll give her this, the crew rather admired it."

Julia groaned softly. "You stood calmly on deck while men were firing cannons."

Brenna nodded thoughtfully. "Well… not entirely calmly."

Julia threw her hands up. "I leave you for a fortnight and you become a spectator at naval warfare."

Reed grinned. "To be fair, we let the *Mercy* limp away."

Julia blinked again. "You what?"

Callum answered quietly. "We had other priorities."

Julia followed his gaze briefly toward Brenna. Understanding flickered. "Oh."

Reed nodded. "Hard to chase pirates when one is busy keeping guests alive."

Julia leaned back slowly, still stunned. "I cannot believe I missed the entire thing."

Brenna smiled. "You were safe on your own ship."

Julia sighed. "Yes, well, next time someone fires cannons near you, I would appreciate a letter."

Reed laughed. "I'll see what we can arrange."

Callum added with a more serious tone, "Pirates are rarely what stories make them."

Brenna glanced at him curiously. "And what are they truly?"

He looked out the carriage window toward the distant road ahead. "Men who believe the world owes them something."

By late afternoon, the carriage turned off the main road toward a small inn nestled between low hills and a cluster of trees. The lantern above the door flickered to life as they approached.

Reed stretched as he stepped down. "Well," he said, "civilization."

Julia brightened immediately. "At last."

Brenna stepped down more slowly, taking in the quiet charm of the place. "It's lovely."

Callum nodded. "It will serve."

Inside, the inn was warm and welcoming, the scent of food and woodsmoke filling the air.

Julia glanced around with approval. “This is already an improvement.”

Reed smirked. “You say that now. Wait until morning.”

Julia turned to him. “What happens in the morning?”

“We leave.”

She frowned. “I was beginning to enjoy it.”

Callum glanced between them. “You’ll enjoy London more.”

Julia smiled. “I intend to enjoy everything.”

The next morning came early. The road resumed. Stories continued.

Julia leaned forward, animated. “And then he truly believed the goat belonged to him.”

Reed shook his head. “That is because you told him it did.”

“I merely suggested it.”

“You insisted on it.”

“It was convincing.”

Callum glanced at Brenna. “She enjoys creating chaos.”

Brenna smiled. “She thrives on it.”

Julia pointed at them both. “I am sitting right here.”

Reed leaned back with a quiet chuckle. “And the entire countryside is grateful for it.”

Laughter filled the carriage as the miles passed more quickly than before.

Even Callum seemed less guarded, his responses easier, his tone less restrained.

Brenna noticed. And said nothing.

By late afternoon of the second day, the road widened. Traffic increased. The distant outline of London began to rise ahead of them.

Julia leaned forward again, though this time her excitement was unmistakable. “Now,” she said, “this feels like an arrival.”

Reed glanced toward the horizon. “Just wait.”

Chapter 20

The tavern sat low against the harbor wall, its windows dim with smoke and lantern light. Outside, the tide crept slowly against the pilings where smaller vessels rocked in the dark water.

Inside, the air smelled of rum, salt, and wet wool. Captain Silas Crowe sat alone at a corner table.

He had chosen the place carefully. Portsmouth held many taverns where sailors drank loudly and questions were rarely asked. This one was quieter, favored by men who preferred their business conducted without witnesses.

Crowe turned the coin on the table slowly with one finger. Gold. Real gold.

A servant had brought it earlier with a short message. *A gentleman wishes to speak with you.*

Crowe smiled slightly. Gentlemen rarely sought out pirates unless the work required something unpleasant.

The tavern door opened. Crowe did not bother looking up immediately. He simply listened. Boots. Measured steps. Not a sailor.

The man approached the table and removed his gloves. "Captain Crowe."

Crowe finally glanced up.

The stranger was dressed well, too well for a dockside tavern. His coat was dark and tailored, his posture confident in the way of men used to being obeyed.

Crowe leaned back in his chair. "That'd depend on who's standin' in front o' me."

The man did not sit. "My name is not important."

Crowe chuckled softly.

The man slid a small leather pouch across the table. The weight of it told Crowe everything. Crowe opened the pouch just enough to see the glint of several more gold coins.

Now he smiled. "Well now," Crowe said lazily, "ye've got my attention."

The gentleman remained standing. "There is a woman."

Crowe raised a brow. "There usually is."

"She has recently arrived in England."

Crowe tapped the pouch lightly. "And I'd say somethin's gone amiss?"

The man's expression tightened. "My first arrangement failed."

Crowe smiled wider. "That happens."

"She was meant to disappear when her ship arrived."

Crowe studied him more carefully now. "But she didn't."

"No."

Crowe leaned forward slightly. "So now ye've come to me."

"Yes." The gentleman's voice lowered. "She must be removed before she reaches Portsmouth again."

Crowe rolled the coin across the table. "So it's blood yer after."

"Yes."

Crowe tilted his head. "Costly, that is."

The gentleman reached into his coat and produced a folded paper.

Crowe recognized the markings immediately. Routes. Ports. Names.

"Her ship," the man said quietly. "And the man she is traveling with."

Crowe looked up. "Ah." A slow grin spread across his face. "Now that's somethin.'"

The gentleman slid a second pouch across the table. It landed with a heavy thud.

Crowe opened it slightly. More gold. Much more. "Ye're a determined one, I'll grant ye that," Crowe said.

"I am a practical one."

Crowe closed the pouch. "And the lady?"

The gentleman's voice hardened. "Brenna Whitmore."

Crowe leaned back again. "She's worth a fair bit o' coin then."

"Yes."

"And why would a man of your sort be payin' to see her gone?"

The gentleman smiled faintly. "That does not concern you."

Crowe chuckled. "No." He pulled the pouch toward himself. "It doesn't."

Crowe stood. "When she makes sail again," he said calmly, "she won't be arrivin' at all."

"See that she doesn't."

Crowe nodded once. "Always a pleasure when the coin's good."

The man paused at the door. "One more thing."

Crowe raised a brow. "Yes?"

"If anyone asks…" The man's fingers turned the signet ring slowly on his hand. "You never met me."

Crowe laughed quietly as the door closed. Crowe looked down at the gold again. Then out the window toward the dark harbor where the *Black Mercy* waited at anchor.

He slipped the pouch into his coat. "Brenna Whitmore," he murmured.

And somewhere in the dark waters beyond Portsmouth, a hunt had just begun.

The townhouse on Brook Street was smaller than the estate on the cliffs but no less refined. Lamps glowed warmly in the windows as their carriage pulled to the curb, the door already opened by a lone footman who had clearly been warned of their arrival.

Callum stepped down first and offered his hand to Brenna.

The house inside bore the quiet order of a residence seldom occupied but well maintained. The staff was small, only a housekeeper, a footman, and a cook, but the table had been set and a simple supper waited.

After weeks of storms, suspicion, and long travel, the meal felt almost peaceful.

Reed stretched his legs beneath the table with a satisfied sigh. "Well," he said, raising his glass, "I'll say this for London. One can arrive half-dead from the road and still eat better than most admirals."

Julia laughed softly. "I suspect that says more about admirals than London."

Callum set down his fork. "You've both traveled the better part of the day," he said to the ladies. "You should rest. Tomorrow will be busy."

Julia lifted an eyebrow. "That sounds suspiciously like dismissal."

"It's sound advice," Callum replied calmly.

Brenna smiled faintly. "I believe he's right, Julia."

Reed nodded in agreement. "And if you intend to face the dressmakers of London tomorrow, you'll need your strength."

Julia stood reluctantly. "Very well. But only because I plan to conquer Bond Street before noon."

The ladies withdrew soon after, leaving the men to finish their wine in quiet conversation.

Outside, London hummed with its usual evening energy. Inside, the townhouse settled into stillness for the night.

The following morning the mood was entirely different.

Julia and Brenna were already awake before the household fully stirred, their excitement filling the breakfast room.

"I cannot remember the last time I looked forward to a dress shop this much," Julia said, smoothing the sleeve of one of her recovered gowns.

Brenna smiled. "And the modistes here are supposed to be the finest in England."

"And the ton," Julia added eagerly.

Callum entered just in time to hear that. "The ton," he repeated.

Julia turned brightly. "Yes. I should like to see what all the fuss is about.

Reed appeared behind him, already looking faintly resigned. "You say that now," he muttered.

The morning in London unfolded with a kind of eager chaos Brenna had not felt in weeks.

Bond Street bustled beneath a pale sky as carriages rolled past and shop windows glittered with silks, ribbons, and polished glass. Julia stepped out of the dressmaker's shop first, a pair of hat boxes balanced in the arms of the footman behind her.

"Well," she said with satisfaction, adjusting the ribbon beneath her chin, "I believe we've made a respectable beginning."

Brenna followed a moment later, the bell above the shop door chiming softly behind her. Another assistant hurried out carrying two more carefully wrapped boxes.

"Respectable?" Brenna repeated with a laugh. "Julia, we have been inside three dressmakers and two milliners before noon."

Julia waved the observation away. "And every one of them has promised delivery by tomorrow evening."

The shopkeeper appeared behind them, bowing slightly. "Lord Ashcombe's deposit ensured our full attention, madam. The gowns will be finished with the utmost priority."

Brenna glanced briefly toward Callum, who stood a short distance away speaking quietly with Reed.

"You truly did not need to do that," she murmured when she reached him.

Callum looked down at her calmly. "You had little choice."

"That does not make it comfortable."

"You may repay me when your funds are restored."

Brenna hesitated. "I will settle the expense promptly, however, our agreement did not extend to you paying for my purchases."

Callum's voice remained even. "The agreement was that you would not place yourself in a vulnerable position while we locate the men responsible."

Reed chuckled quietly beside him. "And I assure you, London dressmakers are quite capable of creating vulnerability."

Julia rejoined them, clearly pleased. "They promised the green silk would be finished first," she announced. "And the pale blue muslin by tomorrow afternoon."

Callum nodded once. "Then we are finished for today."

Julia blinked. "What?"

Brenna frowned. "Finished?"

"Yes."

Julia gestured dramatically toward the street. "We have only visited a third of the shops."

Reed folded his arms. "I counted four shops, three dressmakers, and a milliner who nearly fainted when you described your sleeve preference."

Julia ignored him. "There are at least a dozen more establishments worth visiting."

Callum remained unmoved. "You will have time."

"We have only just arrived," Julia stated.

"And we will be here at least a fortnight," Callum replied calmly.

Brenna paused. "A fortnight?"

"At minimum," he said.

Julia's indignation softened slightly. "Well… when you phrase it that way."

Reed tipped his hat toward the waiting carriage. "Think of it as pacing yourselves."

Julia sighed theatrically but allowed the footman to collect the remaining hat boxes. "Very well," she said. "But tomorrow we begin earlier as we need to have final fittings for our gowns."

Callum opened the carriage door for Brenna.

"Tomorrow," he said.

Brenna stepped inside, glancing back toward the busy street lined with elegant storefronts.

For the first time since the storm, the future felt almost… ordinary.

Once word had begun to ripple through the ton that two of the most eligible bachelors in England had arrived in London during the height of the Season, the invitations began appearing almost immediately.

By the time the carriage returned to the townhouse that afternoon, a small stack of visiting cards already rested neatly on the silver tray in the entry hall.

By dinner, the collection of invitations had grown considerably.

Julia stopped beside the table and lifted the top card with open delight.

"Well," she said, clearly pleased, "London wastes no time." She read aloud.

"Lord Ashcombe is invited to dine Thursday evening…"

Brenna reached for another envelope and broke the seal. "This one invites... Lord Halbrook."

Julia frowned. "I don't believe we know a Lord Halbrook."

Across the room Reed went very still. Callum's eyes shifted slowly toward him.

Julia lifted another card from the stack. "Oh, here it is again."

She read the name carefully. "Lord Halbrook is requested to attend Lady Pennington's evening reception."

Brenna looked up from the table. "Who is Lord Halbrook?"

Reed sighed heavily. "That," he said, reaching for the card, "would be me."

Julia blinked. "You're a lord?"

Reed gave a slight shrug. "Unfortunately," Reed replied.

Callum allowed himself the faintest smile. "I did warn you London would remember."

"You have been traveling about, chasing pirates, pretending to be..."

"I wasn't pretending," Reed interrupted. "Reed is my name."

"That is not the point," Julia said.

"It rather is."

Brenna stepped closer. "You deliberately concealed this."

"I suppose that is true."

"Why?"

Reed leaned back slightly, his expression shifting, less amused now, more thoughtful. "A titled man aboard a ship is not simply a passenger. He is a prize."

Brenna's gaze sharpened. "Ransom."

Reed nodded. "Among other things. Political interference. Attention from the wrong sort of people."

Callum spoke quietly from the mantel. “Smugglers. Pirates.”

Reed glanced at him. “Exactly.”

Julia crossed her arms. “So you simply… stopped being a lord?”

Reed huffed a quiet laugh. “I never stopped being one. I simply chose not to announce it.”

Brenna studied him. “And London?”

Reed’s expression darkened slightly. “London has never quite decided what to do with me.”

“Why?” Julia asked.

Reed was quiet for a moment. “My brother was meant to inherit Halbrook.”

Brenna softened slightly. “But he didn’t.”

“No.” Reed’s gaze drifted briefly to the fire. “He died unexpectedly. Some said illness.” He paused. “Others preferred more interesting explanations.”

“Scandal?” Julia guessed.

Reed gave the faintest nod. “And with his death, the title fell to me.”

Brenna watched him carefully. “And you didn’t want it.”

Reed let out a slow breath. “I grew up watching what that title cost my family. Expectations. Appearances. Endless obligations.”

Julia tilted her head. “That is what society is built upon.”

“Yes,” Reed said simply. “And I found I had no interest in it.”

“So you left,” Brenna said.

“Not entirely,” Reed corrected. “Just enough to keep them guessing.”

Julia’s lips curved slightly. “That sounds like you.”

Reed almost smiled. “I had already spent time at sea, briefly with the navy.”

Brenna's eyes flicked toward Callum. "That's where you met him."

Reed nodded. "Yes."

Callum said nothing, but there was a quiet understanding in his expression.

"And you chose that instead," Julia said.

"I chose to be judged as a man," Reed replied, "rather than a title. Hawthorne needed someone who understood ships. Someone who could keep their mouth shut. Someone who didn't mind sailing outside proper naval command."

Julia lifted a brow. "And you volunteered."

Brenna considered that. "And so the world at sea knows you as…"

"Elias Reed."

Julia glanced down at the stack of invitations again. "And the world here clearly refuses to forget otherwise."

Reed gave a resigned sigh. "They rarely do."

"How many people know the truth?" Brenna asked.

Reed's gaze flicked briefly to Callum. "A very small number."

Callum added quietly, "Fewer than you'd think."

Julia looked between them. "So now?"

Reed leaned back in his chair. "Now," he said, "it would appear I am once again Lord Halbrook."

Julia smiled faintly. "You sound thrilled."

"I assure you," Reed replied dryly, "I am not."

Brenna glanced at Callum. "You both lead very complicated lives."

Callum's gaze met hers. "It keeps things interesting."

Reed huffed a quiet laugh. "That's one way of putting it."

Julia set the invitation back onto the tray and laughed. "Well, Lord Halbrook, it appears society has been waiting for you."

Reed glanced at the growing stack of invitations. "Yes. Halbrook," he said with mild distaste. "A name I only answer to when London insists."

Callum watched them all, knowing full well London was about to become far more complicated than any of them expected.

Chapter 21

The bell above the door chimed softly as Brenna and Julia stepped into Madame Laurent's dress shop on Bond Street. Bolts of silk and satin lined the walls, their colors glowing in the afternoon light that streamed through the tall windows.

Madame Laurent appeared almost immediately from behind a curtain, measuring tape draped elegantly around her neck.

"Miss Whitmore! Miss Fairchild!" she exclaimed warmly. "How delightful to see you again."

Julia smiled. "We have come prepared to test your patience today."

Madame Laurent laughed softly. "My dear, patience is the least of my talents."

She guided them toward the fitting area where several half-finished gowns hung neatly on dress forms. "I have been working very diligently on your dresses," she continued. "Though I must admit, the request for such speed was… ambitious."

Julia glanced toward Brenna. "We had encouragement."

Madame Laurent's eyes sparkled. "Ah yes… Lord Ashcombe." She said the name lightly, but the curiosity beneath it was unmistakable.

Brenna stepped onto the small fitting platform while the dressmaker's assistant began adjusting the gown around her waist.

Madame Laurent circled her slowly, examining the fit. "Such beautiful silk deserves a proper entrance into society," she said thoughtfully. "And of course, everyone is quite eager to see Lord Ashcombe in London again."

Julia tilted her head. "Is he often discussed here?"

Madame Laurent smiled knowingly. "Oh yes." She adjusted a pin along Brenna's sleeve. "A gentleman of his reputation rarely goes unnoticed."

Julia tried to sound casual. "And what reputation would that be?"

The dressmaker raised a brow. "Handsome. Wealthy. Unmarried."

Julia laughed. "Yes, I suppose that would attract attention."

Madame Laurent glanced between the two women. "And now he arrives with two very elegant American ladies."

Brenna smiled politely. "We are merely his guests."

"Of course," Madame Laurent said smoothly.

Her assistant stepped back as she examined the gown again.

"Though I must say, the way he looks at you suggests a rather different arrangement."

Julia looked delighted.

Brenna blinked. Oh?"

Madame Laurent chuckled softly. "My dear, dressmakers observe everything." She stepped closer to adjust the neckline. "And the other gentleman?"

Julia's eyes flicked toward Brenna. "Lord Halbrook?"

"Yes," Madame Laurent said. "He has also been noticed."

Julia tried to sound indifferent. "I imagine London notices many things."

The dressmaker smiled knowingly. "London notices romances most of all."

Julia raised a brow. "And have you discovered one?"

Madame Laurent gave a thoughtful hum. "I have discovered that Lord Ashcombe watches Miss Whitmore whenever she enters a room."

Julia burst out laughing.

Brenna felt her cheeks warm slightly.

"And Lord Halbrook," Madame Laurent added gently, "seems to watch Miss Fairchild in exactly the same manner." Julia tried to hide her smile. "That is entirely his fault." Madame Laurent laughed as she stepped back to admire the finished fit. "Well," she said pleasantly, "London will be very interested to see how this story unfolds."

Julia leaned toward Brenna as the assistant fetched the next gown. "Do you realize we have become entertainment for the entire city?"

Brenna sighed softly. "I had hoped to arrive in England quietly."

Julia grinned. "That was never going to happen."

The ballroom at Lady Pennington's glittered with candlelight and polished mirrors, the air alive with music, silk, and the constant hum of conversation. The ton had gathered in full force, eager to observe the arrival of two of the Season's most intriguing figures.

Brenna and Julia had barely crossed the threshold when whispers began to ripple through the crowd.

"Lord Ashcombe..."

Callum accepted the attention with his usual calm reserve, offering polite bows where necessary. Brenna remained at his side, poised but quietly observant.

Close by, Reed lingered near the edge of the gathering, a glass of wine in hand, doing his best to remain unnoticed.

It was not working.

Julia had just leaned closer to Brenna to comment on the orchestra when a sharp voice cut through the music.

"Good heavens."

Several heads turned.

A stout gentleman near the center of the room squinted toward Reed. “That cannot be…”

Reed closed his eyes briefly.

Too late.

“Lord Halbrook!”

The exclamation carried easily across the ballroom. The effect was immediate. Conversations faltered, fans paused mid-flutter, and a small circle of curious faces turned toward him.

Brenna turned and whispered to Julia, “Lord Halbrook may need assistance” she laughed lightly.

Reed sighed quietly.

The stout gentleman pushed through the crowd with enthusiasm. “I knew it was you! I told them it must be you.”

Reed inclined his head politely. “Lord Denton.”

“Where in heaven’s name have you been hiding?” Denton demanded loudly. “Half of London thought you’d vanished to sea.”

A murmur swept the nearby guests.

“Halbrook…”

“…I heard he rebuilt the estate…”

“…after the debts…”

“…and the tenants…”

Another gentleman joined the circle. “Remarkable business, Halbrook,” he said. “Reclaiming the land like that. New tenants, new mills, turned the entire estate profitable again.”

“And the shipping investments,” someone else added. “Quite clever.”

Julia glanced up at Reed with sudden curiosity. “You rebuilt an estate?” she whispered.

Reed looked faintly trapped. “Circumstances required it.”

Lord Denton clapped him heartily on the shoulder. “The man saved Halbrook lands from ruin, you know,” he told the surrounding listeners. "Reorganized the farms, dismissed half the incompetent stewards, and invested the profits in merchant shipping."

Callum, watching from across the room, lifted a brow slightly.

Reed's expression said plainly that this was not the evening he planned.

"And now," Denton continued loudly, peering around Reed, "where is the fortunate lady?"

Reed blinked. "The lady?"

"Yes, yes," Denton said impatiently. "Surely a man who's restored a fortune must have secured a wife to manage it."

A dozen curious eyes turned expectantly toward him.

For one brief moment Reed considered escape. Then instinct took over. He reached out, gently drawing Julia to stand beside him. Her eyes widened slightly as his hand settled lightly at her arm. "This," Reed said smoothly, his voice calm despite the sudden attention, "is Miss Julia Fairchild."

The crowd leaned closer.

Reed met their collective gaze with practiced ease. "My fiancée."

The silence that followed lasted exactly two seconds. Then the room erupted into delighted chatter.

"Engaged!"

"Well done, Halbrook!"

"When was the announcement?"

Julia stared up at him in astonishment. "Your *what*?" she whispered.

Reed leaned down slightly, his voice barely audible. "I apologize," he murmured. "But it was either that… or explain why I've been sailing under an assumed name for three years."

Across the ballroom Brenna pressed a hand to her mouth to hide a smile.

Callum watched the scene unfold with quiet amusement.

Julia straightened slowly beside Reed, recovering faster than most would have. "Well," she said pleasantly to the gathering peers, slipping her arm neatly through Reed's, "it appears London has discovered us sooner than expected."

Reed exhaled softly. And resigned himself to the role he had hoped to avoid all evening.

The music swelled again as the orchestra struck up the next dance, the polished floor filling quickly with couples. Candles shimmered in the tall mirrors along the ballroom walls, multiplying the movement and color until the entire room seemed alive with silk and laughter.

Callum had scarcely taken his eyes off Brenna since the moment she had stepped down the staircase at the townhouse earlier that evening. It had been the first time he, or Reed, had seen either of the women dressed properly for society since the storm.

He had not been prepared.

The lavender silk of Brenna's gown caught the candlelight with every movement, the fabric flowing easily as she crossed the room. Her hair had been arranged with effortless elegance, leaving the graceful line of her neck exposed. The weeks at sea had not diminished her beauty in the slightest.

If anything, they had sharpened it.

Reed had noticed his silence at the time. "Well," he had said quietly, watching Brenna descend the last step, "that explains a great deal."

Callum had not bothered answering.

Now, standing across the ballroom from her, he was painfully aware that he was not the only man noticing.

More than one gentleman had already asked her to dance. More than one had lingered just a little too long in conversation.

Callum set down his glass. "I believe," he said quietly to Brenna as he approached, "that I have waited long enough."

She turned toward him with a small smile. "You waited?"

"I was observing."

"Of course you were."

He offered his hand. "May I?"

Her smile deepened slightly as she placed her hand in his. "You may."

They moved easily into the forming line of dancers as the music began again. For a moment neither spoke, their steps falling naturally into rhythm with the orchestra.

Callum studied her with quiet appreciation. "You dance exceptionally well."

Brenna arched an eyebrow. "That surprises you?"

"Not precisely."

"Then what does?"

"That you make it appear effortless."

She laughed softly. "My tutors would be very pleased to hear that."

They turned smoothly with the music, her skirts sweeping lightly across the floor.

Across the room Julia watched with great interest while Reed stood beside her looking faintly resigned.

"They look rather good together," Julia said.

Reed watched them. "Yes."

Julia tilted her head toward him. "You sound pleased."

"I am."

"And yourself?"

Reed blinked. "What about me?"

Julia smiled mischievously. "You are also being watched."

Reed sighed. "I feared that, but I do suspect most those eyes are on you."

Meanwhile Callum guided Brenna through the next turnof the dance, his hand steady at hers.

"You seem very comfortable here," he observed.

"I grew up among people like this," she said.

"And yet you seem far more comfortable on a ship's deck."

She smiled slightly. "The sea does not judge quite so loudly."

Callum glanced briefly around the room. Several gentlemen were indeed watching her dance. He did not care for it.

When his gaze returned to Brenna, it held a new intensity. "You have attracted a great deal of attention this evening."

Her lips curved. "I suspect London is merely curious."

"London is rarely merely curious."

They turned again, the orchestra building toward the end of the figure.

Brenna tilted her head slightly. "You sound rather protective."

Callum's expression did not change. "I am."

She held his gaze for a moment longer than necessary. "Of my safety," she said lightly.

"Yes."

But the way he said it made the word feel... incomplete.

The music slowed as the dance drew to a close. He released her hand only when protocol demanded it.

On the other side of the room Julia leaned closer to Reed. "He looks like a man guarding treasure."

Reed nodded calmly. "That is because he believes he is."

Julia smiled. "Well," she said, watching Brenna across the floor, "he may not be entirely wrong."

Chapter 22

The morning after Lady Pennington's ball passed in near silence. Or rather, sleep.

By the time the household stirred again, the sun had long since climbed into the afternoon sky. It was a far quieter scene than the night before, but no less satisfying. An unexpected and thoroughly earned reprieve from the demands of London society.

By mutual agreement, though neither was willing to admit just how necessary it was, the ladies abandoned all ambition for the remainder of the day. Shoes were cast aside, basins of warm water summoned, and aching feet finally given the attention they had long demanded.

By the time they had gathered into the drawing room for afternoon tea, the first stack of invitations had already arrived.

"Another?" Julia asked, holding up a fresh invitation.

Brenna glanced at it. "That makes, how many?"

"Seven," Julia said.

Reed, lounging far too comfortably for a man under scrutiny, lifted a brow. "You should feel honored."

"I feel observed," Brenna replied.

Callum didn't look up from where he stood near the window. "You are."

Julia smiled faintly. "And you, my lord, are the cause of it."

Callum's mouth shifted slightly. "I expected attention."

Reed huffed. "You always do."

"They will find something else to occupy them soon enough," Callum said, remaining composed.

The conversation drifted into lighter banter until dinner was announced.

A comfortable silence fell over the table as they ate.

Having eaten her fill, Julia set her fork aside and gently pushed her plate away with a satisfied sigh. "I have decided," she declared, "that London society is exhausting."

Reed lifted a brow. "You danced every set."

"That is because no one told me it would be a test of endurance."

Brenna gave a knowing smile. "You refused to sit."

"I was committed," Julia replied firmly.

Reed leaned back slightly, studying her. "You were engaged."

Julia stilled.

Brenna's eyes flicked between them. "Oh?"

Reed's mouth curved. "Every gentleman in that room seemed to believe so."

Julia narrowed her eyes. "That is not my fault."

"No?" Reed said lightly. "You did little to correct them."

Julia straightened. "I was being polite."

"You were being encouraging."

Brenna hid a smile behind her glass.

Callum, seated across from her, observed the exchange with quiet amusement.

Julia pointed at Reed. "You didn't correct them either."

Reed's expression didn't change. "I had no reason to."

Julia blinked. "That is precisely the reason to correct them."

Reed shrugged slightly. "I didn't find it necessary."

Brenna set her glass down. "That sounds very much like agreement."

Julia turned to her. "You are not helping."

Callum's voice came calmly from the other end of the table. "I believe the term is… implied understanding."

Julia groaned. "This is intolerable."

Reed smiled faintly. "You'll recover."

The fire burned low as the four of them gathered again in the study, the remains of the evening meal set aside in favor of something far more entertaining.

The growing stack of invitations sat on the table between them.

Brenna picked one up, scanning it briefly. "There are far too many of these."

Julia leaned forward eagerly. "Let me see."

Reed poured himself a glass of brandy. "You've only just arrived."

"And already we are in demand," Julia said brightly.

Callum leaned against the mantel. "You will accept very few."

Julia glanced at him. "That sounds suspiciously like an order."

"It's a recommendation."

"From a man who avoids society entirely."

Callum didn't deny it.

Brenna set one invitation aside. "This one is tolerable."

Julia frowned. "Tolerable?"

"Yes."

Julia snatched another from the pile. "We are not selecting based on tolerable."

Reed took a slow sip. "That seems unwise."

Julia ignored him, opening another. Her eyes widened instantly. "Oh, Brenna look at this one."

Brenna looked up. "What is it?"

Julia didn't answer right away. She simply turned the card toward her.

Brenna read it. "Oh."

Reed sighed. "That does not sound promising."

Julia looked up, barely containing her excitement. "A masquerade."

Callum's expression didn't change. "No."

Julia turned to him. "You haven't even heard the details."

"I don't need to."

Brenna looked at the invitation again, a smile slowly forming. "Lady Carroway."

Reed paused mid-sip. "That explains it."

Julia leaned closer. "It will be magnificent."

"It will be crowded," Callum said.

"Even better."

"It will be unpredictable."

Julia beamed. "Perfect."

Callum exhaled slowly. "No."

Brenna looked up at him. "Yes."

Their eyes met. A familiar tension passed between them.

Reed watched it with interest.

Julia, meanwhile, was already imagining it. "Masks," she said dreamily. "Music. No expectations, no introductions, no rules…"

"Plenty of rules," Callum interrupted.

"None that matter," Julia countered.

Brenna glanced at him. "It's only one evening."

Callum's gaze narrowed slightly. "That is rarely the case in London."

Reed set his glass down. "For what it's worth," he said, "you won't win this."

Callum didn't look at him. "I'm aware."

Julia clapped her hands lightly. "Then it's settled."

"It is not settled," Callum said.

"It is entirely settled."

Brenna folded the invitation carefully. "I think we should go."

Callum looked at her. "You would."

She smiled faintly. "I would."

Reed leaned back slightly. "Well," he said, "this should be interesting."

Callum muttered under his breath. "That's what I'm afraid of."

Julia stood, already energized again. "Oh, it will be wonderful," she said as reached for the next invitation, then another, her brows lifting higher with each. "Another?" she said. "Surely they've run out of reasons by now."

"They don't need reasons," Reed replied from where he sat. "Only interest."

Brenna set her cup down more carefully than necessary. "And we've become… interesting."

Callum, standing near the window, didn't turn. "You've become a subject."

Julia glanced between them. "That sounds worse."

"It is," Reed said lightly.

Julia lifted another card, scanning it. "They're already talking."

Brenna looked at her. "About what?"

Julia hesitated just long enough to make it worse. "That you've secured Lord Ashcombe's attention."

Brenna's expression stilled. "That is not…"

"I know," Julia said quickly. "But that doesn't seem to matter."

Reed exhaled faintly. "It never does."

"They're saying Lord Ashcombe has changed."

Brenna's gaze flicked briefly toward Callum. "Changed."

"Yes," Julia said. "That he doesn't remain in London this long. That he doesn't… linger."

Reed huffed faintly. "That part is true."

Callum didn't respond.

Julia continued. "And that the only reason he has is you."

Brenna's fingers tightened slightly. "That's absurd."

"Of course it is," Julia said. "But they've decided it must mean something."

Reed added, almost thoughtfully, "It always does to them."

Brenna's gaze shifted toward Callum.

Callum finally turned. "They believe what makes sense to them."

"And this makes sense?" she asked.

"To them," he said.

Julia leaned back slightly. "It grows worse."

"How?" Brenna asked.

"They're questioning you."

That drew Callum's attention. "How?"

Julia met Brenna's eyes. "They don't believe you're as unfamiliar with this world as you appear."

Brenna held her composure. "They don't know me." "No," Reed said. "And that's precisely the problem." Callum's voice came low. "Let them speculate." Brenna looked at him. "That's easy for you to say." Callum met her gaze. "It doesn't change anything." "It changes how they see me." Callum's expression sharpened slightly. "How do you know all of this?" Brenna asked, looking at

Julia.

Julia glanced across the room, her expression calm. "Because no one thinks I'm worth lowering their voice for."

Brenna frowned slightly. "That's insulting."

Julia's lips curved in the slightest smile. "It's useful. They never lower their voices quite enough."

Brenna glanced at her. "You were listening?"

"I was standing still," Julia replied. "They did the rest."

She reached for another invitation, her expression shifting. "Well," she said, holding it up, "it seems we've been invited to defend ourselves."

Reed raised a brow. "Where?"

"Lady Ashford's," Julia said. "Two evenings hence."

Callum's expression tightened just slightly. "That will not be a quiet affair."

"None of them are," Reed said.

Brenna looked at the invitation. Another room. Another set of eyes. Another night of being measured. "They will expect us to attend," she said.

"They will," Callum replied.

"And if we don't?" Julia asked.

Reed smiled. "Then they will speak of that instead."

Brenna exhaled softly. "So either way…"

"You're discussed," Reed finished.

Brenna looked toward Callum. "And you are entirely unconcerned."

Callum held her gaze. "No," he said quietly. "I'm very aware."

Something in his tone steadied her more than his words.

Julia set the invitation down. "Well then," she said lightly, "we shall attend."

Reed inclined his head. "Of course we will."

Brenna's gaze lingered on the card a moment longer before she nodded. "Very well."

Callum turned back toward the window, though his voice carried clearly. "Be ready."

Julia smiled faintly. "Oh, we will be."

Reed leaned back in his chair. "This should be entertaining."

Brenna couldn't help but laugh softly. And as the invitation lay between them, the men realized, quite clearly, they had already lost.

Callum didn't respond. But the look in his eyes suggested otherwise. Because by two nights' time, the whispers would no longer follow them. They would be waiting.

Lady Ashford's rooms were already alive with movement when they arrived. Music carried easily through the space, laughter weaving between conversations, and the subtle shift of attention that followed their entrance moved just as quickly as the dancers on the floor.

Brenna felt it. And she chose not to mind.

"Well," Julia murmured beside her, "they're ready for us."

A restrained smile touched Brenna's lips, "Let them be."

Across the room, heads turned. Conversations dipped, then resumed, quieter, more deliberate.

But Brenna didn't slow. Didn't hesitate. Callum noticed. Of course he did.

They had scarcely stepped fully into the room before the first gentleman approached.

"Miss Whitmore," he said, bowing slightly. "May I have the honor of this dance?"

Brenna didn't look toward Callum. She didn't need to. "You may."

Callum's features grew stern as she was led away.

Reed, standing beside him, caught it immediately. "That didn't take long."

Callum said nothing.

Reed's mouth curved faintly. "It seems she intends to enjoy herself."

Callum's gaze remained fixed on the dance floor. "She should."

Brenna moved easily through the steps, her composure steady, her expression relaxed in a way that felt, intentional.

"You are settling into London quite well," her partner said.

"I'm learning," she replied.

"And quickly, it would seem."

Brenna lip's curved in the slightest smile. "I prefer not to struggle in public."

He laughed softly. "A wise approach."

At the edge of the room,

"…that's her…"

"…not at all what I expected…"

"…and Ashcombe lets her…"

"…lets her?"

Callum's gaze flicked briefly toward the voices, then back to Brenna. She was laughing again. Easy. Unbothered.

Reed followed his line of sight. "You could intervene."

Callum didn't look at him. "For what purpose?"

"To remind them."

"Of what?"

Reed's tone sharpened slightly. "That she arrived with you."

Callum's voice was steady. "She is not mine to claim."

Reed glanced at him. "No," he said. "But you're beginning to look like you might want to."

Callum didn't respond.

Julia, meanwhile, found herself just as surrounded.

"Miss Fairchild," a lady began, then paused. "Or should I say, future Lady Halbrook?"

Julia's smile was polite. "Miss Fairchild is fine."

The woman leaned in slightly. "And yet it has been said."

Julia's expression didn't shift. "Then it was said too soon."

"But not without reason," the woman pressed.

Julia's gaze held. "Reason is often assigned where none exists."

The lady smiled. "Of course." But she didn't look convinced.

Reed appeared at Julia's side moments later. "You're being congratulated."

Julia exhaled softly. "I'm being misinterpreted."

Reed's mouth curved. "That tends to happen."

Julia glanced at him. "You're not correcting it."

"They will believe what they want, no matter what is corrected."

By the time Brenna returned from her first dance, another gentleman was already waiting.

"May I?" he asked.

Brenna didn't hesitate. "Yes."

Callum watched. Still. Silent.

Reed exhaled as he stood beside him once more. "This is becoming interesting."

Callum's voice was lower now. "No," he said. "It isn't."

Reed stepped in beside him, voice low. "Two men I don't recognize."

Callum didn't turn. "Where?"

"Near the west corridor. They've changed position twice, without reason."

"Watching?" Callum asked.

"Not openly."

Callum's gaze shifted slightly. "And the others?"

"Unremarkable."

Callum's voice remained even. "Keep them in sight."

Reed inclined his head. "Already done."

Callum's attention remained on Brenna. One dance gave way to the next, each time a different partner, another smile, another quiet exchange.

She moved through it all with ease, no hesitation, no sign of discomfort. As though she belonged there.

Callum's gaze darkened slightly.

"…she's enjoying this…"

"…more than expected…"

"…and Ashcombe, he hasn't…"

"…he hasn't stopped watching…"

That part, was true.

When Brenna finally stepped away from her latest partner, she turned, and found Callum already there.

"You're in demand," he said. His tone was even. Too even.

Brenna lifted a brow. "So it would seem."

Callum's gaze held hers. "You've accepted every dance."

"Yes." Then added, "Is that a problem?"

He didn't answer immediately. "No," he said at last.

Brenna studied him. "But."

His expression didn't shift. "But nothing."

A knowing smile tugged at her lips. "You sound unconvinced."

Callum stepped slightly closer. "I sound observant."

"And what have you observed?"

His voice lowered. "That you're enjoying yourself."

"I am." The answer came easily. Without apology.

Something in his expression tightened. Just enough. "Good," he said.

Brenna held his gaze. "I thought so."

"Will you ask me," she said, "or continue observing?"

That gave him pause. Callum extended his hand.

"Dance."

This time, she let him ask.

As they moved onto the floor, the room seemed to shift again. Not because they had stepped into it, but because of how they did.

"They're still watching," Brenna said quietly.

"They will be."

"And they're still talking."

"Yes."

Brenna met his gaze. "I don't mind."

Callum's brow lifted slightly. "No?"

"No, Should I?"

Callum's voice lowered. "That depends."

"On what?"

His hand tightened slightly at hers. "On how much you intend to give them."

Brenna's expression softened, just slighty. "And what do you think I'm giving them now?"

Callum didn't look away. "Enough. Perhaps too much."

Brenna's breath slowed. "And yet you're the one who asked me to dance."

Callum's voice dropped. "Yes."

"Why?"

The question lingered between them. Not playful. Not light.

Callum held her gaze. "Because I don't intend to stand back while other men enjoy what I've been trying not to."

The words carried weight. Low. Honest.

Too close to what he had been holding back.

Brenna's breath caught, just slightly. But she didn't look away. Didn't step back. Instead, her lips curved, with quiet amusement. "Then perhaps," she said softly, "you shouldn't have waited so long."

The music carried them forward. The room watching. The whispers continuing. But now, the balance had shifted. Because this time, Brenna was no longer reacting to the attention. She was choosing it.

And for the first time, Callum was no longer in control.

Chapter 23

Once again, the morning came later than any of them intended. By the time they gathered in the drawing room, the sunlight had already settled comfortably across the windows, tea long since poured.

Julia sank into her chair with a quiet sigh. “I don’t believe I’ve ever danced that many sets in one evening.”

Reed, far less affected, lifted his cup. “You accepted nearly all of them.”

“I was being polite.”

“You were being thorough,” he corrected.

Brenna smiled faintly into her tea. “It was impressive.”

Julia glanced at her. “And you?”

“I enjoyed it.”

Callum, standing near the window as he so often did, turned slightly at that. “Yes,” he said. “You seemed to.”

Brenna met his gaze. “I wasn’t aware enjoyment required permission.”

“It doesn’t,” he said evenly.

Reed set his cup aside. “Well,” he said, “it seems we’ve successfully established ourselves as a topic of conversation.”

Julia gave a small laugh. “That was accomplished before we arrived.”

Brenna exhaled softly. “They were watching more closely.”

“Yes,” Julia said. “And listening less.”

Reed’s mouth curved faintly. “That tends to happen.”

A brief silence followed before Julia straightened slightly. “I refuse to spend the entire day indoors recovering from it.”

Reed raised a brow. “You have a better plan?”

Julia smiled. "We go out."

Brenna glanced at her. "What do you have in mind?"

Julia's expression brightened. "The theatre."

Reed leaned back again. "That seems rather ambitious."

"It seems necessary," Julia replied. "If we are to be discussed, we may as well be seen."

Callum's gaze shifted between them. "The city will be no quieter than last night."

"All the more reason," Julia said.

Brenna set her cup down. "I think I would like that."

Callum watched her a moment. "Very well."

The theatre was already aglow when they arrived. Light spilled from its tall windows onto the street, carriages lining the front in a slow procession as footmen moved with practiced efficiency, assisting guests down and ushering them inside.

Julia stepped out first, her gaze lifting immediately.

"Well," she said, taking in the façade, "this is already more dramatic than I expected."

Brenna followed, pausing just long enough to study the building before stepping forward "It feels… grand."

Reed offered his arm to Julia. "That would be the intention."

"And does it improve the performance?" Julia asked lightly.

"Rarely," he said. "But it does improve the audience."

Callum glanced at Brenna as he offered his arm. "Shall we?"

Brenna placed her hand lightly against it. "Yes."

Inside, the air shifted at once. Warm. Layered with voices, perfume, candlelight. Brenna slowed as they entered the main hall, her gaze lifting instinctively. The ceiling rose high above them, painted in soft color and gold detail, chandeliers casting lightthat seemed to settle over everything rather than simply illuminate it.

Balconies curved around the room in tiers, filled already with patrons leaning forward, observing not the stage, but each other.

Julia turned slowly in place, taking it all in. "They've arranged it so no one need miss a single thing."

Reed followed her gaze. "Not the performance," he said.

Julia's lips curved. "No," she agreed. "Certainly not that."

They moved toward their box, the murmur of conversation shifting as they passed.

Brenna leaned slightly closer to Callum. "They're watching again."

"Yes."

"Do they ever stop?"

"No."

Brenna's lips lifted slightly. "I'm beginning to appreciate the consistency."

Callum's gaze flicked to her. "That's not the usual reaction."

"No," she said. "But I find I prefer knowing where I stand."

"And where is that?"

Brenna glanced toward the crowd. "Directly in their line of sight."

They reached their box, stepping inside as the view opened fully before them. The stage stretched wide, framed in gold and deep velvet, the curtain still drawn but already hinting at something elaborate beyond it.

Julia moved to the front at once. "Oh, this is better than the ballroom."

Reed raised a brow. "Is it?"

"Yes," she said. "At least here we're expected to stare."

Reed smiled faintly. "That's one way of looking at it."

Brenna stepped forward beside her, her gaze fixed on the stage. "What is it we're seeing?"

Reed leaned slightly against the side. "A tragedy."

Julia glanced at him. "I should have expected as much."

"Would you prefer something lighter?"

"No," she said. "This feels appropriate."

Brenna's brow lifted slightly. "Appropriate?"

Julia gestured toward the room. "Everyone already looks as though they're anticipating something terrible. It may as well be on stage."

The house began to settle, the murmur lowering as more guests took their seats.

Brenna let her gaze drift once more over the theatre, the lights, the movement, the carefully constructed illusion of it all. Faces turning, pausing, recognizing.

But she didn't shrink from it this time. Didn't hesitate. "This is easier," she said quietly.

Callum glanced at her. "Is it?"

"Yes."

"How so?"

Brenna's lips curved faintly. "They're not pretending not to look."

Callum's mouth shifted slightly. "No," he said. "They're not."

For a time, the focus moved elsewhere. Not entirely, but enough.

Julia leaned toward Brenna and said, "And in three days…"

Brenna's gaze remained forward. "The masquerade," she finished.

Julia smiled faintly. "That will be very different."

Reed added quietly, "No expectations."

Callum's voice came lower. "No names."

Brenna turned her head just slightly, catching his profile in the dim light. "And no certainty."

Callum glanced at her. "Perhaps not."

Brenna's breath slowed. "Then perhaps," she said softly, "it will be the first honest evening we've had."

Callum didn't look away.

"Perhaps."

The lights dimmed further. The performance began.

The days following the theatre passed quickly, but not quietly. The ton continued its quiet speculation, invitations arriving in steady succession, each one drawing them further into a world that watched more closely than it revealed.

By the time the evening of the masquerade came upon them, the sense of anticipation had shifted, no longer curiosity, but expectation.

Lady Carroway's townhouse had been transformed entirely for the evening. Lanterns hung from the trees in the courtyard, their soft golden light guiding arriving guests through the garden entrance. Inside, the ballroom glittered with masked figures dressed in elaborate silks, velvet cloaks, and jeweled disguises.

Music floated through the open rooms as laughter and speculation filled the air.

Julia smiled as she took it in. "Well, this was meant to be a quiet evening."

Reed offered his hand. "You don't do quiet."

"That's not the point," she replied, accepting it.

Brenna followed more slowly, her gaze lingering on the entrance before turning to Callum. "What is the point?"

Callum stepped down beside her, offering his arm. "That we proceed as planned."

Julia lifted a brow as she adjusted her gloves. "And that plan would be?"

"To enjoy the evening," Callum said evenly.

Reed's voice came quieter now, just beside her. "And remain aware."

Julia glanced at him, her expression shifting, just slightly.

"Of what?" Brenna asked.

Callum's gaze moved to her, steady. "Anything that requires it."

Brenna studied him a moment. "That sounds like everything."

His voice lowered. "For now, it is."

Brenna's gaze lingered on him. "Do you truly believe we're in danger?" Her voice softened slightly. "Here... of all places?"

Callum's voice lowered. "I believe someone has gone to considerable effort already." His gaze didn't leave hers. "That's reason enough not to dismiss it."

Julia paused near the entrance, adjusting the delicate silver mask tied behind her head. "I do like the idea of a ball where no one knows who anyone is."

Brenna smiled, fastening the last ribbon of her own mask. "London appears to enjoy disguises."

Julia glanced across the ballroom. "Some more than others."

Their gowns had been delivered that morning by the dressmaker in record time thanks to Callum's generous deposit. Brenna wore a pale ivory silk tonight, the fabric catching the candlelight like moonlight on water. Her mask was simple, white with delicate gold trim.

Julia's was far more playful.

Reed turned to them both, dressed in dark formal attire with a black mask that only made his amused expression more obvious. "Well," he said, looking between them, "this may prove dangerous."

Julia raised a brow. "For whom?"

"For every gentleman in this room," Reed replied.

Callum turned slightly toward Brenna, his dark mask lending him a quiet elegance. "You seem to be finding London enjoyable," he said softly.

Brenna smiled. "I admit I didn't expect quite so many dances."

"That problem may worsen tonight."

Across the ballroom several masked gentlemen were already watching her.

Reed leaned closer to Julia. "You see? Dangerous."

"Stay close," Callum said quietly.

Brenna glanced at him. "That wasn't a suggestion."

"No," he said. "It wasn't."

Soon the orchestra began the first set. Masked couples filled the floor as the music carried through the room.

Callum offered Brenna his arm. "Shall we?"

She accepted. They moved easily through the steps, the mystery of the masks adding an unexpected thrill to the evening.

Brenna laughed softly. "I feel like I'm living someone else's life."

Callum studied her. "You seem to be amused by it."

"I am." They turned gracefully through the dance. "But I suspect this room is filled with people who enjoy secrets."

Callum's expression darkened slightly. "You may not be wrong."

Julia stood near the refreshment table when Reed approached.

"Finding this entertaining, are you?" he observed.

Julia smiled. "I like mysteries."

Reed leaned against the column beside her. "London is full of them."

Julia glanced at Brenna and Callum dancing. The orchestra shifted into the next set, the lively rhythm filling the ballroom again as new couples stepped onto the floor.

Julia watched the dancers for a moment before glancing sideways at Reed. "You realize," she said casually, "we have yet to dance."

Reed lifted a brow. "Have we?"

"Yes."

"That seems unlikely."

Julia turned toward him, her eyes narrowing slightly through the silver mask. "You've managed to avoid it rather skillfully."

Reed looked mildly offended. "Avoid?"

"Yes." Julia gestured toward the dance floor. "You've escorted me through crowded rooms, rescued me from overly eager gentlemen, and provided commentary on half the guests in this house… but somehow we have not danced."

Reed considered this thoughtfully. "That does appear suspicious."

Julia crossed her arms. "Very."

Reed studied her for a moment before setting down his glass. "Well."

Julia blinked. "Well?"

He held out his hand. "Shall we correct this oversight?"

Julia tried not to smile too quickly. "I suppose we must."

He led her onto the dance floor just as the next set began.

The steps were simple enough, though the room's swirling lantern light and masked faces gave the entire evening a strange, dreamlike quality.

Julia glanced up at him as they turned through the first figure. "You dance rather well for a man who pretends not to enjoy society."

Reed smiled faintly. "I did not say I disliked dancing."

"You implied it."

"I implied I disliked London."

Julia laughed softly. "That seems more believable."

They moved through another turn.

Reed studied her briefly. "You appear to enjoy it."

"The dancing?"

"Yes."

Julia shook her head. "It's the mystery." She glanced around the ballroom. "No one knows who anyone is tonight."

Reed leaned slightly closer as the music slowed. "I knew who you were immediately."

Julia tilted her head. "Did you?"

"Yes."

"How?"

Reed's voice lowered slightly. "You're the only woman in the room who looks as though she's planning something."

Julia laughed again. "You're not wrong, and here I thought it was due to our arriving in the same carriage together."

Across the ballroom Brenna caught sight of them dancing and smiled knowingly at Callum.

Callum followed her gaze.

Reed and Julia turned gracefully through the final steps of the dance.

Callum nodded slightly. "About time."

Brenna smiled. "I was thinking the same."

Near the shadowed balcony, a man watched the couple carefully. He wore a dark mask and stood slightly apart from the crowd. His eyes never left Brenna.

One of his companions leaned toward him. "That her?"

"Yes."

The man's voice was quiet. "She looks… different than expected."

"She looks wealthy," the other man muttered.

The masked observer said nothing. His gaze remained fixed on the dance floor.

"So that's the famous Ashcombe," his companion said.

The man nodded slightly.

"And the woman?"

"Whitmore, and soon," the masked man murmured softly, "she will belong to no one."

Chapter 24

The final days in London passed far too quickly for Brenna and Julia.

They had grown fond of the lively streets, the endless shops, and the glittering evenings among the ton. Though they knew they would soon return to Portsmouth, the ladies had already begun making plans to spend a full Season in London one day.

For Callum and Reed, however, the days could not pass quickly enough.

London society was exhausting in ways storms and cannon fire never were. With two days remaining before their departure, Brenna appeared at breakfast with a determined expression.
"I should like to visit the shops once more," she announced.

Reed groaned into his coffee. "Again?"

"There were several establishments we did not have time to explore," she said calmly.

Callum looked up from the morning paper. "You said that two days ago."

"And it remains true."

Julia smiled brightly. "I think it an excellent idea."

Callum studied Brenna for a moment, considering. "You will take the carriage," he said finally. "And the footman will accompany you."

Reed raised an eyebrow. "You're letting them loose again?"

Callum's voice remained measured. "We've seen no direct threat since arriving in London." His gaze settled briefly on Brenna. "I believe it safe enough to allow one final visit to

Bond Street. You shall remain on the main streets," Callum replied.

Brenna met his gaze evenly. "We will not stray far."

He hesitated only a moment before nodding. "Very well."

The afternoon carried them once more through the lively bustle of London. Packages accumulated steadily as the ladies visited several familiar shops, their spirits high as the carriage slowly filled with neatly wrapped parcels.

Bond Street was alive with movement, the late morning sun catching on polished glass windows and gilded signage as carriages rolled steadily past. Ladies drifted from shop to shop in silks and ribbons, their laughter mingling with the hum of London society at its finest.

Julia slowed at the next window, pressing her gloved fingers lightly to the glass. "Oh, Brenna, look at that one."

Inside, a gown of pale rose silk shimmered in the light. Brenna glanced at it, then at Julia.

"You don't need another gown."

Julia turned, scandalized. "That is not the point."

Brenna smiled faintly. "You said that about the last three."

"And I meant it every time."

They moved along, pausing next at a milliner's shop where delicate hats were arranged like works of art.

Julia leaned in. "If I am to be a fiancée..."

Brenna gave her a look. "You are not."

Julia lowered her voice, though her grin remained. "If I am to be *believed* to be one, I must look the part."

Brenna shook her head softly. "You seem to be enjoying this far too much."

Julia's smile softened, just slightly. "I didn't say I wasn't."

Before Brenna could respond, a voice called out behind them.

"Miss Fairchild, Miss Whitmore."

Julia and Brenna turned.

"Mrs. Langley," Julia answered.

The woman curtsied lightly, her eyes bright with interest. "We were just speaking of you this morning."

Julia glanced at Brenna briefly before returning the greeting. "I hope only kind things," she teased.

"Oh, the most delightful," Mrs. Langley assured. "Your appearance at Lady Pennington's was quite the topic."

Julia smiled. "That is both flattering and concerning."

Mrs. Langley leaned in slightly. "And your engagement."

Julia stilled.

Brenna watched her carefully.

"Yes," Julia said smoothly.

"How fortunate," Mrs. Langley continued. "Lord Halbrook is considered quite the catch."

Julia's smile didn't falter, but it shifted.

"Yes," she said. "So I've been told."

"And so sudden," the woman added. "How romantic."

Julia laughed lightly. "Yes… sudden."

Brenna caught it then, that small hesitation beneath the ease.

"And when is the wedding?" Mrs. Langley pressed.

Julia blinked. "That has not yet been decided."

"Soon, I should think."

Julia glanced down briefly, then back up. "Perhaps."

Mrs. Langley smiled knowingly. "Well, we shall all be waiting eagerly."

After a few more pleasantries, she drifted away.

Julia remained still for a moment.

Brenna tilted her head. "You handled that well."

Julia exhaled softly. "I nearly committed myself to a date."

Brenna smiled faintly. "That would have been inconvenient."

Julia looked down at her hands. "Yes."

A brief silence passed as the noise of the street carried around them.

Brenna said in a lowered voice, "You didn't deny it."

Julia glanced up. "I couldn't."

"You didn't want to."

Julia hesitated. Just for a moment. "I don't know," she admitted.

Brenna studied her. "That's new."

Julia gave a small, almost reluctant smile. "Yes."

They resumed walking, slower now. More thoughtful.

"He didn't correct them either," Julia added after a moment.

Brenna's lips curved slightly. "No."

Julia glanced at her. "That feels like part of the problem."

"Or part of the answer."

Julia didn't respond.

But something in her expression softened.

They turned toward another shop, fine gloves displayed neatly in the window.

Julia paused again, though her attention had shifted elsewhere entirely. "He makes things… uncomplicated," she said quietly.

Brenna looked at her. "That's not a word I would use for him."

Julia smiled faintly. "No," she said. "But it is when he's with me."

Brenna said nothing. Because she understood that feeling far more than she cared to admit.

Julia straightened slightly, shaking off the moment. "Well," she said, brighter now, "if I am to be a fiancée, I require gloves suitable for the role."

Brenna laughed softly. "Of course you do."

And as they stepped into the shop, neither of them noticed how closely they were being watched.

By late afternoon the sky had softened into a pale gold, and the streets were thick with pedestrians finishing their errands before evening.

The ladies paused at the curb as their carriage drew up behind them, the footman already stepping down to assist. The last of their parcels were gathered and secured inside. Ribbons and fine paper shifted softly as each package was arranged with care.

Julia allowed herself one final, satisfied look before turning. "Well," she said lightly, "that was entirely productive."

Brenna gave her a look. "That was entirely unnecessary."

"Details."

The footman offered his hand. Julia stepped up first, settling into her seat with ease before Brenna followed, the door closing firmly behind them.

For a moment, the carriage remained still.

Julia turned toward her, studying her with a knowing expression. "You've been smiling more."

Brenna frowned slightly. "I have not."

"You have." Julia leaned back, folding her hands with quiet satisfaction. "And very specifically," she added, "when Lord Ashcombe is in the room."

Brenna's expression stilled. "That is not true."

Julia's brow lifted. "No?"

Brenna looked away briefly, adjusting her gloves. "You imagine things."

Julia smiled. "I observe things."

Brenna met her gaze again. "You exaggerate them."

"Only slightly." Then Julia's voice softened, just enough to be sincere. "You like him."

Brenna didn't answer immediately.

Outside, the carriage began to move.

"That is... a very bold conclusion."

Julia tilted her head. "Is it incorrect?"

Brenna's gaze shifted toward the window. "I hardly know him."

Julia watched her a moment longer. "That has not stopped you from smiling."

Brenna exhaled quietly. "That proves nothing."

Julia's smile lingered. "No," she said. "But it does suggest something."

Brenna didn't respond. But the faint warmth in her expression gave her away more than words ever could.

As their carriage rolled slowly along one crowded avenue, Brenna suddenly leaned forward.

"Oh!"

Julia looked up. "What is it?"

Brenna pointed through the window. A flower vendor stood at the corner, his cart overflowing with bright bouquets, roses, lavender, and fresh greenery.

Brenna smiled. "Mrs. Pembroke."

Julia blinked. "The housekeeper?"

"Yes," Brenna said warmly. "She mentioned the other evening how much she misses fresh flowers in the house."

Julia remembered. "With his lordship away most of the year, they don't keep them," she said.

"Exactly."

The carriage slowed slightly with traffic.

"I'll only be a moment," Brenna said, reaching for the door.

Before Julia could protest, she had stepped down onto the street.

The crowd moved thickly around the flower stall as Brenna approached the vendor.

Julia watched through the window at first, smiling faintly as Brenna began selecting bouquets. But the street was busy. Carriages rolled past. People crossed constantly between stalls and storefronts.

Within moments Brenna disappeared behind a cluster of shoppers. Julia leaned forward slightly, trying to catch sight of her again. A minute passed. Then another.

Julia frowned. “That’s taking longer than it should.”

She opened the carriage door and stepped down onto the pavement.

“Miss Fairchild?” the footman asked.

“I’ll fetch her,” Julia said quickly.

She moved toward the flower stall, weaving carefully through the dense crowd.

“Brenna?” she called quietly.

There was no answer. The vendor was now serving another customer. Julia’s unease deepened.

She stepped farther down the street, scanning faces and bright gowns moving through the afternoon bustle.

“Brenna?”

Still nothing. A cold feeling crept slowly into her stomach. She turned to retrace her steps, and suddenly felt something hard press against her side.

A voice spoke close behind her. Low. Controlled. “Do not make a sound.”

Julia froze. The pressure at her ribs shifted slightly, unmistakable now. A pistol.

“Walk with me,” the man said quietly.

Julia’s pulse thundered.

“If you value your friend’s safety,” he continued softly, “you will come with me out back.”

The crowd continued moving around them, completely unaware. Julia forced herself to breathe slowly.

"And do not make a scene."

She swallowed. Then, very carefully, she began to walk. The carriage had not moved from its place along the curb.

Packages from the day's shopping still sat neatly stacked inside, ribbons and paper catching the fading afternoon light. The footman stood beside the door, scanning the crowd with growing unease.

Miss Fairchild had stepped down to fetch Miss Whitmore. That had been several minutes ago. Too many minutes.

He craned his neck again toward the flower stall. The vendor was serving another customer now, cheerful and oblivious. Neither lady stood nearby.

The footman's stomach tightened. He moved forward into the crowd, trying not to appear alarmed. "Miss Whitmore?" he called quietly.

No answer.

"Miss Fairchild?" Only the noise of the street answered him, carriages rolling, vendors shouting, laughter drifting between shop doors.

A terrible realization crept slowly over him. Something was wrong. He pushed farther through the gathering of shoppers, scanning every face he passed.

Nothing. No blue silk gown. No familiar figure. The unease hardened into certainty.

Without another moment's hesitation he turned and hurried back toward the carriage. The driver looked down at him.

"Find them?"

"No," the footman said sharply. "And we are not waiting here any longer."

Within moments the carriage wheels were rattling hard across the London streets, turning sharply toward Brook Street.

Chapter 25

Back at the townhouse, Callum stood near the study window reviewing a letter when the front door burst open below.

Boots struck the marble entry with unmistakable urgency.

Callum looked up immediately.

The footman appeared in the doorway moments later, breathless. “My lord,”

Callum’s expression changed instantly. “What is it?”

The man swallowed hard. “The ladies… they’re gone.”

Reed, who had been seated near the fireplace, was on his feet before the sentence finished. “Gone?”

“They stepped out of the carriage near a flower vendor, sir,” the footman said quickly. “Miss Whitmore first, then Miss Fairchild when she could not find her.”

“How long?” Callum asked sharply.

“Ten minutes, perhaps fifteen before I realized neither had returned.”

Reed’s jaw tightened. “And the crowd?” “Thick, sir. Busy street.” Callum was already moving. “Where?” The footman gave the location quickly. Reed grabbed his coat. “I knew London was too quiet,” he

muttered.

Callum stopped only long enough to collect the pistol from the desk drawer.

His voice was calm. Too calm. “No one leaves this house,” he told the footman.

“Yes, my lord.”

Reed met his gaze. “You thinking what I’m thinking?”

Callum's eyes had gone cold. "If the men behind this have taken them…"

Reed nodded once. "We'll find them."

Callum stepped toward the door. "We will."

And this time… He had no intention of letting anyone limp away.

Brenna had only meant to be gone from the carriage a moment.

The flower vendor's stall overflowed with bright color, roses, lavender, small bundles of greenery tied with twine. She selected three bouquets quickly, already imagining Mrs. Pembroke's surprised smile when the flowers appeared on the breakfast table.

Then the voice came from behind her. "Do not react."

The words were quiet enough that only she could hear them. At the same instant something hard pressed firmly against her side beneath the man's coat.

A pistol.

Brenna's fingers tightened slightly around the flowers, but her face remained perfectly composed.

"Walk," the man said softly.

He steered her away from the busy front of the stall toward a narrow passage behind the row of shops. The crowd swallowed them almost immediately, and within seconds they had slipped out of sight of Bond Street.

The alley smelled faintly of damp brick and horse tack.

"Where are we going?" Brenna asked calmly.

"You'll see soon enough."

They moved quickly through the back lanes until they reached another street farther down where traffic bustled just as loudly as before.

Brenna's mind raced. She could not run. The pistol never left her side. As they stepped out into the crossing crowd, the man beside her leaned closer.

"You'll behave," he murmured. "Unless you fancy another swim."

A chill slid down her spine.

"Last time you had luck," he continued quietly. "This time no one will be there to drag you out of the sea."

So. Portsmouth. They were taking her back to the water.

They had just begun crossing the busy street when a cheerful voice called out.

"Miss Whitmore!"

Brenna's head turned instinctively.

"Oh! Miss…!"

The dressmaker from Bond Street hurried toward her, stopping just short as she recognized Brenna in the crowd. "Well, what luck," the woman said breathlessly. "I had meant to send word to the house."

The pistol pressed harder into Brenna's side. "Do not linger," the man beside her whispered.

Brenna forced a pleasant smile. "I'm afraid we are in something of a hurry," she said politely.

"Yes, of course," the dressmaker replied. "I only wished to mention that you left a small parcel at the shop last week. A shawl and a pair of gloves."

Brenna inclined her head slightly. "How careless of me."

The woman glanced at the gentleman beside Brenna, clearly curious but too well-mannered to ask questions. "I had intended to deliver it myself."

"That would be very kind," Brenna said smoothly. "If you might drop it by the estate in the morning."

The dressmaker brightened. "Certainly."

Brenna shifted the flowers in her arms, keeping her voice light. "My cousin and I are getting underway shortly."

Brenna met her eyes briefly.

The dressmaker blinked slightly at the phrase but nodded politely. "Of course, Miss Whitmore."

The man at Brenna's side tugged her forward. "Come along."

Brenna offered the woman a quick smile. "Thank you again."

"Enough," the man said quietly. "Move."

They left the busy street quickly, cutting through narrower roads where the crowds thinned and the noise of Bond Street faded behind them. By the time they reached the edge of the city, the buildings stood farther apart and the road had grown quiet.

A waiting carriage stood near the trees. The man pushed her toward it.

Inside, another man waited. "Is this her?" the second asked.

"Think so."

Brenna was shoved inside before she could protest. Rough hands seized her wrists, binding them tightly with cord before she could resist.

The carriage lurched forward almost immediately. For a few minutes there was only the rattle of wheels and the steady pounding of Brenna's heart.

Then the carriage slowed again. Voices outside. A door opening. Another figure pushed inside, and Brenna's breath caught.

"Julia?"

Julia froze as she was forced onto the opposite bench. "Brenna?"

Shock flashed across both their faces. But the deeper feeling came just as quickly. Dread.

The man sitting beside them shut the carriage door hard. "Both of them?" he muttered irritably toward the driver.

A voice outside answered. "You said the one in blue was Whitmore."

"Well they were together, weren't they?" The man inside sighed.

"Blast it. We weren't told which one was which."

"Doesn't matter," another voice said from outside. "We've got both now."

The carriage jolted forward again, faster this time.

Brenna's stomach dropped. They had taken Julia by mistake. Or perhaps simply out of caution. Either way, Julia was now trapped with her.

Across the narrow space Julia stared back at her, eyes wide but steady.

Neither of them spoke.

The man seated beside them watched closely, one hand resting near the pistol tucked beneath his coat.

Any attempt to whisper would be noticed immediately. So they sat in silence.

The carriage sped along uneven roads, each jolt sending painful shocks through Brenna's tied wrists. Hours seemed to pass. The ride grew rougher the farther they traveled, the wheels bouncing hard over rutted ground.

Brenna shifted uncomfortably against the bench. It was, without question, the most miserable carriage ride she had ever endured. But she forced herself to remain still.

Callum would understand the message. He had to. Because if he didn't, they were sailing into the dark with men who had no intention of letting them go.

By the time the carriage finally slowed, the sky had settled into its deepest hour, well past midnight of the following day. Brenna had lost count of the turns and miles, but the scent of salt in the air told her everything she needed to know.

Portsmouth.

The door was yanked open and rough hands hauled her out before she could steady herself. Lanterns flickered along the dock, casting long shadows over unfamiliar masts and rigging.

Brenna looked toward the harbor instinctively. But the ship waiting there was not one she recognized.

Not a vessel from her father's fleet. And certainly not the *Hawthorne*.

"Move."

The pistol appeared again, guiding her forward up the gangplank. The crew that met them said very little. Their eyes lingered on the women with the detached curiosity of men who had been paid not to ask questions.

Brenna's and Julia's wrists were still tied as they were pushed down the narrow ladder below deck. A small cabin waited for them, bare, dim, and already smelling of damp wood and salt. The door slammed shut behind them.

Outside, boots moved across the deck above. Voices barked orders. About an hour later came the unmistakable groan of ropes loosening. Moments later the ship shifted beneath them. Sails unfurling. Lines cast off.

The vessel was leaving port. Only then did the door open again. One of the men stepped inside and cut the ropes binding their wrists.

"Don't get clever," he warned.

Then he stepped out and locked the door behind him.

The two women sat in silence for a moment, rubbing life back into their hands. The deck rolled gently beneath them as the ship gathered speed.

Julia flexed her wrists and let out a slow breath. "Well," she said quietly, "this is not how I imagined my evening."

Brenna looked down at the rope marks still circling her wrists. "This is my fault."

Julia blinked. "What?"

"I should never have stopped for those flowers."

Julia shook her head immediately. "No."

"If I hadn't stepped away from the carriage.."

"Brenna," Julia said firmly, "listen to me."

Brenna met her eyes reluctantly.

"They were watching us," Julia continued. "They knew exactly where we were."

Brenna said nothing.

"They would have taken you eventually," Julia added gently. "Flower stall or no flower stall."

Brenna leaned back against the cabin wall, the weight of the situation pressing heavily on her chest. "They didn't even know which one of us was Miss Whitmore," she said quietly.

Julia gave a small humorless smile. "Apparently they decided it was safer to take both."

Brenna's expression tightened. "I never meant to drag you into this."

Julia reached across the small space and squeezed her hand. "You didn't."

For a moment the only sound between them was the creaking of the ship and the distant rush of wind against the sails.

Then Brenna spoke again. "I may have left Callum a message."

Julia looked up quickly. "You did?"

Brenna nodded. "The dressmaker from Bond Street ran into me in the street."

Julia frowned. "The one from the shop?"

"Yes."

"What did you say?"

"I told her to deliver a forgotten parcel to the estate in the morning."

Julia tilted her head. "That doesn't sound like much of a clue."

Brenna's lips curved faintly. "I told her we were getting underway."

Julia blinked. "A sailor's phrase."

Brenna nodded. "Callum would never ignore that."

Julia's expression softened slightly. "You're certain he'll understand?"

Brenna looked toward the small porthole where the dark sea was beginning to stretch endlessly around them.

"Yes."

The ship rolled gently beneath them as it moved farther from shore.

"Because if anyone in England understands what that means…" Her voice quieted. "It's him."

Chapter 26

By the time Callum and Reed reached Bond Street, the last light of evening had faded from the sky. The street still bustled with traffic and late shoppers, but the place where the carriage had waited felt suddenly ordinary, too ordinary for the violence Callum knew had occurred there.

He stepped down from the carriage before it had fully stopped. "Here?" he asked the footman.

"Yes, my lord," the man said nervously. "Just there by the flower cart."

The vendor was still present, though the flowers now looked wilted beneath the lantern light.

Reed approached him first. "You sold flowers to a young lady earlier this afternoon," he said calmly.

The vendor nodded. "Several."

"This one wore blue silk."

Recognition flickered. "Yes, I remember her. Bought three bouquets."

"Did you see where she went afterward?" Callum asked.

The vendor shook his head slowly. "No, sir. The street was crowded."

Reed exchanged a look with Callum. Not good.

For the next several hours they searched. They questioned shopkeepers, carriage drivers, stable boys, and street vendors. They walked every alley within three blocks of the flower cart. They checked the backs of warehouses and narrow passages where a carriage might have waited unseen.

Nothing. No witnesses. No sound of struggle. No trace of the women.

By midnight the city had grown quieter, but the answers had not come. Reed leaned against a lamppost, frustration etched across his face. “They vanished.”

Callum stared down the dark street where the carriage had once stood. “Not vanished.”

“Taken, then.”

“Yes.”

Reed exhaled slowly. “They knew exactly where to find them.”

Callum said nothing. The realization had already settled heavily in his mind. Someone had been watching.

They returned to Ashcombe’s London townhouse long after the city had gone still.

The housekeeper met them anxiously in the entry hall. “Any news, my lord?”

Callum shook his head once. “No.”

Reed poured two glasses of brandy in the study, handing one silently to Callum.

Neither man slept. The night stretched long and restless. Maps of London lay spread across the desk. Names of possible suspects were written and crossed out. Every lead Reed had gathered in Portsmouth was reconsidered, every rumor examined again.

But the hours passed without progress. Morning arrived gray and cold. And with it, a letter.

Mrs. Pembroke brought it in on the breakfast tray. “There is no seal, my lord,” she said nervously. “A boy left it at the door.”

Callum took the envelope. The handwriting was unfamiliar. Reed watched silently as he opened it.

The message inside was brief. Cold. Direct. Callum read it once. Then again. His jaw tightened.

Reed held out his hand. “Let me see.”

Callum passed him the paper.

Reed read aloud quietly.

Donot attempt to find them.

Unless you wish to be exposed.

Along with your mate you will do as instructed.

No loose ends.

Once the signature is complete they will be released.

This time there will be noone to rescue them.

Silence filled the study. Reed folded the paper slowly. "They know who we are."

"Yes."

"And they know what we do."

Callum's eyes hardened. "Which means they've been watching us for some time."

Reed looked toward the window, the gray London streets beyond. "So what now?"

Callum took the letter back. "They want a signature."

"Yes." Reed studied him carefully. "You're not considering it."

Callum folded the paper once. Then again. "They believe we will stop searching."

Reed shook his head slowly. "They don't know you very well."

Callum's voice was quiet. "No." His gaze lifted toward the door. "They don't."

The morning had worn on in a tense, heavy silence when the front bell rang sharply through the townhouse.

Reed looked up from the desk where he had been studying the threatening letter for the tenth time.

Callum didn't move.

A moment later hurried footsteps crossed the entry hall, followed by the housekeeper appearing in the doorway.

"My lord," she said, slightly breathless, "there is a lady here insisting she must speak with you immediately."

Callum's eyes lifted. "Who is she?"

"She says she is the dressmaker from Bond Street."

Reed straightened. "That's interesting."

"Send her in," Callum said.

A moment later the woman swept into the study in a swirl of fabric and nervous energy. She was clearly flustered, clutching a carefully wrapped parcel against her chest.

"Oh, thank heavens," she exclaimed. "I was so afraid I might miss you before you returned to Portsmouth."

Callum remained standing behind the desk. "You wished to see me?"

"Yes, my lord, terribly sorry for the intrusion," she said quickly. "I've come about Miss Whitmore."

Reed and Callum exchanged the faintest glance.

The woman hurried forward, placing the parcel carefully on the desk. "She forgot these when she collected her gowns last week," the dressmaker continued breathlessly. "A shawl and a pair of gloves. I had meant to deliver them earlier, but business was dreadful and, well…"

She paused, catching her breath. "But then I ran into her yesterday evening," she added brightly.

The room went still.

Reed spoke first. "You saw Miss Whitmore yesterday?"

"Yes," the woman said. "Quite by chance. She seemed to be in a dreadful hurry."

Callum's voice was quiet. "Where did you see her?"

"Just off Bond Street, near the carriage stands."

Reed leaned forward slightly. "She spoke with you?"

"Oh yes," the woman said. "She apologized terribly for the oversight and asked if I would kindly bring the items here today."

Callum's expression did not change. "And she was alone?"

The dressmaker hesitated. "Well… no."

Reed's voice sharpened. "No?"

"She was with a gentleman," the woman said. "She introduced him as her cousin."

Silence dropped into the room.

Callum's gaze darkened.

The study had only just fallen quiet after the dressmaker's hurried explanation when Callum asked gently, "Did Miss Whitmore say anything else to you?"

The woman clasped her hands nervously. "Well, not much, my lord. She only seemed eager to be on her way."

Reed leaned against the desk. "Eager how?"

"She said they had to leave immediately," the dressmaker replied. "That they were, what was the phrase…" She paused, thinking. "Oh yes, she said they were getting underway directly."

The room went still.

Callum folded his arms slowly, his gaze sharpening. "Miss Whitmore chose those exact words?"

"Yes, my lord."

The dressmaker looked between them, clearly unsure why the phrase mattered. "She also asked if I would kindly bring the parcel here this morning," the woman added. "Said she might not have the chance to return for it herself."

Callum's expression did not change, but something colder settled behind his eyes.

Reed exhaled softly. "She knew."

Callum nodded once. "She knew we would question you."

The dressmaker blinked. "I beg your pardon?"

Callum stepped closer to the desk. "She expected you would be asked exactly what she said."

Reed gave a quiet, impressed huff of breath. "And she left us a message."

Callum looked down at the parcel lying on the desk. "Getting underway," he repeated.

Reed's voice was low now. "Not a gentleman's phrase."

"No." Callum's gaze lifted toward the window, toward the distant direction of the Thames "It's a sailor's."

Reed nodded grimly. "And if they're getting underway…"

Callum finished the thought. "They're leaving by water."

For the first time since the letter had arrived, they had a direction. And Brenna had made sure they would understand it.

The dressmaker clasped her hands nervously. "Is something wrong?"

Callum ignored the question. "Tell us about this cousin."

The woman blinked. "Well, he was tall."

Reed moved closer. "How tall?"

"About your height," she said, gesturing uncertainly toward him.

"Hair?"

"Dark."

"Age?"

"Perhaps thirty. Maybe older."

Callum's voice remained steady. "Did he give a name?"

"No."

"Accent?"

She thought for a moment. "He didn't speak much. Not a London laborer, certainly."

Reed paced slowly across the room.

"Clothing?"

"Dark coat," she said. "Very respectable looking."

Callum's jaw tightened slightly. "And Miss Whitmore herself?"

"She seemed, hurried," the dressmaker admitted. "But she did not appear frightened."

Reed muttered under his breath. "She wouldn't."

Reed's eyes lifted slowly toward Callum. Neither man answered immediately.

At last Reed gave her a polite smile. "You've been very helpful."

The woman nodded nervously. "I only meant to return her things."

Callum lifted the parcel slowly from the desk.

"You may have done far more than that."

As the dressmaker was escorted out, Reed turned back toward Callum. "Well," he said quietly. "That answers one question."

Callum unwrapped the parcel without speaking.

"And raises ten more," Reed added.

Callum stared down at the shawl inside.

"Not cousin," Reed muttered.

"No." Callum folded the fabric carefully. "Captor."

Chapter 27

They did not wait for the carriage.

The moment the realization settled, *getting underway,* Callum was already moving. “Horses,” he said sharply.

Reed was beside him before the word finished.

The horses were brought around before the sun had fully risen. Mist still clung low to the ground, curling across the drive as though reluctant to release the night. The stable hands moved quickly under Callum’s instruction, though neither man needed to be told what urgency looked like.

Reed adjusted his gloves as he stepped toward his horse. “You intend to ride straight through.”

Callum didn’t look at him as he tightened the saddle strap. “Yes.”

Reed exhaled quietly. “That will shave time.”

“It will.”

“It will also leave the horses half-dead.”

Callum swung up into the saddle in one clean motion. “Then we change them along the way.”

Reed followed a moment later. “And if we don’t find fresh ones when we need them?”

Callum finally glanced at him. “Then we don’t stop.”

Reed’s mouth curved faintly. “Of course we don’t.”

Within minutes they were riding hard out of London, the road south stretching long and dusty beneath the late afternoon sun. Neither man wasted breath on conversation. The urgency of the message Brenna had left them pressed forward like a rising wind.

If the kidnappers meant to leave by water, then Portsmouth was their only real chance.

Callum urged his horse faster.

Reed rode beside him, grimly focused.

"Think they're heading for the Channel?" Reed asked at last.

"They'll want distance," Callum replied. "And a ship no one will question."

Reed nodded. "Smugglers, then."

By midmorning, the mist had burned away, replaced by clear skies and a road that had grown busier the closer they drew to the main route.

They did not slow. A cart ahead was forced aside. A rider turned sharply to avoid them.

Callum didn't acknowledge either.

Reed followed close behind, his expression tightening as they pushed forward. "If they left ahead of us…"

"They did," Callum cut in.

Reed adjusted his grip on the reins. "Then we're already behind."

Callum shook his head once.

"Not by much." Callum studied the road ahead a moment before speaking. "If they left ahead of us, I'd say we're perhaps half a day behind, no more."

Reed glanced over. "Assuming they didn't lose time."

Callum nodded once. "That depends on how they traveled. If they took a carriage, it would slow them considerably, likely costing them a full day."

"And if not?"

Callum's gaze sharpened. "On horseback, they'd move faster. In that case, we're closer than they think."

They changed horses just past noon. The stop was brief, too brief. Water. Fresh mounts. Nothing more.

Reed swung back into the saddle with a quiet breath. "You're driving this harder than necessary."

Callum didn't respond.

Reed studied him a moment. "This isn't just about the Crown."

Callum's jaw tightened. "No."

Reed nodded slightly. "I didn't think so." Then added, " She matters to you."

Callum didn't answer. But he didn't deny it either.

Reed let out a quiet breath. "That complicates things."

"Yes."

"And yet," Reed added, glancing ahead, "you're not slowing."

Callum's voice was steady. "No."

The afternoon stretched long and relentless.

Dust rose beneath the horses' hooves, clinging to boots and coats as the miles passed beneath them.

They spoke little. Didn't need to. Every moment carried the same weight. Every mile, not fast enough.

By late afternoon, the road narrowed, turning rougher as they pushed closer toward the coast.

They rode harder. Pushing the horses again, ignoring the strain now evident in every movement. They rode until the sky began to deepen toward evening, the air turning cooler as the scent of salt finally reached them.

The wind picked up as the land opened ahead of them. And then, the first glimpse of water.

Distant. But there.

Callum leaned forward slightly. "Portsmouth."

Reed followed his line of sight. "Aye."

The final stretch came fast. The road gave way to the outer edges of the port, activity increasing, voices carrying, the distant creak of ships already reaching them.

Callum pulled the horse up sharply as they reached the rise overlooking the harbor. Reed reined in beside him. Both men looked out. Ships. Too many. Movement everywhere.

Reed exhaled. “They could be anywhere.”

Callum’s gaze sharpened. “They won’t be for long.”

Reed glanced at him. “You have a plan.”

Callum didn’t look away from the harbor. “I always do.”

Then he turned the horse again, already moving.

“Let’s hope,” Reed muttered as he followed, “this one works.”

Callum’s voice carried back, low and certain, “It will.”

By the time they reached the docks the sun was sinking low over the harbor. Ships rocked gently against their moorings, masts creaking softly in the wind. Lanterns had begun to glow along the quay as sailors finished their day’s work.

The *Hawthorne* sat exactly where she had been left.

Callum swung down from the saddle before the horse had fully stopped. Several of the crew still aboard straightened in surprise.

“Captain?”

Callum’s voice carried across the deck. “Where’s the rest of the crew?”

One of the men hesitated. “Some ashore, sir. Taverns mostly.”

Reed climbed the gangplank behind him. “Then start running.”

The sailors exchanged quick glances.

Callum’s tone left no room for doubt. “Find them,” he ordered. “Every man you can. I don’t care if they’re sober or sleeping.”

One of the deckhands hurried forward. “Sir?”

“We sail tonight.”

The man blinked. “Tonight?”

"Posthaste."

Within moments the quiet harbor erupted into motion. Men were sent racing into the streets and taverns along the waterfront, shouting orders and dragging reluctant sailors from their drinks.

Reed watched over the sudden flurry of activity while waiting for the harbor master.

Callum's gaze remained fixed on the darkening horizon.

Below them the crew scrambled to ready the brig. Lines were checked. Lanterns lit. Sails loosened.

And somewhere out on the water, Brenna had trusted they would understand her message. Now it was up to them to reach her and Julia in time.

The harbor master's lantern cast long wavering shadows across the dock as Callum and Reed met up with him to glance over the man's ledger.

Callum's finger traced the most recent entry. A single ship. Departed that morning.

"Which way?" Reed asked.

"South-southeast," the harbor master replied, adjusting his spectacles. "A merchant brig. Cleared early morning with the tide."

Callum's jaw tightened. Morning. They had already lost hours.

Reed studied the page again. "You're certain?"

The harbor master nodded. "Only vessel to depart since dawn."

Reed exhaled slowly. "They're ahead of us."

Callum closed the ledger with quiet finality. "Not for long."

The harbor master blinked as Callum turned away without another word.

Reed followed him down the dock toward the *Hawthorne*, the ship already alive with motion.

Lanterns swung from rigging. Crewmen rushed along the deck hauling lines and shouting orders as more sailors arrived at a run from the taverns and alleys of Portsmouth.

One man stumbled aboard half-laced and still breathless. "Captain, heard we're sailing?"

Callum stepped onto the deck. "We are."

"How soon?"

"Now."

The man grinned. "Thought you'd say that."

Reed leaned against the rail as another group of sailors clambered aboard. "Looks like we found most of them."

"Enough," Callum said.

The boatswain called out from the quarterdeck. "Stores checked, sir!"

While the ship had remained in harbor the previous weeks, the crew had quietly restocked her, fresh water, salted provisions, powder, and shot.

The *Hawthorne* was ready.

Reed nodded approvingly. "Well, that's one less worry."

Callum turned toward the assembled crew, his voice carrying across the deck. "Listen carefully."

The sailors fell quiet.

"Two women have been taken."

A low murmur rippled through the men.

"Miss Whitmore and Miss Fairchild," Reed added.

Several of the crew exchanged glances. They had met the women. They liked them.

Callum continued. "A brig left Portsmouth this morning. They are likely aboard."

"And we're chasing them?" one sailor asked.

Callum's eyes hardened. "Yes."

Another voice called out. "How far ahead are they?"

"Hours."

The crew shifted uneasily.

Reed spoke calmly. "But they're not sailing the *Hawthorne*."

Grins began to spread among the men. They knew their ship. And what she could do.

Callum's voice lowered slightly. "They have a head start." He looked out across the dark water where the last light of day was fading. "But we are faster."

The boatswain shouted from the bow. "Lines ready!"

Callum stepped to the helm. "Cast off."

Ropes splashed into the water. The sails climbed the masts as the crew moved with practiced speed. Within minutes the brig slipped free of the dock and turned toward open water.

Reed stepped up beside Callum as the *Hawthorne* leaned into the wind, her sails filling cleanly as the harbor lights of Portsmouth began to fade behind them.

He watched Callum for a moment, the set of his shoulders, the fixed line of his gaze on the dark horizon. "You look like a man determined to outrun the wind itself."

Callum didn't glance away. "I intend to."

Reed folded his arms against the rail as the brig surged forward, cutting cleanly through the growing swell. "They've half a day on us," he said.

Callum adjusted the wheel slightly as the sails strained with the strengthening wind. "Less."

Reed lifted a brow. "You're assuming they're not pushing hard."

"I'm assuming they don't know we're coming."

Reed nodded slowly. "That helps."

The deck tilted as the ship caught a stronger gust, the rigging humming overhead.

A crewman hurried past hauling a line, the men already settling into the rhythm of pursuit.

Reed watched the sails climb higher. "She's hungry tonight."

Callum's voice remained quiet. "So am I."

Reed followed his gaze out across the dark water. "You think they're heading for France?"

"Or anywhere they think we won't follow."

Reed gave a low chuckle. "That's optimistic of them."

Callum finally spoke the thought both men carried. "They won't expect us to sail this soon."

"No."

"They won't expect us to sail this fast."

Reed looked up at the taut canvas overhead, the brig already gathering speed. "No one does."

The wind strengthened again, the *Hawthorne* responding eagerly beneath their feet.

Reed pushed off the rail and straightened.

"Well," he said, glancing back toward the darkening horizon behind them, "I suppose we should give them something worth running from."

Callum's eyes remained fixed ahead. "They already have."

And somewhere beyond the darkening sea, the chase had begun.

Chapter 28

Brenna woke to the dull, rhythmic knock of wood striking wood. For a moment she lay still, unsure where she was. The events of the previous day pressed in slowly, the carriage, the ship, the locked cabin.

The vessel rolled gently beneath them. Beside her, Julia still slept, curled awkwardly against the thin mattress of the bunk.

She drew in a quiet breath. "Julia," she whispered.

A slight shift beside her. "I'm awake," Julia murmured back, her voice rough with sleep. "Though I rather wish I wasn't."

Brenna let out a soft breath of relief. "We're at sea."

Julia was quiet for a moment. "Yes," she said finally. "I thought as much."

The ship creaked again, a deeper roll beneath them.

Brenna shifted slightly, wincing. "I don't think I've ever been so uncomfortable in my life."

Julia gave a faint huff of agreement. "That carriage ride alone was punishment enough."

Brenna closed her eyes briefly, the memory settling in. "They didn't stop," she said quietly. "Not properly."

"No," Julia agreed. "Only long enough to change horses."

"And the privy."

Julia made a face in the dim light. "I'd rather not relive that part."

Brenna almost smiled. "They gave us food."

"Barely."

"With our hands tied," Brenna added.

Julia shifted beside her. “That was particularly thoughtful of them.”

Brenna exhaled slowly. “The place we stopped…” She trailed off.

Julia nodded, though Brenna couldn’t fully see it. “Not an inn.”

“No.”

“Too quiet,” Julia said. “And the caretakers…”

“…didn’t ask questions, ” Brenna finished.

“Which is worse,” Julia muttered.

Brenna’s voice lowered. “They knew.”

“Yes.”

Silence settled briefly between them, broken only by the steady movement of the ship.

Brenna shifted again, trying to ease the stiffness in her arms. “I don’t think I can feel my legs.”

Julia let out a quiet breath. “That makes two of us.”

“Sharing a bench with one of them didn’t help.”

Brenna’s voice sharpened slightly. “Not at all.”

“He didn’t say a word,” Julia added.

“That doesn’t make him less unpleasant.”

“No,” Julia agreed. “Just quieter about it.”

Brenna leaned her head back against the wall behind her. “It was well into the night when we reached the harbor,” she said softly.

Julia nodded again.

Brenna’s brow furrowed slightly. “We must have slept after they brought us aboard.”

Julia shifted beside her. “I don’t remember lying down.”

“Neither do I.”

Another long creak of the ship filled the space.

“We’re further out now,” Brenna said quietly.

Julia was silent for a moment.

Brenna turned her head slightly toward her. "I still feel this is all my fault."

Julia's response was immediate. "No."

"I stopped," Brenna said. "For the flowers. If I hadn't…"

"They would have found another moment," Julia cut in.

Brenna shook her head faintly. "You don't know that."

"I do." Her voice was steady.

"They were watching us, Brenna. This wasn't chance." Julia continued, softer now, "you didn't cause this, and you are not going to carry it."

Brenna let out a slow breath. "You're very certain."

"Yes."

A faint smile touched Julia's voice. "I refuse to let you be miserable about it."

Despite everything, Brenna felt the smallest hint of warmth at that. "You always do."

"It's one of my better qualities."

Brenna shifted again, testing the space around them. "We need to think, once we know more."

Julia exhaled. "And once we can feel our legs again."

Brenna almost laughed. Almost. But instead she steadied herself, listening to the ship around them. To the movement. To the unknown ahead.

"We'll get out of this," she said quietly.

Julia didn't hesitate. "Yes," she said. "We will."

Time stretched unbearably, until at last, Brenna caught the sound of faint noises creeping closer. She nudged Julia.

Julia answered with a quiet groan. "What is it…?"

"Listen."

The knocking came again. Wood against wood. Then footsteps outside their door.

Julia pushed herself upright, blinking away the last of her sleep.

The lock outside their door scraped. Both women stiffened.

The door swung open. "Up," one of the sailors ordered.

They were ushered roughly up the narrow ladder toward the deck. Brenna went first. The early dawn air struck her face as she stepped outside. Then she saw it.

And gasped.

Another ship sat directly alongside theirs. The rising light revealed the dark hull clearly now, scarred timbers, black paint, and the familiar lines Brenna recognized instantly.

The *Black Mercy*.

Massive iron hooks held the two ships together while a rough plank walkway bridged the narrow gap between their rails.

Julia stared in stunned disbelief. "I've never seen anything like this," she whispered.

The men behind them gave no time for questions. "Move."

They were shoved toward the plank. The sea rolled gently beneath the narrow boards as they crossed, the water far below shifting darkly between the two hulls.

Brenna's heart pounded. As soon as they stepped onto the *Mercy's* deck, the men there seized them quickly.

"…you have them," one of the men from the first ship said, low and uneasy.

The captain stood opposite him, unbothered. "I do." His gaze flicked briefly toward the women. "One was the agreement, and now you've brought me two."

The words were said lightly. Too lightly. The man's jaw tightened.

"I delivered what was arranged."

"No," the captain said calmly. "You delivered more."

Silence stretched between them. The sea shifted beneath the hulls.

The man didn't reach for additional coin. Didn't ask. Because there was nothing to be given.

Brenna watched the understanding settle across his face, not outrage, not surprise, just calculation.

The captain stepped closer, his voice lowering just enough to carry weight. "I was paid to have one disposed of and I intend to see that done."

The man hesitated. "And the other?"

The captain's mouth curved faintly. "What is one more?" Then added, "A gift for the crew."

No answer came. None was needed. After a long moment, the man gave a single, tight nod.

A decision made. No further argument.

"Pleasure doing business," the captain said.

The man said nothing. He turned back toward his ship.

Julia's voice came quietly beside her. "They knew."

Brenna didn't answer. Because she did too. This wasn't desperation. It wasn't confusion. It was transaction.

The captain turned toward them then, his full attention settling at last. He approached slowly, as though inspecting cargo. "Welcome aboard the *Mercy*. You may call me Crowe," he said, voice low and steady. "Captain of this vessel, and the last voice you'll be hearing."

Circling them with an easy stride, he continued, "well now, the tide's turned in our favor."

Julia straightened slightly. "For you."

Crowe glanced at her, faint amusement touching his expression. "Indeed."

He stopped in front of her. Julia didn't look away.

The captain's grin spread slowly, revealing teeth stained dark with rot. "I was paid in gold," he said. "That tends to cover a great many inconveniences."

"And as I said," he added lightly, "what is one more?" The casual cruelty of it settled heavily.

Julia's hand tightened faintly against Brenna's.

Crowe studied them both, considering. "I could hand you over to the crew," he said thoughtfully.

Julia stiffened.

"They would find you very… entertaining."

Brenna's voice was steady. "And if that proves inconvenient?"

His gaze sharpened just slightly. "Then I dispose of you sooner."

The sea moved around them, endless and indifferent.

He turned then, gesturing lazily to the men nearby. "Put them below."

Julia resisted instinctively. "Wait…"

A hand caught her arm.

Behind them, the hooks securing the ships were already being released. Lines splashed into the water. The vessels began to separate.

Brenna turned just in time to see the other ship slowly turning away. In the opposite direction. Her stomach dropped.

If Callum had received her message… He would be following the wrong ship.

The crew aboard the *Mercy* watched them with a colder stare.

Brenna moved with her, refusing to be separated as they were forced toward the hatch.

Behind them, the captain's voice followed, almost absent, "I'll decide shortly."

They were pushed down below deck and into a small room, the air closing in around them as the door shut behind them, bolted from the outside. Darkness. The steady creak of the ship. The sound of the sea. For a moment, neither spoke.

Brenna's thoughts had shifted. "These men are far worse than on the other ship," she said quietly. She stared toward the faint line of light above. "The others needed something from us. These men have already been paid, they don't need us alive."

Silence fell heavier than before.

Julia's voice dropped. "I'm scared, Brenna," she confessed.

"Yes." Brenna closed her eyes briefly, the truth settling fully now. They hadn't just been taken. They had been sold. And now, they were waiting to be disposed of.

This cabin was darker. No lantern had been left.

Brenna suspected their captors feared exactly what desperate prisoners might do with fire aboard a ship. A single small window let in just enough early afternoon light to reveal the room. The cabin was bare in the way most crew quarters were.

Two narrow bunks fixed against opposite walls. A small table bolted to the floor. A few hooks for coats. At the far end of the lower bunk sat a small trunk. It had been bolted down, likely to keep it from sliding during rough seas.

Brenna moved toward it slowly. "What are you doing?" Julia whispered.

"Looking." She lifted the lid.

Inside were clothes. Simple garments, shirts, trousers, a few loose jackets. Clearly meant for crewmen. But there were enough pieces to serve as disguises.

Julia stared at the contents in horror. "You cannot be serious."

Brenna looked up. "I am."

"You're suggesting we wear those?"

"Yes."

Julia shook her head slowly. "That's not the part that concerns me."

Brenna began sorting through the garments quickly. “We leave our dresses on the bunks.”

Julia blinked. “What?”

“It will look as though we’re still here.”

Julia stared at her friend as though she had finally lost her mind. “And when someone discovers we are not?”

Brenna picked up one of the heavier shirts, testing the fabric. “When someone enters the cabin.”

Julia’s eyes widened. “You plan to attack them?”

“Yes.”

“With what?”

Brenna glanced around the small cabin. The table was bolted down. The trunk was bolted down. But one object sat loose upon the floor. A heavy wooden stool.

She picked it up slightly, testing the weight. “This.”

Julia looked from the stool to Brenna with growing alarm. “And after we strike the unfortunate sailor?”

“We escape.”

Julia gestured vaguely toward the walls of the ship. “To where, precisely?”

Brenna walked toward the small porthole and looked out at the endless gray water rolling beneath the morning sky.

Julia folded her arms. “You do realize we are currently in the middle of the ocean.”

Brenna turned back toward her. “Yes.”

Julia waited. “And?”

Brenna set the stool quietly beside the door. “Then we improvise.”

Julia stared at her for several long seconds. Then sighed deeply. “Well,” she muttered. “At least this time I’ll know when the battle begins.”

Chapter 29

The *Hawthorne* cut cleanly through the water, her sails straining full against the steady wind as she gained speed with every passing mile.

Callum stood at the helm, his eyes fixed on the horizon.

Reed leaned against the rail beside him, watching the same stretch of sea.

"Captain!" The lookout's voice carried down from the mast. "Ship ahead!"

Callum didn't move. "Bearing?"

"North by west, coming toward Portsmouth!"

Reed lifted his spyglass and climbed a few steps up the rigging to get a better look. A faint shape appeared against the pale morning sky.

A brig. And she was indeed sailing toward them.

Reed studied her for several long seconds. Then lowered the glass slowly. "She's slowing," he said.

Callum's gaze sharpened. "Slowing?"

Reed handed him the glass.

Callum raised it to his eye. The other ship's sails had eased. Not turning. Not running. Waiting. Almost as if… Expecting to be stopped.

Callum lowered the glass. "They want us to board her."

Reed nodded. "That's what it looks like."

The decision hung between them. If the women were aboard, they could not let the ship pass.

But if it was the wrong vessel, boarding her would cost precious time.

Callum looked again toward the distant brig. She wasn't circling back toward Portsmouth. She was simply drifting closer. Inviting inspection.

Reed watched him carefully. "What does your gut say?"

Callum's jaw tightened. "They want us delayed."

Reed nodded slowly. "That was my thought."

Callum lifted the glass again. The other vessel had slowed even further now. Too convenient.

Reed gave a short huff of breath. "They're practically waving us over."

Callum lowered the glass. "And if we stop? We lose the wind and the distance."

Reed folded his arms. "They're counting on you to hesitate."

Callum studied the brig one final moment. Then he handed the glass back. "Helm steady."

Reed smiled faintly. "Thought so."

Callum's voice carried across the deck. "Do not slow."

The crew glanced briefly at one another but obeyed without question. The *Hawthorne* held her course, sails full and driving hard through the water.

As they closed the distance, the other ship's intent became even clearer. She had slowed nearly to a crawl. Waiting.

Reed shook his head. "It's a bluff."

Callum nodded once. "Keep our speed."

The brig slipped past them slowly on the port side, her crew watching with quiet tension. But the *Hawthorne* never altered course. Never slowed.

Reed leaned over the rail as they passed. "They were hoping we'd take the bait."

Callum's eyes never left the open sea ahead. "We don't have time for games."

Behind them, the decoy ship faded into the distance. Ahead, the real hunt continued.

The cabin was quiet except for the steady creak of the ship and the low rush of water against the hull.

Brenna and Julia waited.

The dim gray light from the small porthole barely reached the bunks, leaving most of the room in shadow. Brenna had arranged the dresses carefully. One on each bunk, stuffed loosely with the pillow and folded blanket beneath the fabric to give the illusion of sleeping figures.

In the faint light it looked convincing enough. Or so she hoped.

Julia crouched beside the door, gripping the heavy wooden stool with both hands. "How long do we wait?" she whispered.

"Until someone checks," Brenna murmured.

Julia exhaled slowly. "I never imagined kidnapping would involve this much patience."

Footsteps approached. Both women froze. The lock scraped. The door opened.

The sailor stepped halfway into the cabin, glancing toward the bunks. From the doorway it would have looked exactly as Brenna intended, two women lying quietly where they had been left.

He took two steps forward.

Julia swung. The stool connected with a dull, decisive crack.

The man collapsed instantly.

Julia stared down at him, breathing hard. "Well," she said quietly. "That was satisfying."

Brenna quickly knelt beside the unconscious man, searching his pockets. "Key."

Julia grinned. "Kind of him."

They slipped out into the narrow passageway, Brenna closing the door behind them before locking it again. The man lay inside the cabin now instead.

"Should buy us a little time," Julia said.

Brenna nodded. "But not much."

She glanced down the corridor. The layout of the ship had been forming in her mind since the moment they were first forced aboard. Years spent around ships, her father's ships, had taught her to notice things quickly. Where ladders were placed. Where cargo was stored. Where crew moved most often.

"This way," she whispered.

Julia followed as Brenna moved carefully along the passage. They avoided the ladder leading directly to the deck. Too exposed.

Instead Brenna guided her deeper toward the midsection of the vessel.

"Where are we going?" Julia whispered.

"To hide first."

They slipped into a larger cargo hold partially filled with stacked crates and coils of rope.

Brenna crouched beside a pile of bundled canvas. "Ships always keep spare sailcloth here," she said quietly.

Julia ducked beside her. "And then?"

Brenna studied the hold. "There will be a longboat."

Julia blinked. "Of course there will."

"All ships carry one."

"And you plan to steal it."

Brenna nodded. "When night comes."

Julia stared at her. "You've thought this through."

"I've sailed enough to know where things are kept."

Julia glanced around nervously. "And how do we reach this longboat without being seen?"

Brenna's eyes flicked toward the ladder leading upward from the hold. "There's usually a maintenance hatch near the bow."

Julia groaned softly. "Usually?"

Brenna gave a small shrug. "Ships are predictable."

Julia leaned closer. "And what if this one isn't?"

Brenna looked toward the dim ladder again. "Then we improvise."

Julia sighed. "I had a feeling you were going to say that."

Not knowing how much time they had before the sailor was discovered, Brenna moved quickly. "Come," she whispered. They slipped deeper into the hold, weaving between crates stacked nearly to the beams overhead. Coils of rope and bundled sailcloth filled the spaces between them, leaving narrow passages just wide enough to pass through.

The ship rolled gently beneath their feet. Somewhere above, boots crossed the deck. Brenna's pulse thudded in her ears. They did not have long.

She guided Julia toward a shadowed corner near the bow where spare some of the rigging and folded canvas had been stored. Brenna pushed several loose coils aside, creating a hollow space just large enough for them both to crouch inside.

"Stay here," she whispered.

Julia grabbed her sleeve. "Where are you going?"

"I need to see the layout."

"Brenna…"

"If they find the empty cabin before we know our way around this ship, we'll be caught in minutes."

Julia reluctantly released her. "Be careful."

Brenna nodded and slipped out from their hiding place, moving quietly along the dim passage between cargo stacks.

Her father's ships had looked much like this. Every vessel followed the same practical logic. Cargo toward the center. Crew quarters toward the stern. Storage and maintenance areas forward.

Which meant the hatch she needed should be somewhere near the bow. She paused at the end of the hold, listening. Footsteps overhead. Voices carried faintly through the planks. But no one below.

She moved farther forward, her hand brushing along the wall of the hull until she found what she expected. A narrow ladder.

It climbed toward a smaller compartment just beneath the deck, likely where rigging tools and spare tackle were kept. Exactly the sort of place where a maintenance hatch might exist.

Brenna climbed halfway up, careful not to let the ladder creak. At the top she pushed gently against the small door. It opened just enough to reveal another cramped space filled with tarred rope, iron hooks, and rigging tools.

And above it, a square wooden hatch.

Her breath caught. Fresh air seeped faintly through the cracks. The bow.

If she could reach that hatch after dark, they might slip onto the forward deck unseen. From there they could reach the longboat tied along the rail.

Brenna lowered the hatch again carefully. For the first time since being taken, a thin thread of hope tugged at her chest.

She climbed back down the ladder and hurried quietly toward their hiding place.

Julia looked up anxiously as she returned. “Well?”

Brenna crouched beside her again. “I found it.”

“The hatch?”

“Yes.”

Julia exhaled in relief. “And the longboat?”

“Should be tied along the starboard rail.”

Julia gave her a doubtful look. “Should be.”

Brenna smiled faintly. "Ships are predictable."

Julia leaned back against the crate behind her. "And how long until someone realizes we're missing?"

Brenna glanced toward the ladder leading above them. "Not long."

The ship rolled again beneath them as the wind shifted in the sails. "So we wait," Julia said.

Brenna nodded. "Yes."

Julia crossed her arms. "I'm beginning to think your plans involve a lot of waiting and a great deal of improvising."

Brenna's voice softened. "Only until we reach the longboat."

Julia looked at her carefully. "And then?"

Brenna listened to the wind filling the sails above them. "Then we disappear."

They crouched in silence, the ship creaking around them, the slow roll beneath their feet a constant reminder of where they were.

Julia exhaled softly. "Well," she murmured, "this is not how I imagined the evening ending."

Brenna let out a quiet breath. "No."

After a few minutes of silence, Julia shifted slightly, her shoulder brushing Brenna's. "If this is it…" she said, softer now.

Brenna turned toward her. "It isn't."

Julia gave a faint, almost amused breath. "You always say that."

"Because it's true."

Julia was quiet for a moment. "If it were not," she said, her voice lowering, "I would be very cross with myself for not saying certain things."

Brenna frowned slightly. "Such as?"

Julia hesitated, just a fraction. Then smiled faintly in the dark. “For instance, Reed is entirely too handsome for his own good.”

Despite everything, Brenna huffed the smallest breath of laughter. “That is what you would choose to confess?”

“It seems relevant.”

Brenna shook her head faintly. “You’ve been thinking about him.”

Julia didn’t deny it this time. “He’s… different.”

Brenna glanced at her. “In what way?”

Julia’s voice softened, losing its usual playfulness. “He doesn’t try to correct me,” she said. “Or quiet me. Or decide things for me.” A small pause. “He listens.”

Brenna studied her. “And that’s enough?”

Julia smiled slightly. “It’s more than enough.” Then Julia turned her head toward Brenna “And you?”

Brenna stilled. “What about me?”

Julia’s voice was gentler now. “You’re not thinking about the danger.”

Brenna didn’t answer.

Julia continued, “You’re thinking about him.”

Silence settled.

“Yes.”

The word was quiet. Julia’s smile returned, softer this time. “I knew it.”

Brenna exhaled slowly, her voice low. “He’s impossible.”

Julia let out a faint breath of amusement. “That sounds familiar.”

“He assumes too much,” Brenna continued. “Decides things without asking. Expects me to follow along as though I have no say in it.”

“And yet…” Brenna hesitated. “And yet,” she said quietly, “he would let me walk away.”

Julia stilled at that. "He would?"

"Yes." Brenna's voice softened further. "He said as much."

"And that matters," Julia said.

Brenna nodded faintly. "Yes."

The ship creaked again, louder this time. Brenna leaned back slightly, her gaze unfocused in the dark. "He unsettles me," she admitted. "In a way I don't entirely understand."

Julia smiled softly. "I think you do."

Brenna didn't argue. "If we get out of this," she said.

"When," Julia corrected.

Brenna almost smiled. "When," she agreed, "I don't think I can pretend this is nothing."

Julia's voice warmed. "Good." She shifted slightly closer. "Because I have no intention of pretending anything where Reed is concerned."

Brenna let out a quiet breath. "I gathered that."

Julia's smile lingered, even in the dark. "And you?"

Brenna didn't hesitate this time. "I will see him again."

Julia nodded, satisfied. "Yes," she said softly. "You will."

Chapter 30

The sun was dropping toward the horizon when the lookout's voice disrupted the steady motion of the ship.

"Sail ahead!"

Every man on deck lifted his head.

Callum turned toward the bow immediately. "Where away?"

"Off the starboard quarter!"

Reed was already climbing the rigging with the spyglass in hand. The wind snapped hard through the sails as the Hawthorne drove forward across the darkening water.

Reed steadied himself against the mast and lifted the glass. For a long moment he said nothing. Then slowly he lowered it. "Well," he muttered.

Callum didn't need to ask. "The *Mercy*?"

Reed nodded once.

Black hull. Low in the water. Running fast but not fast enough. Callum had expected it. Still, seeing the ship there, real and reachable, sent a cold focus through him.

He stepped forward onto the quarterdeck. The crew had already begun to sense it. Something had changed.

"What is it, Captain?" one of the sailors called.

Callum pointed toward the distant ship. "There."

The lookout shouted down again. "Black brig!"

A murmur rippled across the deck. Several of the crew remembered the name well enough. The ship that had fired on them weeks earlier.

Reed dropped back onto the deck beside Callum. "She's pushing hard."

Callum's eyes never left the horizon. "So are we."

The distance between them was closing slowly now. The *Hawthorne* had the wind. And she was faster.

Callum turned to the helmsman. "Give her everything she's got."

The man grinned and adjusted the wheel. The sails strained harder, the brig leaning sharply as she surged forward.

Reed watched the black hull growing clearer. "You think they know we're here yet?"

"They will."

Reed nodded. "And when we catch them?"

Callum's voice was quiet. "We hook up."

Reed smiled grimly. "And then?"

Callum's gaze hardened. "We board."

The wind roared louder through the rigging as the *Hawthorne* gained speed.

"And then," Callum finished, his voice carrying just enough for the nearby sailors to hear,
"We find what's ours that they stole."

Reed glanced sideways at him. "And the *Mercy*?"

Callum's answer came without hesitation. "We sink her."

Around them the crew moved faster. Cannons were checked. Lines prepared. Men grinned with the eager tension of sailors about to fight.

Ahead of them the black hull of the *Mercy* cut through the water. But the distance between the ships was shrinking. Fast.

Brenna and Julia had lost all sense of time.

They crouched in the cramped hollow behind the stacked sailcloth, hardly daring to breathe. The ship creaked steadily around them as it cut through the water, the dim light from the hold shifting slowly as the sun dropped lower outside.

At first there was only the normal activity of the vessel. Boot steps overhead. The occasional shouted order. The steady rush of wind through the sails.

Then suddenly, a shout. Another voice answered it. Boots pounded across the deck above them.

Julia lifted her head slightly. “Did you hear that?”

Brenna nodded slowly.

The noise above grew louder. Men running. Voices shouting. But the words themselves were lost in the echo of the ship.

Julia strained to listen. “What are they saying?”

Brenna shook her head. “I can’t tell.”

Another shout rang out. Louder this time. One word carried clearly through the chaos “Ship!”

Julia frowned. “Did he say ship?”

Brenna’s eyes sharpened. Above them the deck erupted into activity. Commands were being shouted now, urgent, rapid. Men running in every direction. Canvas snapping overhead.

Julia blinked in confusion. “That doesn’t sound like they’ve discovered we escaped.”

Brenna listened carefully. The sounds were wrong. This wasn’t the quiet alarm of missing prisoners. This was something else entirely.

Battle preparation. Another voice barked a command. Then another.

Julia whispered, “What’s happening?”

Brenna slowly leaned back against the crate behind her. “I think…” She paused. A small smile touched her lips despite everything. “I think someone found us.”

Julia’s eyes widened. “You think it’s…”

Brenna nodded once. “Callum.”

Another shout carried through the hull above them. This one unmistakable. “Ready the guns!”

Julia stared at her. "You're certain?"

Brenna pushed herself quietly to her feet. "If it is him," she said calmly, "then we have a very small window before things become... loud."

Julia looked up nervously toward the deck above. "And our brilliant plan to steal a longboat?"

Brenna brushed dust from her hands. "Change of plans."

Julia blinked. "What plan is that?"

Brenna glanced toward the ladder leading upward. "We get to the deck."

Julia stared at her in disbelief. "To the deck?"

Brenna nodded. "If Callum is here, that's the safest place on this entire ship."

Julia sighed. "Well," she muttered as she stood, "I suppose that does sound slightly better than rowing into the open ocean."

Above them the *Mercy's* crew rushed frantically across the deck. And somewhere just beyond the hull, the *Hawthorne* was closing fast.

The *Hawthorne* closed the distance like a hunting hawk. Wind screamed through the rigging as Callum drove the brig harder, the black hull of the *Mercy* growing rapidly in the fading light.

Reed lowered the spyglass. "That's her."

Callum needed no confirmation. The scarred black hull was unmistakable. "Helm steady," he ordered.

The crew moved quickly now, the tension of battle humming through the deck. Cannons were run out. Powder carried up from the magazine.

But Callum raised a hand. "No guns."

The men paused.

Reed glanced sideways. "You're serious?"

"The women could be aboard."

Reed nodded grimly. "So we board."

Callum pointed forward. "Prepare the hooks."

The distance shrank rapidly. The *Mercy*'s crew had spotted them now. Men ran across her deck shouting warnings. Swords flashed into hands.

Within minutes, they reached the *Mercy*.

"Brace!" someone yelled.

The ships slammed together with a violent crack of wood. Hooks flew. Iron bit into railings. Lines were pulled tight. The two vessels groaned against each other as the gap vanished.

"Board!"

The *Hawthorne's* crew surged forward like a wave. Steel rang instantly as blades met. The deck erupted into chaos. Pirates lunged across the rails. Sailors answered with equal fury. Men fought across rigging lines and cannon carriages while the wind tore at the sails overhead.

Callum moved through the battle like a storm, blade flashing as he drove toward the center of the enemy deck. Somewhere on this ship, Brenna was waiting.

Below deck Brenna and Julia climbed the ladder cautiously. The sounds of battle exploded around them the moment they reached the deck. Steel clanged. Men shouted. Boots pounded across the planks.

Julia stared. "Good heavens."

Pirates and sailors crashed together in brutal close combat.

But Brenna only glanced once before pulling Julia forward. "Stay close."

Julia looked down at the rough crew clothes they wore. "You're certain we won't be noticed?"

"In this chaos?" Brenna ducked under a swinging sword. "No."

They moved quickly across the deck, blending into the commotion of the fight.

Brenna's eyes scanned everything. The rigging. The distance between ships. The lines holding the vessels together. Then she stopped.

Julia nearly ran into her. "What..."

Brenna pointed upward. The rigging stretched between the ships like a web.

Julia followed her gaze. Then looked back at Brenna slowly. "No."

Brenna smiled slightly. "Do you remember when we used to swing from the rope in your father's orchard?"

Julia blinked. "Why are you bringing this up now?"

Then she saw where Brenna was looking. The rope. Swinging just far enough to reach the other ship. "Oh no."

Brenna grabbed the line.

"No, no, no."

"It's the only way," Brenna said.

Julia looked at the havoc below. Men fighting. Blades flashing.

"You said you wanted adventure."

Julia stared at her. "This is not what I meant."

Brenna was already climbing the rigging. "Up."

Julia sighed. "This is how I die."

They climbed quickly through the ropes until they reached the swinging line stretched between the ships.

Brenna turned to her. "You first."

Julia blinked. "Why me?"

"Because if you fall I can still go," Brenna said, trying hard not to laugh.

Julia glared. "That is a terrible argument." But she grabbed the rope anyway. For one brief moment she hesitated. Took a deep breathe and then she swung.

The rope carried her across the narrow gap between ships, and directly into the path of an unsuspecting crewman. Just as she reached the deck, her grip faltered, and she slipped, crashing into him and sending them both sprawling. She looked up and found herself staring directly into Reed's eyes.

Reed lay there for a moment, wind knocked from his lungs as the world spun.

Then he grabbed the person who had just knocked him flat.

He froze. "Well," he muttered hoarsely, still flat on his back, "this is becoming a habit."

Julia pushed herself upright. "Reed!"

Across the chaos of the battle Callum had seen the swing. He forced his way through the fighting sailors toward them.

"Julia!" He reached her in seconds. "Where's Brenna?"

Julia turned instinctively toward the rigging where she had just come from. "She was right behind me."

The rope still swayed between the ships. Julia frowned. "Brenna?"

Callum followed her gaze. No one swung across. No one climbed the line. The rope moved once more in the wind. Empty.

Julia's stomach dropped. She leaned over the rail, scanning the deck of the *Mercy* through the upheaval of fighting men.

"I..." Her voice faltered. "She was right there."

Callum's expression hardened.

Julia looked again. And then she saw it. A glimpse of her on the other ship. A man dragging someone toward the companionway.

Julia's voice dropped to a whisper. "Oh no."

Chapter 31

Brenna had nearly made it. Julia's swing carried her cleanly across the gap. Brenna reached for the rope, and something seized her ankle.

Hard.

She lost her grip instantly. The world tilted. She fell. The impact knocked the air from her lungs as she hit the deck of the *Mercy* with brutal force. For several seconds she could do nothing but gasp, the fight above her blurring into noise and motion.

Boots approached. "Tryin' to make a run for it, were ye?"

A rough hand seized her arm and hauled her roughly to her feet. Pain shot through her ankle and ribs as she struggled to breathe. The man holding her was exactly what she expected a pirate to look like.

Grubby beard. Tar-stained coat. Eyes that carried none of the discipline she had seen in the other crew.

"Well now," he said with a crooked grin. "Aren't you a valuable little prize."

Brenna tried to pull free. She could feel his stale breath on her as he bent closer.

His grip tightened painfully. "Move along, the captain'll be wantin' a word with ye."

He dragged her toward the companionway ladder. The battle still raged above them, steel ringing, men shouting, the two ships grinding together in the water.

He shoved her down the ladder and into the dim corridor below deck. "Captain!" the pirate called.

A door opened ahead. Inside stood a tall man in a dark coat, studying a chart spread across the table. He looked up slowly as Brenna was dragged inside.

For a moment he simply stared. Then a slow smile crept across his face. “Well now,” he drawled. “What have we here?”

Brenna straightened, forcing her breath to steady.

Crowe’s gaze flicked briefly past her, toward the passage she had come from, then back again. “Out of your cabin,” he said. “And wanderin’ about my deck.”

After a pause he continued, “Tryin’ to slip away, were ye?”

Brenna lifted her chin. “I needed air.”

Crowe let out a low chuckle. “Aye,” he said. “I’m sure ye did.”

He took a slow step toward her.

Brenna didn’t move.

“Funny thing,” he continued, “my crew don’t tend to leave doors open by accident.”

His eyes narrowed slightly. “So either ye’re very lucky…” Another step. “Or very clever.”

Brenna held his gaze. “I wouldn’t know.”

Crowe’s mouth shifted, almost a smile. “I think ye would.”

A brief silence passed, the creak of the ship filling the space between them.

Then his eyes dropped, to her attire. That smile deepened. “Well now,” he murmured. “That’s interestin’.”

Brenna’s pulse quickened, but she didn’t let it show.

Crowe’s gaze lifted again, sharper now. “Where’s the guard?”

No answer. Brenna didn’t speak.

Crowe studied her a moment longer. A quiet laugh. “Ah.” Understanding settled in. “He won’t be wakin’ soon, then.”

Brenna said nothing still.

Crowe stepped closer, close enough now that she could see the wear in his coat, the faint scars along his jaw. "Bold," he said. "I'll give ye that." A slight pause again. "Foolish."

Brenna's voice was steady. "You were going to kill us anyway."

Crowe's brow lifted slightly. "Was I?"

"Yes."

He studied her, weighing something. "Hadn't quite decided," he said lightly. "But ye've made it easier."

The words landed cold. Brenna didn't flinch. "Then why hesitate?"

"Because," he said, almost thoughtfully, "sometimes it's worth seein' what else a thing might bring."

Brenna's gaze hardened. "We're not cargo."

"No," Crowe said softly.

His eyes darkened. The ship shifted beneath them. Crowe straightened slightly, his tone sharpening. "Well then," he said, stepping back just enough to signal the end of the moment, "this little excursion ends here."

His gaze flicked once toward the man who had taken hold of her arm. "Move along."

"The captain's got more than a word for ye now," he said, leaning in near her ear, before exiting.

Brenna didn't move right away.

Crowe's smile returned, slow, dangerous. "Or," he added, "we can make this unpleasant."

Brenna held his gaze one moment longer. She stepped forward. But her mind was already moving. Because now, she knew exactly what kind of man she was dealing with, and there would be no mercy on the *Mercy*.

"I've been told quite a lot about you," he continued. "And paid very handsomely to dispose of you."

His hand seized her arm. “Unfortunately for your friends above,” he said calmly, “they arrived a little too late.”

He began pulling her deeper into the cabin. “Once the ships separate, the matter becomes very simple.”

Brenna’s mind raced. The room was small but functional, chart table, lantern hooks, weapons rack, and something else. Mounted along the wall beside the companionway was a heavy iron belaying pin. The kind used to secure rigging lines. Solid. Loose. Close enough to reach.

Brenna’s eyes flicked to it and a plan began to form.

The deck of the *Mercy* had become a storm of steel and shouting men.

The *Hawthorne’s* crew surged across the rails in waves, blades flashing in the dim light as the two ships ground together. Callum cut his way through the fight with relentless focus, barely aware of the men falling around him.

“Clear the quarterdeck!” someone shouted.

But Callum wasn’t looking for the quarterdeck. He was looking for her.

Reed appeared beside him for a moment, parrying a blow and sending a pirate sprawling. “She’s below!” he shouted over the noise.

Callum didn’t wait. He shoved past two sailors and reached the companionway ladder, descending two steps at a time.

The sounds of battle dulled as he reached the dim corridor below deck.

Then he heard a voice. “…paid very handsomely to dispose of you.”

Callum’s grip tightened on his sword. He moved silently toward the open cabin door. Inside, a tall man had Brenna by the arm, dragging her deeper into the room.

"Once the ships separate," the man continued calmly, "this becomes very simple."

Callum stepped into the doorway. "I'm afraid it just became complicated."

Both of them turned. For a heartbeat the pirate captain simply stared.

Then he laughed. "Well now." He tightened his hold on Brenna. "Lord Ashcombe himself."

Callum's eyes never left Brenna. "Release her, Crowe."

The man smiled thinly. "Ye don't seem to grasp your position here." His hand moved toward the pistol at his belt.

Callum moved faster. Steel flashed.

Crowe barely had time to draw before Callum's blade knocked the weapon aside. The pistol clattered across the floor as the two men collided in a brutal clash of swords.

Callum drove forward fast, precise.

Crowe met him easily. "Well now," Crowe drawled, parrying with a lazy twist of his wrist, "the gentleman pirate's come to take what he thinks is his."

Callum didn't answer. His blade struck again, harder.

Crowe stepped back, boots sliding slightly across the salt-stained planks, a grin splitting across his face "Ah," he said. "So it's not business."

Another clash. Callum pressed him. "It never was," he said quietly.

Crowe's eyes flickered. "That so?"

Their blades locked briefly, close enough now that Crowe could see the intent in Callum's expression. "Then this must be personal."

Callum shoved him back. "It is now."

Crowe laughed, circling.

The cabin was too small for elegance. The fight was savage and close. Crowe swung hard, forcing Callum back a step.

"Ye should have stayed in Portsmouth," the man snarled.

Callum drove forward again, forcing the other man toward the wall. "You should have left her alone."

Crowe studied him as they circled again. "Ye've been huntin' men like me a long while now." he said.

"Perhaps."

"And yet," Crowe added, tilting his head slightly, "you never quite stop."

Callum's gaze didn't waver. "I suppose that's true."

"Why is that, I wonder?"

Callum stepped forward again, forcing Crowe back. "Because men like you keep existing."

Crowe laughed, the sound sharp against the wind. "Ah," he said, "so it's a calling."

Callum's voice dropped. "It's a reckoning."

Their blades collided again, hard enough to jar through the arm.

Crowe's grin faded slightly now. Just enough. "Ye think you're better," he said.

Callum didn't hesitate. "I know I am."

Crowe's expression darkened once again. "Dangerous thing, certainty." He attacked again, faster now, less careless.

Callum met him head-on. Steel rang. Boots scraped. The deck shifted beneath them.

Crowe pressed harder this time. "Ye crossed a fair stretch o' sea for 'em, didn't ye?" he said between strikes.

Callum didn't answer.

Crowe smirked. "That one," he added, nodding faintly toward where Brenna had been taken. "It's her that brought ye here, isn't it?"

Callum's next strike came sharper. More force. Crowe caught it, but barely. "There it is," Crowe murmured. "Thought as much."

Callum stepped in close, their blades locked again. "You chose the wrong ship," he said.

"I chose the gold, same as always."

Callum's voice lowered. "You chose the last one."

Crowe's smile returned, thin now as he broke the lock, striking again with renewed force. "Let's see about that."

Callum's blade drove him back again, "Who sent you after her?"

Crowe's eyes flickered, just for a moment. "Someone who wanted her out o' the way."

"That narrows nothing."

Crowe laughed once.

Callum's gaze hardened. "You're already dead."

Crowe's smile returned, thin, defiant. "Then I've no cause to give ye anything, do I?" Crowe's eyes flickered. Then hardened.

"Though," Crowe added, breath rougher now, "ye're nearer than ye know."

Callum didn't respond. He moved. Fast. Decisive. Steel drove forward, and this time it did not stop.

Steel clashed again and again, faster now, the rhythm shifting from measured to relentless. Crowe lunged recklessly. It was the mistake Callum needed. His blade struck cleanly, sending the man crashing backward into the chart table.

Crowe's breath caught, the grin faltering as the strength left his body. For a moment, he just stared at Callum. Then his knees gave, collapsing against the wall before sliding down to the floor.

Callum stepped back, blade lowering slightly.

Crowe coughed once, blood dark against his lips. His head tilted faintly, eyes unfocused now. "Mar…"

The word barely formed. Cut short. His body slackened. Still.

The lantern swayed overhead. And whatever name he had meant to give, died with him.

The fight ended as quickly as it began. Silence filled the cabin except for the distant roar of battle above.

Callum turned immediately. "Brenna."

She stood near the wall, still gripping the iron belaying pin she had nearly used as a weapon herself. For a moment neither of them spoke.

Then Callum crossed the room in two strides and pulled her into his arms. The force of it nearly lifted her off the floor.

Brenna clung to him instinctively, relief flooding through her. "You came," she breathed.

Callum's voice was rough against her hair. "Of course I came."

She leaned back slightly, studying his face. "I wasn't entirely certain you understood my message."

"The dressmaker was very helpful."

A faint smile touched her lips. "I hoped she would be."

Callum brushed a loose strand of hair from her face, his expression shifting from relief to quiet intensity. "Are you hurt?"

"My pride perhaps," she admitted.

"Your ankle?"

"Sore."

"Anything else?"

Brenna tilted her head slightly. "You sound very concerned."

"I am."

Above them the battle still raged.

Reed's voice echoed down the corridor. "Hawthorne!"

Callum glanced toward the doorway. “Hold fast!” He called back. Taking Brenna’s hand firmly he asked, “Can you walk?”

“Yes.”

“Good.” He led her toward the ladder. “We need to go.”

Brenna paused once at the threshold and glanced back at the pirate captain slumped against the wall. “Well,” she said quietly, “As Julia would say, that was satisfying.”

Callum allowed the faintest hint of a smile. “Wait until you see what happens to the ship.”

Chapter 32

The cabin door flew open, the noise of battle crashing back in at once, shouts, steel, boots pounding across the deck.

Callum caught Brenna's arm. "Stay with me."

"I am," she said, breath quick but steady.

He moved first, pulling her into the chaos. A man lunged toward them. Callum turned, blade flashing, driving him back with a hard strike.

"Keep moving," he said.

"I am moving," Brenna shot back, keeping pace despite the uneven deck.

They pushed forward, bodies colliding, the air thick with smoke and salt.

Another sailor crossed their path, Callum shoved him aside with his shoulder, clearing space.

"Head for the rail," he said.

"I see it."

The gap between the ships came into view, men still crossing, ropes straining, the *Hawthorne* just beyond.

Brenna hesitated for half a breath as the deck lurched.

Callum's grip tightened. "Don't stop."

"I'm not stopping."

A crewman from the *Hawthorne* reached toward them. "Over here!"

Callum guided her forward. "Go."

Brenna stepped onto the plank, steady despite the sway. "Callum…"

"I'm right behind you."

She didn't argue. Didn't look back. She crossed, boots striking the *Hawthorne's* deck as strong hands caught and steadied her.

"You're safe, miss."

She turned immediately. Callum was still on the *Mercy*. Fighting.

He drove another man back, clearing his path, then moved for the crossing.

"Captain!" one of his crew shouted.

Callum didn't slow. "Hold your positions!" He crossed in two strides, landing hard on the *Hawthorne's* deck.

The moment his boots hit wood, he turned. His fingers lifted to his mouth, and he gave a sharp, ear-piercing whistle.

It cut through everything. The fight. The shouting. The sea.

It rang out across the *Mercy*, reaching every crewman of the *Hawthorne* now on her deck. They responded without hesitation.

"Back to the *Hawthorne*!" one shouted.

"Move!"

Lines were seized, men disengaging with practiced precision, falling back toward the crossing.

Reed appeared at the rail, blade still drawn. "You took your time," he muttered.

Callum didn't look at him. "Get them across."

Reed nodded once.

The two ships still ground together in the swell, their hulls groaning as the hooks held them locked side by side.

The moment his crew was back on deck, and both Brenna and Julia were safely away from danger, Callum's expression hardened again.

"Cut the hooks!" he shouted.

Sailors rushed to obey. Axes swung and iron bit into rope. One by one the grappling lines dropped into the sea.

"Back us clear!" Callum ordered.

The helmsman spun the wheel as the *Hawthorne* drifted away from the wounded *Mercy*. The gap widened slowly between the two ships. The crew moved with tense anticipation. They had been waiting.

Callum turned toward the gun deck. "Run out the cannons!"

The heavy guns rolled into place. "Load!" Powder and shot were rammed home with practiced speed. The moment the ships cleared each other's reach, Callum's

voice cut across the deck "Fire."

The cannons thundered. The blast tore through the side of the *Mercy*, splintering wood and ripping open the hull. Men on the *Hawthorne* quickly pulled Brenna and Julia down behind the rail as debris exploded outward across the water.

"Reload!" Callum barked.

The crew moved instantly, working the guns again with brutal efficiency. The *Mercy* staggered in the water, her hull already sagging where the cannonballs had struck.

"Ready!" Callum didn't hesitate. "Fire."

Another deafening volley roared across the water. This time the damage was fatal. The black brig lurched violently as water rushed through the shattered hull. Her mast tilted as the ship began to sink.

The *Mercy* never fired a shot.

Within minutes her deck slipped beneath the waves. A roar of triumph erupted from the *Hawthorne's* crew. Cheers echoed across the water as the last of the black hull vanished beneath the sea.

Several of the pirates who had boarded the *Hawthorne* made their choice quickly. They dove over the rail and disappeared into the water rather than face the crew's justice.

The battle was over. The wind settled back into the sails as the men slowly returned to their duties.

But Callum hardly noticed. He had only one thought left in his mind. Brenna. He crossed the deck toward her where she stood beside Julia, still catching her breath after the chaos of battle.

For a moment he simply looked at her. Then he pulled her into his arms and kissed her. The kiss was fierce and unrestrained, the fear of losing her still burning through him. Brenna clutched his coat instinctively, returning the kiss with equal intensity.

Across the deck Julia smiled quietly.

Reed leaned beside her, watching the scene with mild amusement. “About time.” He gave a quiet chuckle.

Julia nodded. “Quite.”

At last Callum pulled back, resting his forehead briefly against Brenna’s. “You frightened me,” he said quietly.

Brenna smiled faintly. “I had a feeling you would catch up.”

The *Hawthorne* turned slowly back toward Portsmouth. This time there was no urgency in her sails. The ship moved at an easier pace across the water while the crew cleaned the deck and tended to the minor wounds left from the battle.

The tension that had driven them south had begun to fade. But the emotions aboard the ship remained high. They had nearly lost far more than a fight that day.

The *Hawthorne* sailed steadily north, the worst of the excitement behind them now. The wind had softened, and the crew moved about their duties. Bits of charred splinter and powder had been washed from the deck, though the faint smell of cannon smoke still lingered in the air.

Callum stood near the helm with Reed, one hand resting along the rail. Blood had darkened his sleeve at the arm, and a deeper stain marked his shirt across the chest, subtle, but not unnoticed.

Reed glanced at him. “You should have that seen to.”

“It can wait.”

Reed exhaled. “Of course it can.” The added, “Those pirates will not be troubling anyone again.”

Callum nodded once, though his expression remained thoughtful. “He said someone paid him.”

Reed’s gaze sharpened slightly.

Callum’s voice dropped. “He started to say a name.” He looked back over the water. “Mar…”

Reed frowned. “Could be a dozen names.”

“It’s enough,” Callum said. “Or it will be, not many with reason to want Brenna dead.”

Reed considered that carefully. “The Whitmore fortune.”

Callum nodded. “And the betrothal.”

Reed gave a quiet sigh. “So someone stood to gain if Brenna never reached England.”

Callum’s face grew unreadable. “Or if she disappeared shortly after arriving.”

Reed folded his arms. “You think the same man who sent the letter?”

“Yes.”

Reed nodded slowly. “Then he is not finished yet.”

His voice lowered. “He will be.”

Reed smiled slightly. “Protective already.”

Callum did not deny it. “She nearly died once because of this man.”

Reed nodded. “That will not happen again.”

Callum’s eyes returned to the horizon. “No.”

A shift of movement behind them drew both men's attention. They turned, and paused.

Brenna and Julia had come up from below.

Brenna was mid-sentence, her voice carrying just enough for him to hear. "…and the deck runs the full length, there's a second level beneath, but you wouldn't notice it unless you knew where to look. It's…" She stopped when she realized they were no longer alone.

Julia's gaze moved across the deck, taking it in again, quieter now. "It is rather impressive," she said.

Still dressed in the crew's borrowed clothes, loose shirts, sleeves rolled, hair pulled back just enough to keep it from their faces.

The effect was… noticeable. The crew slowed. Then stared. One man nearly missed securing a line entirely.

Reed blinked once. "You should be below."

Julia smiled. "I have been below."

"That was not a suggestion."

"Nor was this," she returned.

Brenna's gaze found Callum immediately. She stepped closer, her eyes narrowing slightly as she took in the blood along his arm. "You're injured."

Callum's attention shifted back to her. "You're unhurt?"

"I am."

His gaze moved briefly, taking in the absence of injury for himself. Then settled again."Good."

Callum straightened just slightly, the movement controlled despite the injury.

Brenna noticed immediately. "You should sit," she said.

"I'm fine."

"You're not."

Callum held her gaze. "It's nothing I haven't had before."

"That doesn't make it acceptable."

For a moment, neither of them looked away.

Callum glanced at her. "It's nothing."

Her eyes dropped briefly, just enough to catch the faint stain at his chest as well."That," she said quietly, "is not nothing."

Callum held her gaze. "It looks worse than it is."

Reed muttered beside him, "That is rarely true." He glanced between them, then away again, as though he had no interest in the outcome. "Right," he said lightly. "Well." He gestured toward the deck. "At least the ship remains intact."

Julia looked out across the water, then back again. "It is a remarkable vessel."

Callum inclined his head slightly. "It does its job."

Brenna's gaze lingered on him. "Yes," she said quietly. "It does."

Julia glanced between them, then toward the crew, who were making a very poor effort of appearing occupied.

"Oh," she said, amused, "we seem to be causing trouble."

"You are," Reed said flatly.

Julia tilted her head. "I don't see how."

Reed gave her a look."That is precisely the problem."

Julia stepped forward first, entirely unconcerned.

Callum's gaze lingered a moment longer than necessary. "You both look…" he paused, choosing the words carefully, "… well suited to crew attire."

Reed's mouth curved faintly. "That's one way to put it." He glanced between them "Though I believe that makes another set of dresses lost."

Julia exhaled softly. "I'm beginning to think that may become a pattern."

Brenna shook her head faintly. "I would prefer it didn't."

"Right," Reed said under his breath. "That's enough of that."

He turned toward the crew again. "Back to work."

Movement snapped back into place instantly.

Julia glanced around, amused. "Was that necessary?"

"Yes," Reed said.

Callum added, without looking away from Brenna, "Very."

The moment stretched, quiet, steady. The wind filled the sails again, pushing the *Hawthorne* steadily toward Portsmouth, and toward the next answer waiting there.

Chapter 33

By the following evening, the sea had been replaced with polished silver and candlelight, but the unease had not left them.

The meal had been laid with its usual precision, the candles steady, the setting untouched by the unrest of the past few days, yet none of it felt entirely normal.

Conversation had begun lightly enough. It did not stay that way. The clink of silverware had long since faded into something hollow, a pretense none of them bothered to maintain.

Brenna set her fork down first. “It was not random,” she said quietly. “It could not have been.”

Across from her, Julia’s hand tightened around her glass. “They did not even know which of us was Miss Whitmore at first. They took us both to be certain.” Her voice wavered, then steadied. “That means someone told them enough to make us worth taking.”

Reed leaned back slightly, his gaze shifting between them. “Or told them just enough to be dangerous.”

Callum had not touched his wine. His attention was fixed entirely on Brenna. “The trustees,” he said at last.

The word seemed to settle over the table like a weight. Brenna’s breath caught, but she did not look away. “They are the only ones who knew the full arrangement. The timing, the voyage, the… value of it.” Her lips pressed together. “And they waited until the last possible moment to tell me.”

“As if they needed you in motion before anyone else could interfere,” Reed added.

Julia shook her head faintly. “But why risk something so… crude? Kidnapping in the middle of London.”

"Because subtlety failed them," Callum cut in, his voice low. "Or because they believed they no longer required it."

Brenna looked down at her hands. "You think they meant to force the marriage."

"I think," Callum said carefully, "they intended to ensure it."

Reed exhaled through his nose. "And when they lost control of the situation, they sought to regain it by whatever means remained."

Julia let out a quiet, disbelieving laugh. "By having us dragged through a market like parcels?"

"No," Callum said. His gaze sharpened. "By making certain you could not refuse whatever came next."

That stilled her.

Brenna lifted her head again, something steadier in her expression now. "Then this is not finished."

"No," Callum agreed. "It is not."

Reed set his glass down with a soft but deliberate sound. "Which means we should not be having this conversation in a room full of doors and servants."

Callum gave a slight nod. "Agreed." He rose first, the decision made in the movement. "My study."

Julia pushed back her chair almost immediately, though her hand brushed briefly against Brenna's arm as she stood, seeking, or offering, reassurance.

Brenna followed, slower, her thoughts clearly still turning.

Reed lingered just long enough to ensure the door to the corridor was clear before stepping aside, gesturing for the women to go ahead.

The study door closed with a quiet, solid finality behind them. The atmosphere shifted at once. No candlelight softness. No pretense of civility. Just purpose.

Callum crossed to the desk, one hand braced against its edge as he looked back at them. "Now," he said, his voice lower, more direct, "we speak plainly."

Reed took up position near the door, as if by instinct, his posture relaxed but watchful.

Julia moved nearer the hearth, though she did not sit. "You already believe the trustees are behind this."

Callum's expression remained controlled. "I'm certain they know more than they've said."

Brenna's fingers tightened slightly against the shawl she had wrapped around her. "My father trusted them."

"I believe," Callum replied, "they are either directly responsible… or they have lost control of something they set in motion."

Brenna stepped further into the room, drawing his attention again. "And which is worse?"

His gaze held hers. "The first," he said. "Because it means they will not stop."

"And the second?" she asked.

Reed answered that one. "Means someone else knows your worth."

Brenna straightened slightly. "Then we must find out which it is."

Callum nodded once. "We will. But we do nothing blindly."

Julia folded her arms, her expression tightening. "And what does 'nothing blindly' look like, exactly?"

Callum's tone sharpened just a fraction. "It looks like control. Information. And making certain that the next move, whoever makes it, is one we are prepared for."

Reed glanced toward Brenna, then back to Callum. "Which means we start by determining who among the trustees benefits most from forcing this through… now."

Brenna's voice came quieter, but firmer than before. "Ican tell you that."

All eyes turned to her.

She met them steadily. "Talbot."

Julia blinked. "Talbot? No… Brenna, he would not…"

"He would," Brenna said, the words cutting through gently but without doubt. "He already has."

The room stilled. "He was the one who delayed telling me of the betrothal," she continued. "The one who assured me everything was in my best interest." A faint, bitter breath. "All the while ensuring I had no time to question it."

Reed's expression darkened. "That is not guidance. That is manipulation."

"Yes."

Callum watched her closely. "You trusted him."

"I did, that was my mistake."

Julia stepped closer. "And now?"

Brenna lifted her chin. "Now I understand what he is willing to do to see this through."

Reed stood at the window overlooking the dark grounds while Callum paced slowly near the fire. Brenna and Julia sat nearby, the weight of the evening's revelations still lingering in the room.

Callum stopped at last. "Crowe said someone paid him."

Reed nodded. "And he started to give a name."

Callum stared into the fire. "'Mar…'"

Julia frowned slightly. "That could be several names."

Reed turned from the window. "Not many with reason to want Brenna dead."

Brenna sat very still. "The Whitmore fortune," she said quietly.

Julia's eyes widened. "And the betrothal."

Callum looked up sharply. "Yes."

Reed crossed the room slowly. "An English lord eager to see the Whitmore inheritance fall conveniently into his control."

Julia frowned. "Someone who knew about the betrothal."

Brenna's thoughts moved quickly now. Someone who knew. Someone who had sent the letter that lured her to England. Someone who had been watching her in London.

Her breath caught suddenly. "The masquerade."

Callum looked at her. "What about it?"

"There was a man watching me."

Julia nodded immediately. "Yes, near the gallery."

Reed's brow furrowed. "Did either of you recognize him?"

Brenna shook her head slowly. "No."

Callum spoke quietly. "But he recognized you."

Silence settled over the room. Then Brenna spoke again. "There was a man introduced briefly at Lady Pennington's ball a few nights before."

Callum's gaze sharpened. "Who?"

Brenna searched her memory. "Lord Marcus Dalridge."

Reed went very still.

Callum noticed instantly. "You know him."

Reed exhaled slowly. "Yes."

Julia looked between them. "And?"

Reed spoke carefully. "Dalridge is heavily in debt."

Brenna nodded. "I remember hearing rumors of that."

Callum's expression darkened. "He could gain control of the Whitmore shipping fortune through marriage."

Julia's voice dropped. "But Brenna never accepted the betrothal."

"No," Callum said quietly.

"But if Brenna disappeared before reaching England…"

Reed finished the thought. "The estate would fall into trusteeship."

"And eventually into Dalridge's hands," Callum said.

Julia looked stunned. “He tried to have you killed.”

Brenna nodded slowly.

Callum’s voice turned cold. “Yes.”

Reed crossed his arms. “And if Crowe had finished the name…”

Julia whispered, “Mar…”

Brenna looked up. “Marcus.”

Silence filled the room.

Callum’s eyes hardened with quiet certainty. “Marcus did not act alone.”

Julia frowned. “He had men. We saw that.”

“Yes,” Callum said. “But I’m not referring to hired hands.”

Brenna’s gaze lifted. “You mean someone told him where to be.”

Callum nodded once. “He knew too much.”

Reed pushed off the window slightly. “The docks,” he said. “He was there before the ship even fully came in.”

Julia’s expression tightened. “He knew I was arriving.”

“And which ship,” Brenna added quietly.

Reed nodded. “And that wasn’t the only time.”

Callum’s gaze moved to Brenna. “He knew your movements in London.”

Brenna’s brow furrowed. “I hadn’t even settled in before…”

“Before he began closing in,” Reed finished.

Julia leaned forward. “That isn’t coincidence.”

“No,” Callum said. “It’s information.”

Brenna spoke first. “He would need access to both sides.”

Reed’s eyes sharpened. “Exactly.”

Julia looked between them. “Both sides?”

Reed gestured slightly. “You,” he said to Brenna. “Your arrival. Your movements. Your supposed betrothal.” Then nodding toward Callum, "And him. His estate. His schedule. His absence from Portsmouth."

Brenna's gaze narrowed. "That isn't information someone overhears."

"No," Callum said. "That's information someone provides."

Julia's voice lowered. "Someone close."

Reed exhaled slowly. "Well," he said, "that confirms it."

Brenna sat back slightly. "The trustees."

No one disagreed.

Chapter 34

Two days later, afternoon sunlight filled the room. The study door closed with a quiet, deliberate finality. No witnesses. No interruptions. Only men, and the truth that had been circling them for days.

Callum did not immediately turn. Instead, he crossed the room at an unhurried pace, one hand resting briefly on the back of the chair at his desk before he moved past it. He let the silence stretch, long enough to remind his guests that this was not their ground.

Talbot stood near the hearth, composed as ever, his hands loosely clasped behind his back. Avery lingered a step behind him, less at ease, though doing his best not to show it.

Reed remained by the door. Watching. Waiting.

At last, Callum turned. Across from them, Mr. Talbot and Mr. Avery stood together. Two trustees. Two estates. Not quite united. But not opposed either.

Callum's voice broke the silence. "You're going to explain it."

Talbot exhaled slowly. "There is nothing to explain that you have not already concluded."

Reed gave a short, humorless laugh. "That's rarely a promising start."

"I'll ask this once," he said evenly. "And I expect a direct answer."

Talbot inclined his head. "Of course."

Callum's gaze did not soften. "The betrothal agreement. It was dissolved," he continued. "Years ago. By my instruction."

Talbot's hands folded neatly in front of him. "That is not how it appears in the records."

Callum's jaw tightened slightly. "I am not asking how it appears."

"I am telling you what was done." Talbot held his gaze. "And I am telling you what remains."

The air in the room shifted. Reed's attention sharpened.

Callum stepped forward. "You're suggesting my directive was ignored."

Talbot did not hesitate. "I'm stating that the agreement was never formally removed."

Avery cleared his throat softly. "There may have been, confusion in the filing."

Callum's gaze snapped to him. "There was no confusion."

Silence. Avery faltered. Talbot did not. "The documentation," Talbot said carefully, "was incomplete."

Callum's voice lowered. "My instructions were not."

Talbot's composure held. "Without the proper filings," he said, "the agreement remained valid."

"No," Callum said quietly. "It was convenient."

Avery shifted. "It was binding on paper."

Reed's gaze sharpened. "Because it was never updated."

Talbot didn't respond.

Callum's eyes locked on him. "You were responsible for that."

"Yes."

"And you failed to file the dissolution." Callum's voice raised, "You expect me to believe," he said, "that an agreement of that magnitude remained in place due to clerical error." Talbot's expression did not change. "I expect you to understand that such matters require precision."

Callum took another step closer. "And yet, precision failed…or was it withheld?"

Avery looked between them, tension tightening his posture.

Talbot remained still. “Are you implying intent?” he asked.

Callum held his gaze. “I’m asking you to account for it.”

The room went quiet. “The agreement benefited multiple parties,” Talbot said.

Reed’s brow lifted slightly. “So that’s what it comes to.”

Callum did not look away. “And my decision to end it?”

Talbot’s voice remained measured. “Was not formally executed.”

Callum’s tone sharpened ,“It was given directly, and not recorded.” Silence. Heavy. Deliberate. Callum’s hand tightened slightly against the chair. “You received that instruction.”

Talbot hesitated. Only for a fraction. “I did.”

“And you chose not to act on it.”

Talbot’s gaze did not waver. “I chose to ensure the matter was handled correctly.”

Reed let out a quiet breath. “That sounds very much like not acting at all.”

Avery shifted again. “There were… complications.”

Callum cut him off. “There were no complications.” His voice dropped. “Only a failure to follow instruction.”

Talbot’s expression hardened, just slightly. “You were not present.”

Callum’s gaze sharpened. “I didn’t need to be. I gave the order.”

Talbot leaned forward a fraction. “And then you disappeared.”

Reed straightened slightly.

Callum did not react immediately. “I left the matter in capable hands.”

Talbot’s voice cooled. “And yet it was not completed.”

Callum stepped closer still. “No,” he said quietly. “It was not.”

A long silence stretched between them.

"And now," Callum continued, "that same agreement has resurfaced, conveniently, just as Miss Whitmore is brought to England."

Avery's head lifted. "That was not..."

Reed spoke first this time. "Careful."

Avery stopped.

Talbot remained composed. "The timing," he said, "is coincidental."

A muscle flickered in Callum's jaw. "No," he said. "It isn't."

"You had knowledge of her location."

Talbot's gaze held steady. "The estate is not difficult to track."

"That's not what I asked," Callum said. "You had contact."

Talbot did not answer immediately.

Avery looked distinctly uncomfortable now.

Reed's attention sharpened further.

Callum took another step. "Did you," he asked quietly, "or did you not initiate communication with her household?"

Talbot's voice lowered slightly. "There were inquiries made."

Reed's mouth curved faintly. "Inquiries."

Callum's tone sharpened. "And a letter."

Talbot's gaze did not break. "Correspondence occurs in such matters."

Callum's voice dropped. "I never sent it."

That shifted the room. Avery looked up sharply. Talbot stilled.

"Then someone did," Talbot said.

Callum's gaze hardened. "Yes."

"Which brings me," Callum said, his voice quiet now but far more dangerous, "to the question you have yet to answer."

Talbot held his gaze. "And that is?"

Callum did not hesitate. "Why." The word lingered. Heavy. Unavoidable.

"Why," he repeated, "was an agreement I dissolved kept active?" A step closer. "And why was she brought here under it?"

Avery shifted again, clearly unwilling to meet anyone's eyes now.

Talbot remained composed. But not untouched. "There were interests to consider," he said at last.

Reed let out a quiet, humorless breath. "Always."

Talbot inclined his head slightly. "I chose not to file it."

The room stilled.

Reed let out a slow breath. "That's a very deliberate failure."

Talbot's voice hardened. "It preserved stability."

"It preserved control," Reed corrected.

Callum stepped forward. "You and Avery are related."

Avery stiffened. "Distantly."

"Closely enough," Reed muttered.

Callum's gaze didn't waver. "You worked together."

Avery hesitated.

Talbot did not. "Yes."

Callum's voice dropped. "You waited."

Talbot's expression didn't change. "It was a matter of timing."

Reed's brow lifted. "That's one way to describe it."

Callum's eyes darkened. "You waited for her father to die."

Talbot's jaw tightened. "It was inevitable."

"Was it?"

The question hung in the air. Avery looked away first. Talbot kept eye contact.

Callum took another step forward. "When did he fall ill?"

Talbot didn't answer.

Reed's tone sharpened. "That's not a difficult question."

Talbot exhaled slowly. "After a meeting."

"With you."

"Yes." The admission settled heavily.

Callum's voice remained steady. "What happened at that meeting."

Talbot's hands tightened at his sides. "He had taken to port that night."

Reed went still.

Callum didn't. "And?"

Talbot hesitated. For the first time, uncertainty touched his composure. "It was not immediate."

Reed's voice cut in. "That's not what he asked."

Talbot looked between them. Then, quieter, "It weakened him."

Silence again filled the room.

Callum's gaze hardened. "You poisoned him."

Talbot's expression didn't flinch. "I assisted what was already in motion."

Reed scoffed sharply. "That's a convenient way to describe murder."

Avery stepped forward. "It was controlled…"

Callum turned on him. "Be very careful."

The room went cold. Avery stopped speaking.

Talbot continued, as though the words had already been decided long ago. "He was declining."

"You ensured it," Reed said.

Talbot didn't deny it.

Callum's voice dropped lower. "You accelerated his death to enforce an agreement you knew had already been abandoned."

Talbot met his gaze. "It secured the outcome."

Callum held his stare a long moment. "No." The word was quiet. Final. "You secured nothing."

Reed exhaled slowly, running a hand along the back of his neck. "And Brenna?" he asked. "She believes the agreement was legitimate."

Talbot said nothing. Avery didn't answer.

Callum's gaze shifted briefly toward the door. Toward the rest of the house. Toward her.

"She saw her father's signature," Reed continued. "She had no reason to question it."

"No," Callum said quietly. "She didn't."

Another silence.

Then Reed looked at him. "You intend to tell her."

It wasn't a question.

Callum didn't answer immediately. His jaw set slightly. His gaze distant now, not on the men before him, but somewhere else entirely. Weighing. Calculating.

Reed watched him carefully. "She deserves the truth."

Callum's voice came low. "She deserves peace."

Reed frowned. "That isn't the same thing."

"No," Callum agreed.

Reed studied him. "You're deciding for her."

Callum's gaze returned, sharp now. "I'm protecting her."

Reed didn't argue. But he didn't agree either.

Then Callum turned back to Talbot and Avery. "And as for you…" His voice carried something far colder now. "This ends here."

No raised tone. No threats spoken aloud. But none were needed. Because for the first time, the men who had orchestrated everything understood they no longer held any power at all.

Chapter 35

Callum had also sent for Lord Marcus Dalridge, who had been out of town during the trustees' visit, despite having been originally summoned to attend alongside them.

"Dalridge had sent word of his intention to arrive by noon today. He arrived at precisely a half an hour past one, offering some excuse for the delay, though he seemed far from apologetic.

Mr. Carrington showed him into the study where Callum stood waiting near the fireplace, hands clasped behind his back.

Dalridge removed his gloves slowly, glancing around the room with mild curiosity. "Lord Ashcombe," he said pleasantly. "Your message sounded rather urgent."

Callum did not return the pleasantry. "Thank you for coming."

Dalridge did not waste time on pleasantries. As he settled back into the chair opposite Callum, his fingers began turning a heavy signet ring slowly around his finger. "I assume this concerns Miss Whitmore. I hear your return was not without incident," he said. "A pirate vessel, was it? Sunk, I believe."

Callum did not immediately respond. He noticed the motion immediately. Once. Twice. Again. The same restless motion Julia had described. "Sunk," he repeated at last, his tone even. "That is a very specific detail."

Dalridge gave a faint shrug. "Word travels."

"Yes," Callum said. "Though not usually with such precision."

A pause stretched between them.

Callum leaned back slightly, his gaze never leaving Dalridge's face. "Tell me," he said quietly, "who told you that?"

Dalridge smiled. But it did not answer the question.

And in that silence, Callum no longer wondered.

Dalridge sighed theatrically. "A tragic situation, that voyage of hers. Pirates everywhere these days."

Callum stepped closer. "The captain of the *Mercy* said something interesting before he died."

Dalridge's expression remained calm, though the ring continued its steady turning. "Oh?"

"He said he was paid."

Dalridge folded his hands casually. "I imagine pirates are frequently paid."

Callum watched him carefully. "He began to say a name."

A pause stretched between them.

Dalridge leaned back comfortably in his chair. "And?"

"Mar…"

The ring stopped turning. The smile on Dalridge's face did not disappear, but it had grown colder. "You must have been mistaken."

Callum stepped forward slowly. "The letter sent to Brenna. The one that lured her to England."

Dalridge said nothing.

"You knew about the betrothal," Callum continued. "You knew the Whitmore fortune would follow it."

Dalridge's eyes narrowed slightly. "Careful, Ashcombe."

"And when Brenna arrived safely," Callum said quietly, "you arranged for her to disappear."

The room grew very still.

Dalridge rose slowly from the chair. "You have no proof."

Callum met his gaze evenly. "No."

Dalridge's stood slowly from the chair, sliding the ring back into its usual position as though nothing at all had happened. "Then this conversation is finished."

Callum did not move. "Except for one thing."

Dalridge paused at the door.

"If Brenna Whitmore were to die," Callum continued calmly, "the Crown would become extremely interested in the matter."

Dalridge said nothing.

"Especially after learning a titled lord hired pirates to murder her."

Dalridge's fingers returned to the ring. Turning once more. "You wouldn't."

Callum's voice remained quiet. "I would."

The room fell silent.

Dalridge's expression darkened. "You're bluffing."

Callum stepped closer. "Try me."

For the first time, Dalridge looked uncertain.

Callum continued. "You will leave England."

Dalridge's eyes snapped up. "You have no authority to…"

"You will sell what remains of your estate and disappear quietly to the continent."

Dalridge's voice hardened. "And if I refuse?"

Callum held his gaze. "Then the Crown learns everything."

The threat hung heavily in the room.

Dalridge stared at him for several long seconds, then gave a thin smile. "You have a theory, Ashcombe. Nothing more."

Callum said nothing.

Dalridge finally reached for his gloves and turned toward the door. "You've wasted my time."

Callum's answer came cold and steady. "No."

"You did that yourself."

Dalridge walked toward the door, stopping briefly before leaving. "You are a very dangerous man, Ashcombe."

Callum did not deny it. "Yes."

Dalridge opened the door.

"And if I ever see you near Brenna again," Callum added quietly, "I will finish what the sea began."

Dalridge left without another word.

The door closed behind him.

In the entryway, Brenna had just come down the staircase, drawn by the sound of voices from the study.

Mr. Carrington stood quietly nearby, hands folded behind his back as always.

Dalridge emerged from the study doorway. He nearly walked past her before his eyes flicked briefly in her direction.

For a moment neither of them spoke. Then Dalridge inclined his head politely, as though greeting a stranger at a dinner party. "Miss Whitmore."

His voice was smooth. Controlled.

Brenna stared at him.

He stepped toward the front door as Mr. Carrington opened it.

Callum emerged from the study seconds later. He immediately saw Brenna standing motionless in the entry hall. "What is it?"

Brenna looked toward the door where Dalridge had just left.

She turned slowly toward him. "That was Lord Marcus Dalridge."

Callum nodded once. "Yes."

Brenna glanced back at the door again, still unsettled. Her brow furrowed slightly as the memory settled more firmly. "I didn't realize that night at Lady Pennington's he had anything to do with any of this." Her voice lowered. "And now that I've seen him again… I'm quite certain he knew exactly who I was when we were introduced."

Reed stepped out from the adjoining room where he had been listening the entire time.

"Well," Reed said. "That went better than expected."

Callum exhaled slowly. "Did it?"

Reed nodded. "No bloodshed."

"No," he replied as he turned back toward Brenna. "That part comes later."

That evening, once dinner had ended and the house had settled, Callum and Reed knew there was no delaying it any longer, it was time to tell the ladies everything. Yet even then, Callum hesitated, still weighing whether Brenna should learn the truth of her father's death, and how it had been quietly hastened.

The door closed behind them, shutting out the formal quiet of the dining room for something far more honest.

Reed moved toward the side table, pouring a measure of brandy without asking.

Julia and Brenna settled nearby, the tension no longer disguised.

Callum remained standing.

Reed handed him a glass. "Well," he said, "let's say it plainly."

Callum remained standing near the desk, the brandy Reed had poured untouched in his hand. The room had gone still again. "I sent word to one of my trustees," Callum said at last.

Reed glanced over to the women. "Avery."

Brenna watched Callum closely. "You trust him."

"I did."

The slight shift in phrasing did not go unnoticed. Julia leaned forward. "What do you mean?"

A quiet, heavy understanding settled over the room. "When I sent word for Avery," he said, "I expected him alone."

Callum set the glass down without drinking. "Avery has been with my estate less than five years," he said. "Newer than the others, but deliberately chosen."

Reed's brow lifted slightly. "You vetted him."

"Extensively." Callum's voice remained even. "He represents the firm I've long relied on to supply trustees. They're trained, discreet, and meant to be beyond reproach."

Brenna's gaze sharpened. "And you still conducted your own inquiries."

"Yes."

"And he came back clean?" Brenna asked.

"He did."

Julia tilted her head. "But not anymore."

Callum's jaw tightened just slightly. "Recent events suggested otherwise."

Reed leaned back against the wall.

"So I looked again." Callum said. "More thoroughly this time."

Brenna's voice lowered. "And?"

Callum's gaze moved between them. "And I discovered something Avery failed to mention."

Silence settled in the room, then he added, "He has a cousin, in the Americas."

Brenna stilled. "A cousin."

"Yes."

Reed's expression sharpened. "Who is also a trustee."

Julia's voice came quieter now. "For which estate?"

Callum didn't look away. "The Whitmore estate."

Brenna's breath caught, just slightly.

Reed exhaled slowly. "That's not coincidence."

"No," Callum said. "It isn't."

Brenna's voice was steadier than she felt. "And his name?"

Callum's expression hardened. "Talbot."

Silence followed.

Callum's voice dropped. "And when I sent for Avery, he did not arrive alone."

Julia's eyes widened. "Talbot."

"Yes."

Brenna shook her head faintly. "He was already here."

"Or close enough to arrive with him," Reed said.

Callum nodded. "Which means he knew."

Julia frowned. "Or was told."

Callum's gaze hardened. "He came because he was already involved."

Brenna looked between them. "They positioned themselves on both sides."

Julia looked between them. "You think they were working together from the beginning."

Reed gave a quiet, humorless laugh. "I think they were waiting."

Brenna's eyes flicked between Callum and Reed. "For what?"

Callum answered. "For the right moment."

Brenna frowned. "My father's death." The understanding settled.

Reed continued. "Talbot controls the American estate," he said. "Avery controls the estate side here."

"And together," Callum said, "they control the agreement."

Brenna's voice came quieter now. "And Marcus?"

Reed's mouth curved slightly. "He's was the bridge."

Julia tilted her head. "Meaning?"

"He moves easily in society," Reed said. "Knows who's arriving. Who's expected. Who's vulnerable."

Callum added, "And he's not questioned."

Brenna's expression darkened. "So they fed him information."

"Yes."

"And he acted on it."

Reed nodded. "With enthusiasm."

Julia folded her arms. "That still doesn't explain how he knew *everything*."

Callum's gaze shifted slightly. "He didn't know everything."

They all looked at him. "He knew enough."

Reed's brow lifted. "Because someone was giving it to him."

Callum nodded. "Regularly."

Then Brenna said it. "He was watching us before we even knew we were being watched."

Reed exhaled slowly. "That's the sort of thing that takes planning."

Callum's voice dropped. "Years of it."

Reed nodded. "They panicked."

"So Talbot sails over immediately." Brenna's voice sharpened, "to control the narrative."

"Exactly."

Julia shook her head. "And instead they walked into the truth."

Reed's mouth curved slightly. "That does happen."

Callum pushed off the desk slightly. "They needed someone who could move in both worlds," he said. "Business and society."

Brenna's gaze steadied. "And they chose Marcus."

Reed added quietly, "Which was their first mistake."

Callum didn't disagree.

Julia let out a slow breath. "So this was never just about a betrothal."

Brenna's voice followed, steady now. "No."

Her eyes met Callum's. "It was about control."

Callum held her gaze. "Precisely."

Silence settled again. But this time, everything made sense.

Chapter 36

The tension of the past week had finally begun to ease, replaced by something far more welcome, quiet, warmth, and the rare absence of danger.

Reed stood near the window, a glass in hand, watching the last of the light fade over the grounds. Callum leaned against the mantel, while Brenna sat nearby, the calm of the room settling around her.

The door opened. Julia entered without announcement. As usual.

"You all look entirely too relaxed," she said.

Reed glanced over. "I was enjoying the unfamiliar experience."

"That won't last."

"I suspected as much."

Julia crossed the room, pausing near the desk as though something had just occurred to her. "Oh."

Reed's eyes narrowed slightly. "That is never a reassuring tone."

Julia smiled. "I forgot to mention something."

Reed didn't move. "I'm already concerned."

She turned toward him, entirely unbothered. "On that last trip to Bond Street…"

Brenna's attention lifted immediately.

Reed sighed softly. "Yes?"

"Every shopkeeper we visited insisted I place everything on your account."

Callum's brow lifted.

Reed blinked once. Slowly. "My account."

Julia nodded, entirely composed. "Yes."

Reed said hesitantly, "You don't have access to my accounts."

Julia waved a hand lightly. "They didn't seem troubled by that."

Callum let out a quiet breath that might have been a laugh.

Reed stared at her. "You allowed them to believe…"

Julia tilted her head. "You had already made that quite clear yourself."

Brenna pressed her lips together, trying not to smile.

Reed's expression flattened. "I did no such thing."

Julia's brow lifted. "No?" She stepped a little closer. "At the ball… at dinner… in nearly every conversation since."

Reed opened his mouth. Closed it again.

Callum's voice came dryly from the mantel. "You did introduce her that way."

Reed shot him a look. "That was situational."

Julia smiled sweetly. "And I simply continued the situation."

Brenna let out a soft laugh.

Reed exhaled slowly, setting his glass down. "How extensive is this… situation?"

Julia considered. "A few gowns."

Brenna coughed softly into her hand.

Reed didn't react.

"And hats," Julia added.

Callum turned slightly away, shoulders tightening with suppressed amusement.

"And gloves."

Reed's expression went completely still. "Of course."

Julia brightened. "They were very persuasive."

"I'm sure they were." Then Reed crossed his arms. "And you intend to repay this… how?"

Julia looked at him as though the answer were obvious.

"I assumed you would pay it."

Brenna's composure slipped entirely now, a smile breaking through.

Callum's mouth curved faintly.

Reed stared at Julia. "Of course you did."

Julia stepped a fraction closer, her voice softening just slightly. "You didn't correct them," she said.

Reed met her gaze. "No."

The word settled between them. Quiet. Certain. A brief silence followed.

Callum glanced between them, then toward Brenna, something thoughtful shifting in his expression.

"Well," he said lightly, "that seems to have resolved itself."

Brenna smiled. "It does seem so."

Reed let out a slow breath, some of the tension giving way. "Well," he said, reaching again for his glass, "I suppose it's fortunate I can afford it."

Julia's smile softened. "I thought you might say that."

Reed shook his head. "You are entirely impossible."

Julia tilted her head. "And yet…"

Reed glanced at her. "And yet," he repeated.

Neither of them looked away.

Across the room, Callum studied Brenna for a moment, something more serious settling behind the ease. He crossed the room without hesitation, coming to stand before her.

Then, quietly, "Walk with me."

Brenna looked up at him. His tone had shifted. "Now?"

"If you will."

Brenna gave Callum a questioning look as she rose.

Julia watched them with interest.

Reed said nothing.

But as Callum offered Brenna his arm and led her toward the door, his voice lowered just enough for her alone. "We should discuss our betrothal agreement."

Brenna's expression changed. The lightness of the room lingered behind them, but what waited ahead was something far more important.

The evening air had cooled just enough to carry the faint scent of the gardens, the last of the light fading into a soft blue dusk.

Brenna drew the shawl closer around her shoulders as they walked, her fingers brushing the familiar fabric.

Callum noticed. "You kept it." Brenna glanced down at it briefly. "It seemed… worth keeping." Then added, "It reminds me of where this began."

Callum's gaze lingered on her a moment. "A strange beginning."

"Yes," she said quietly. "Not one I would have chosen."

"No," he agreed. "Nor I."

They walked a few steps further in silence, gravel shifting softly beneath their feet.

"The agreement," Brenna said after a few minutes of silence.

Callum exhaled lightly. "Yes."

She stopped walking. "So this is where you tell me what is expected of me."

Callum turned to face her. "No."

The answer came without hesitation. Brenna's brow lifted slightly. "No?"

"No," he repeated. "This is where I tell you I want nothing to do with it."

The words settled between them.

Brenna searched his face. "You would cast it aside so easily?"

"There is nothing easy about it," Callum said. "But I will not have you bound to me because of something arranged without your knowledge, or mine."

Brenna's fingers tightened slightly against the shawl. "It bears your name."

"It does."

"And yet you reject it."

"That's right."

Silence lingered. Then Brenna asked softly, "Why?"

"Why?" Callum stepped closer, not enough to crowd her, but enough that she could not mistake the shift in his tone.

"Because if you marry me," he said, "it will be because you choose it."

Brenna stilled. Not just in movement, but entirely. For a moment she said nothing. Couldn't. The words didn't feel like part of the conversation they had been having. They landed differently. Heavier. Closer.

Her fingers tightened slightly against the shawl at her shoulders, the familiar fabric grounding her as something unsettled rose beneath the surface.

"Marry you," she repeated, though the words came softer than she intended.

Callum didn't look away. "Yes."

Brenna let out a slow breath, but it did little to steady her. "That is not a casual suggestion."

"No."

Her gaze dropped briefly, not in avoidance, but in thought, in the sudden weight of what he was asking.

"You ask as though I can separate this moment from everything that brought me here," she continued. "From the agreement. From my father. From…" she hesitated slightly, "… from what I thought my life was meant to be."

Callum's voice lowered. "I'm asking you to choose whatit could be."

That unsettled her more than anything else. Brenna looked away again, her thoughts shifting faster now, harder to keep in order.

She took a step back, not retreating, but needing space from the closeness of it. "You make it sound as though it's that easy."

"I don't think it is."

"Then you understand why I hesitate."

Callum nodded. "I do."

Brenna studied him, searching, not for charm, not for persuasion, but for truth.

"And if I say no?"

Callum's answer came steady. "Then nothing changes."

Her brow knit slightly. "Everything changes."

"For you," he said. "But not for me."

Callum stepped closer, not enough to corner her, but enough to be heard clearly. "I don't say anything I don't mean."

Brenna felt it then, not just the weight of his words, but the sincerity behind them. And that was far more dangerous.

She drew a slow breath. "And what is it you want, then?"

Callum's voice lowered. "You."

The word was quiet. Certain.

She turned back to him. "That is not a small answer."

"No," he said. "It isn't."

A pause stretched between them. Then Callum's expression shifted, just slightly, something lighter threading through the weight of the moment.

"So," he said, "tell me what it would take"

Brenna blinked faintly.

"To convince you."

Her lips pressed together, though there was the faintest hint of something softer beneath it "I'm not certain that's something that can be purchased."

Callum's mouth curved slightly. "No?" He took another step closer. "A garden of your own, then."

Brenna's brow lifted. "I already have one."

"A better one."

She almost smiled. "That seems unlikely."

Callum continued, unbothered. "A new carriage."

"I don't require one."

"A ship, then," he said, watching her closely now. "A new one. Built for you."

That caught her. Her fingers stilled against the shawl. "For me."

"For us," he corrected.

A quiet moment passed. Brenna looked out toward the horizon, though the sea was far from sight.

"You think that would convince me."

"I think it might make you consider it."

She glanced back at him. "And if it doesn't?"

Callum's voice softened. "Then I will find something that does."

Brenna studied him, something shifting behind her expression. "You are very certain."

Callum held her gaze. "Yes."

"Why?"

"Because no one has ever affected me the way you do."

The words settled into the quiet around them.

Brenna's breath caught, just slightly. "You barely know me."

Callum's mouth curved faintly. "I know enough."

Brenna looked down at the shawl again, her fingers brushing the fabric.

"This began on your ship," she said quietly.

"Yes."

"In the middle of something neither of us expected."

"Yes."

She lifted her gaze. "And now you're asking me to choose."

Callum didn't hesitate. "I am."

Brenna exhaled slowly. "That is a dangerous thing."

Callum's voice lowered. "So is not asking."

The faintest smile touched her lips then, brief, but real. "You make a compelling argument."

"I intend to."

Brenna met his gaze, something steadier settling in her expression. "I won't be persuaded by promises," she said.

Callum nodded once. "Good, then I'll have to prove it."

The words lingered between them.

Brenna's breath caught, just slightly. "Callum..."

She meant to say more. She didn't. Because he stepped closer. Slowly this time. Deliberately. Giving her time to move away. She didn't.

Her fingers tightened in the shawl at her shoulders as he stopped just in front of her, close enough that she felt the warmth of him, the steadiness of his breath.

"Tell me to stop," he said quietly.

Brenna looked up at him. Her answer never came. Because she didn't want him to.

And he saw it. That was all it took. His hand lifted, brushing lightly against her cheek before settling there, steadying, not claiming.

Then he kissed her. Not rushed. Not uncertain. But held, like something he had been denying himself for far too long.

Brenna's breath faltered as she felt it, her hand rising instinctively to his coat, gripping it as though to keep herself grounded.

For a moment, everything else disappeared. The garden. The agreement. The expectations waiting beyond them. All of it gone.

There was only this, and the undeniable truth of it.

When he drew back, it was only just enough to find her eyes again. And for the first time,
there was nothing restrained in his expression. Only certainty. Only her.

The evening settled deeper around them, the last of the light slipping away as they stood there, no longer bound by an agreement.

But something far more uncertain.

And far more real.

Epilogue

One Year Later

"Brenna!"

Callum's voice carried easily through the halls of Ashcombe Estate. "We are going to be late if you do not hurry."

From the top of the staircase Brenna appeared at last. Callum stopped speaking mid-sentence.

She looked… breathtaking.

Nearly a year of marriage had not dimmed the effect she had on him. If anything, it had only deepened it. Brenna moved with the same grace and confidence that had first captivated him, though now there was a warmth about her that filled the great house with life.

Ashcombe Estate had changed since she arrived.

The rooms no longer felt like a place visited only in passing. Brenna had filled them with laughter, light, and the quiet strength of someone who belonged there completely.

Callum crossed the entry hall and offered her his arm. "Beautiful as ever," he murmured.

Brenna smiled. "Flattery will not make the carriage arrive any sooner."

"It might make you move faster."

She laughed softly as he escorted her outside.

The carriage waited at the front drive, horses stamping impatiently as the coachman held the reins.

Callum assisted Brenna carefully up the step before climbing in after her.

As she settled into the seat across from him, the soft curve of her gown revealed the gentle rounding of her belly.

Callum's eyes softened. "Well," he said, leaning forward slightly, "how is my son today?"

Brenna lifted an eyebrow.

"Your daughter," she corrected calmly, resting a hand against her stomach. "Is growing stronger every day."

Callum smiled. "If you give me a daughter, I will be just as happy." He reached across and covered her hand with his. "We will simply keep trying until we have a son."

Brenna shook her head, though she could not hide her amusement. In truth, she knew how deeply Callum already loved the child they had yet to meet. Whether son or daughter mattered very little in the end.

He would be a devoted, and likely very protective, father.

The carriage moved smoothly along the road, the late afternoon light stretching long across the countryside, though her attention had long since drifted from the view outside.

"I've been hearing things," she said at last.

Callum glanced at her. "That rarely bodes well."

Her lips curved faintly. "No," she agreed. "It doesn't."

"About Talbot," she added.

That drew his full attention.

"And Avery."

Callum's expression sharpened, just slightly. "What sort of things?"

Brenna tilted her head, studying him as though deciding how much to say. "That neither of them has been seen in some time."

Callum didn't respond immediately.

"They were last known to be working together," she continued. "Quite closely, it would seem."

A faint shift in his posture. "And now?"

Brenna's voice softened. "Now they've both… disappeared."

The word lingered. Callum's gaze held hers. "That's a strong conclusion."

Brenna lifted one shoulder slightly. "It's the word being used."

"Talbot never returned to Boston," she added. "Which, given his, interests, seems unlikely."

Callum's tone remained even. "Men leave their affairs unfinished more often than they should."

"Not men like him," Brenna said quietly.

The carriage continued on, the steady rhythm of the wheels filling the brief silence between them.

Callum studied her. "You sound as though you've already drawn your own conclusions."

Brenna's lips curved faintly. "I have questions."

"And answers?"

"Not yet, though the timing is curious."

Callum's gaze shifted briefly toward the window, then back to her. "Yes," he said. "It is."

Brenna watched him a moment longer. "And then there's Dalridge."

That name did not pass as easily. Callum's expression didn't change. "What about him?" Brenna's voice remained calm. "I heard he met with an unfortunate accident. A carriage, I believe."

Callum inclined his head slightly. "That's what was reported."

"Two months ago," she added.

"Yes."

Brenna's gaze didn't waver. "That's quite a number of unfortunate circumstances in a very short span of time."

Callum held her gaze. "Circumstances tend to cluster."

Her lips curved again, faint, knowing. "How convenient."

Callum's mouth shifted slightly. "Or inevitable."

Brenna leaned back just slightly, studying him with quiet interest. "You don't seem surprised."

Callum's voice lowered. "I've learned not to be, especially where men like that are concerned."

Brenna considered that. "Do you think anyone will go looking for them?"

Callum didn't hesitate. "No."

"Why not?"

"Because men like Talbot and Avery," he said evenly, "tend to leave behind more questions than anyone is willing to follow."

Brenna's gaze softened, just slightly.

"And Dalridge?"

Callum's expression remained steady. "Accidents happen."

The words were simple. Too simple.

Brenna held his gaze a moment longer. "Of course they do."

A quiet understanding passed between them.

Callum leaned back against the cushions, changing the subject, "Reed tells me we had better not arrive late."

Brenna laughed. "Julia would never forgive us."

"Julia?" Callum asked.

"She would not dare marry Reed without me present."

Callum chuckled. "That would be a brave decision indeed."

Brenna gazed out the window as the estate disappeared behind them, the morning sunlight stretching across the fields.

One year.

A year filled with danger, discovery, and more happiness than she had ever expected. She glanced back at Callum, who watched her with the same steady warmth that had carried them through everything.

Brenna smiled softly as the carriage rolled forward. "I still can't believe they're doing this so quietly."

Callum glanced at her. "That surprises you?"

"A little," she admitted. "Julia has never done anything quietly in her life."

Callum's mouth curved slightly. "She has Reed now."

Brenna's smile deepened. "That explains it."

A brief pause passed before she added, "They suit each other."

Callum nodded once. "Yes."

Brenna glanced at him. "When did that happen?"

Callum considered it. "Gradually."

She tilted her head. "That's not very helpful."

"They met in the middle of a problem," he said. "And neither of them ran from it. Somewhere between danger, laughter, and shared defiance, it had quietly become inevitable.

Brenna smiled faintly. "That sounds familiar."

Callum didn't argue.

Reed's name lingered between them a moment before Brenna spoke again. "He lets her be exactly as she is."

Callum glanced at her. "They are meant for each other."

And as the carriage came to a gentle stop, Callum reached for her hand once more, and Brenna knew she was exactly where she was meant to be.

Reed stood at the front, the quiet of the small gathering pressing in around him in a way no storm ever had.

For once, he had nowhere to go. No escape into duty. No distance to hide behind. Only this moment. Then the doors opened. He turned.

And everything else fell away. Julia stepped inside, light catching in her hair, her expression brighter than he had ever seen it, unrestrained, certain, entirely herself.

Not dressed for society. Not performing for anyone. Just Julia. Walking toward him.

Reed exhaled, though he hadn't realized he'd been holding his breath. For all the years he had spent avoiding titles, expectations, the weight of a name, this was the first time any of it felt… right.

Because it led to her.

Julia reached him, her eyes lifting to his. "You look entirely too serious," she murmured.

Reed's mouth finally curved. "I'm considering my options."

Her smile widened. "And?"

Reed took her hand. "I find I have none."

And as he looked at her, Reed Halbrook did not feel like a title. He felt like a man who had finally chosen exactly where the path had always been leading.

AUTHOR BIO

Wendy Hamilton has always believed in the power of stories. After decades of setting aside her dream of writing, she has returned to it with renewed purpose, bringing to life the characters and worlds she first imagined years ago.

With a passion for both art and storytelling, Wendy writes historical fiction that blends adventure and romance into stories that carry the thrill of the journey while remaining free of explicit content and language.

When she's not writing, Wendy works as a dental hygienist and lives along the Oregon coast with her husband and their three dogs, drawing daily inspiration from the sea and the quiet beauty around her.

Made in the USA
Coppell, TX
28 April 2026

76284755R00194